THRONE
OF WINTER
FIRE FAE BOOK ONE
SOPHIE DAVIS

Throne of Winter
Sophie Davis

Cover design Jamie Dalton at Magnetra's Designs

Interior design by Breakout Designs

FOR A.J.,
GONE BUT NEVER
FORGOTTEN

THRONE OF WINTER

BOOK ONE

TABLE OF CONTENTS

PROLOGUE

FIVE YEARS AGO FAE CANYON, FREELANDS OF THE AMERICAS

ONCE IN A FAE'S lifetime, she might be lucky enough to see a night where four different elemental moons shine in the sky simultaneously. Or unlucky enough, as the elders claim, to witness a quartet of fire orbs among the stars on Night of Four Moons….

Silly superstition, I thought, staring out my bedroom window at the collection of glowing orange moons. *How can anyone believe something so pretty is such a bad omen?*

Where others saw misfortune, I saw hope. Life. Color. The moons transformed our frozen world from a desolate landscape sketched in shades of gray to one painted in rich crimson, magenta, and violet. In my fifteen years on this earth, I had never seen something so breathtakingly beautiful, so purely magical.

Come morning, the dull sun would rise and wash away the color with pale, white light. Only the Goddess knew when the next Night of Four Moons would occur. Chances were high that night wouldn't include a single fire moon, let alone four. At least, that was how I justified defying my father's order to remain inside our house, tucked safely behind the wards until morning.

"This is a once in a lifetime opportunity," I whispered aloud, stealing a glance at my brother Illion asleep in the bed on the other side of the small room. "I can't miss it."

With the dying embers of a fire smoldering in the hearth, I folded back the quilt and swung my legs over the side of the bed. Illion's head poked out from beneath a woolen blanket, his small thumb stuck between his lips. Careful not to wake him, I smoothed his dark-blond locks back from his forehead and kissed my brother softly on the cheek. He smelled like the cinnamon tonic my father insisted we all drink before bed.

"I'll be back soon," I promised Illion.

My running clothes were stacked neatly in the cupboard beneath the bathroom sink, sneakers on top. I layered two pairs of pants and three shirts under a heavy down jacket. Woolen gloves and a matching hat, handcrafted by our next-door neighbor, came next. I checked the time—just before midnight. Sienna and Gregory were probably already waiting for me at the bottom of Fae Canyon.

The front door squeaked a little when I pushed it open. Freezing, I listened with bated breath. Neither Dad nor Illion stirred. I slipped out into the frigid night.

Wards weren't visible to the naked eye, but there was a palpable change in the atmosphere when I crossed outside the ring of protection. A lump formed in my throat.

Is this a stupid idea?

It was. My father would ground me until I turned eighteen if he found out.

If he finds out. Don't get caught, and he will never find out.

I started down the canyon at a light jog to warm up my stiff muscles. The moons illuminated the road, but shadows moved among the trees. *No patrols tonight,* I reminded myself. Though, if anything, that fact made my ears more sensitive, my eyes keener. The nights when the guards weren't on duty made sneaking out too tempting, but also very dangerous.

Nothing ever happens in Fae Canyon, I told the pixies fluttering about in my stomach.

That was true enough. The canyon was secluded, isolated even. The next closest community was hundreds of miles away. Dark creatures didn't bother with us, not when they could hunt in densely populated cities or pick off lone fae families without a powerful council of elders to protect them. Hell, even the shifter colonies were easier targets than Fae Canyon.

Still, I picked up the pace. My nerves would calm once I met up with Sienna and Gregory. They always did.

The air tasted crisp and fresh as I jogged down the winding road. Frozen earth crunched beneath my soles, and my breath came out in little clouds tinged orange by the moons. Wind whipped the hair sticking out from beneath my hat and stung my eyes. I wasn't bothered, though. Having grown up in a frozen world, the cold was a constant companion.

I reached the bottom of the canyon.

"Brie! Over here!" Sienna called softly.

Adrenaline erased lingering doubts. Confidence in my decision to sneak out grew by leaps and bounds. I squinted in the direction of her voice and found her huddled together with Gregory in the shadows behind the sign for Fae Canyon. He waved one mitten-clad hand. I returned the gesture and hurried over to join them. Both my friends were red-faced and shivering, eyes sparkling bright with excitement.

"Am I super late? How long have you guys been waiting?" I asked, jogging in place to keep my blood pumping.

Gregory shrugged. "Nah, you're good. I got here early, and Sienna just showed up." He blew into his covered hands to warm them. "So, where to, ladies?"

Sienna and I exchanged glances. "The beach?" we replied in unison.

He grinned with noticeable effort, facial muscles likely frozen. "Like you were reading my mind."

The three of us set off across the deserted stretch of road that separated the canyon from the beach.

"Did anyone see you guys?" I asked.

"Not me." Sienna shot a look at Gregory.

He sighed. "My sister got up to use the bathroom right as I opened the window to climb out." Gregory's sister was the same age as Illion. They were in the same year at school and friendly with one another. "It's fine," he added hurriedly. "She won't tell on us."

"You sure?" I arched an eyebrow in his direction. "You know my father. He's a stickler for the rules. And he forbade me to leave the house tonight."

"Elder Hawkins *makes* the rules," Sienna laughed.

"Exactly. Which is why he gets so pissed when his daughter breaks one," I reminded her.

The air smelled of salt water as we approached the ocean. I longed for the days before the Freeze, when living at the beach meant surfing and sunbathing, picnics and barbeques, waterskiing and sailing. Not that I had firsthand knowledge—the world turned to a frozen wasteland long before I was born. Those were just the types of activities the people in my favorite books always did.

"She won't say anything," Gregory promised.

We stopped at the water's edge and admired the view. Frozen sand glistened like an endless sea of diamonds. The moons' orange glow mixed with the blue ocean water beneath a layer of ice to create a vast expanse of magenta.

"Wow. It's so pretty," Sienna breathed.

Gregory wrapped one of his long arms around her waist and the other around my shoulders. Pulling us both into his sides, we made a small huddle for warmth. Even with all my layers of clothes, the additional body heat was welcome.

The three of us had been a trio practically since birth. Over the years, Sienna and I had both had a crush on Gregory at some point. She'd been his first kiss, and he'd been mine. But now, we were just three best friends and partners in crime.

"Why do the elders say fire moons are bad luck?" Gregory wondered.

"Fire moons aren't bad luck," I corrected as we started walking along the shoreline. "It's only bad luck when there are four of them at once."

"Like tonight," Sienna added.

"Okay. But why?" Gregory pressed.

"Fire's destructive," I said. "And since Night of Four Moons signals the start of a new crop season, the elders believe all the crops will die if the harvest season begins with only fire moons."

"Has that ever actually happened?" Sienna asked.

"Don't you guys pay attention in history class?" I teased.

"No," they chorused.

"Right. Stupid question." I rolled my eyes and shook my head. "Once. Sort of. Way back in the day. Right after the Freeze. But back then a lot of the crops died every season. They hadn't evolved yet to withstand the cold. It had nothing to do with the fire moons, though they were still blamed for it, and the superstition was born."

Gregory kicked a patch of seagrass. The frozen spikes shattered into hundreds of tiny green ice chunks and scattered like marbles on the beach ahead of us.

"Sooooo," he began, drawing out the single syllable.

There was no point pretending like I didn't know where the conversation was headed.

"I don't know, guys," I hedged, eyes trained straight ahead.

"Come on, Brie. Please?" Sienna broke apart from our

huddle, turned to face me, and began walking backward. "This will be our last chance for months." Batting her long lashes, she added, "Pretty please?"

I smiled despite my growing unease. I'd known they would ask. More often than not, it was the sole reason we snuck out.

"Months? That's a slight exaggeration, don't you think, Sienna?" I countered, buying myself a few extra seconds to decide.

"Sugar fruit is a night harvest crop," Gregory pointed out. "Pickers will be all over the canyon once harvest season begins. No way we'll be able to sneak away without being seen." He gave me an encouraging squeeze and shot that smile that made so many fae putty in his hands. "We're over halfway there already. And you know you want to."

"Peer pressure much?" I grumbled.

Sienna clapped her hands in delight. "Is that a yes?" she squealed.

I sighed. "Yes. Okay. Let's go."

With a graceless little jump and twirl, Sienna whooped excitedly and took off at a dead sprint up the beach. Laughing at her silliness, Gregory and I raced after her.

Approximately three miles from the base of Fae Canyon, bluffs jutted out into the sea. Between two rock faces was a narrow passage only accessible from the water. Gregory went first. Holding his arms parallel to the ground for balance, he stepped gingerly onto the icy ocean surface. Salt water didn't freeze completely, so there was always a risk of falling through the ice. But Gregory was a water fae, capable of solidifying a path to minimize the danger.

"Follow directly in my footsteps," he called over his shoulder.

Rolling my eyes at the instruction—this wasn't my first rodeo—I stepped onto the ice. Sienna waited until I was several feet from the shore before following behind me. Up ahead, Gregory reached the opening and turned sideways to shimmy through. My jacket caught on something when I did the same. I didn't want to rip the fabric—Dad would definitely ask questions if he noticed a tear—but the gloves made my fingers too thick to be nimble.

"Damn it," I swore, removing my gloves with my teeth. There wasn't much light or room in the passage. I felt around for whatever had snagged my jacket.

"Need help?" Sienna asked, sidling up beside me.

"I think I've got.... Shit!" The pointy rock that had caught my jacket sliced across my palm.

"You okay?" Gregory called. He was through the passage and waiting for us in the cavern on the other side.

The cut smarted, but there didn't appear to be too much blood. "Yeah, just a scratch," I called back, slipping on my gloves.

I started moving again and managed to make it through without further incident, Sienna only a few steps behind. I blew out a long breath. The temperature inside the cavern was noticeably lower than outside. But there was no wind, so that was a bonus. Not that it would matter soon.

"We still have wood. Good," Gregory remarked, gesturing to a pile of sticks and tree limbs in the corner.

"And snacks," Sienna added, grinning broadly. She bent and began untying her boots.

"Wait. Let me start a fire first," I told her.

There was still a ring of stones with charred wood in the center from our last late-night outing. Gregory piled fresh sticks inside the ring. Once again, I removed my gloves, this time summoning my magic. Two baseball-sized fireballs appeared, one in each of my palms. I tossed them both onto the wood pile and stepped back, watching as bright-orange flames cast dancing shadows on the rounded cavern walls. The air temperature increased instantly.

"So much better," Sienna said. She finished removing her boots and placed them against one wall, away from both the fire and the frozen pool in the center of the cavern.

I knelt beside the pool, placing both palms flat against the ice. Even with the fire, it was dark enough to see the faint orange glow on my hands as the skin heated. It took several minutes, but eventually I melted two holes in the top layer of ice.

"How much longer?" Sienna asked, teeth chattering.

I scowled at her over my shoulder. Sienna had stripped down to her underwear already, her clothes piled on her jacket at her feet. Beside her, Gregory was still partially dressed in socks, long underwear, and a thermal undershirt. He leaned over and rubbed his hands up and down her bare arms to create friction. I shrugged out of my jacket and rolled up my sleeves.

"I'm going as fast as I can," I said, plunging my arms, up to the elbows, into the holes I'd made.

Closing my eyes, I tilted my head back and felt the power build in my belly. One of the reasons we preferred this cavern, over the several others we'd found, was the small opening directly above the center of the pool, like a skylight. Some nights, the moon was just barely visible through the crevice. Tonight was one of those nights. I imagined the fire moons giving me strength, intensifying my natural abilities.

Steam warmed my face and arms as the water heated and thawed the rest of the ice from below. I opened my eyes and smiled. Mist hung in the air over the pool. I pulled my arms out of the water and sat back on my haunches as Gregory's undershirt landed on my head. Water splashed over the side of the pool and soaked through the knees of my pants when he and Sienna leapt in.

"Jerks," I teased, laughing as I undressed hurriedly.

By the time I slid into the steaming pool with my friends, the water was gurgling and bubbling like a hot tub. But this wasn't due to jets or natural hot springs, only an air fae—Sienna. The warm water felt amazing swirling around my tired muscles. I stretched my arms out along the edge of the pool and sighed contentedly.

"Glad we came?" Sienna asked, splashing water playfully toward my face.

"You know I am," I replied grudgingly.

"This is the life," Gregory mused.

The pool wasn't big enough to swim laps, but it was plenty big for the three of us to move around without knocking into one another. An interior rock ledge circled the perimeter at waist height, providing seats. They were needed since the pool was too deep for Sienna and me to stand. Gregory could manage on his tiptoes except in the very center.

After a while, we busted out the snacks and made smores over the fire. We drank spiced avocado wine from ice goblets that Gregory made. Every time one of us grew cold, I summoned my magic and reheated the water.

"There's no way that's true!" Sienna exclaimed, smacking the water and splashing Gregory.

He'd just finished telling us about the fae girl his older brother had supposedly met at the last Freelands Fair—an annual bazaar where people came from all over the Americas to sell and exchange goods. Each year, the elders selected an envoy to go on behalf of the canyon. I'd always hoped to go, but my father thought it was too dangerous.

"I swear." Gregory made an 'X' over his heart. "George told me that she told him that the fighters in the capital are treated like royalty. So are the palace fae, the ones who serve—or should I say, service—Queen Lilli." He wiggled his eyebrows suggestively. "Living under a dome doesn't sound so bad to me. You get to live in the sunshine, eat fresh meat and vegetables, and hang with a royal family? Sign me up."

Sienna laughed. "Me, too. Except I'd want to be Prince Kai's personal fae."

I shook my head. "Not me. I'd much rather have freedom than fresh salmon or whatever."

"It's different than serving just any caster family, Brie," Gregory countered. "There's a big difference between being just any old fae under the dome and being one of the fae who gets to entertain or serve the royal family."

I arched an eyebrow. "Is it? Just because palace fae live in a castle and get pretty clothes and fancy food, that doesn't make it any better. They aren't free to leave. Witches and warlocks need us—our magic anyway—to live. That's why the monarchs of the Americas created the Fae Fidelity Act. They had to *force* fae into service as magic feeders. No one wants to be a Caster power source, that's gross."

Sienna's eyes went wide. "Wait, what? That's what the Fae Fidelity Act is?"

"You really need to start paying attention in school," I said dryly.

"We aren't forced to share our magic," Gregory argued.

"No, you're right," I conceded. "The domed fae are just forced to choose between sharing their magic with casters and cleaning toilets for them. Either way, fae under the dome aren't free to come and go as they please."

Our night of risky frivolity suddenly didn't seem like so much fun anymore. Fae Canyon was in the Freelands of the Americas—areas not under the rule of caster kings and queens who held court and made laws from beneath their biodomes. Only fae and shifters lived in the Freelands. Casters were delicate and unable to survive the cold on their own. Vampires could live outside the domes, though most just chose to keep their residences inside of them.

In the Freelands, government officials didn't journey

from door to door to force fae and shifters into service like what happened in the kingdoms. We might live in a frozen wasteland, but at least we were free to use our magic how and when we pleased.

"George said the girl—"

A thump from above cut off Gregory midsentence. All three of us fell silent. My heart thudded painfully in my chest. I looked up. The natural skylight was clear, nothing and no one obstructing the moonlight. That fact did not make me feel any better.

A shower of small rocks and ice came through the opening, sizzling when they hit the hot water. Sienna, Gregory, and I exchanged glances.

"We need to go," Sienna mouthed. No further discussion was necessary. We hurried from the pool, not bothering to be quiet about it. There was no point; if someone was outside the cave, they already knew we were inside.

I pulled my shirts over my head in record time. My pants, however, proved a little more difficult. Between my wet skin and the fact that my pants were still wet from earlier, I had trouble getting the material up my legs. So much so that I didn't bother with more than one pair before wedging my feet into my sneakers.

"Hello," came a cold, flat voice from the cave's entrance.

In the canyon we called them cowboys, but the name never made much sense to me before that night. They didn't ride horses. They didn't wear spurs. Their hats were not of the ten-gallon variety. Cowboys were a type of vampire who hunted fae and shifters and sold them into service to the casters.

"What're three faelings doing out here all by themselves?" asked the cowboy.

Five feet from where I stood, his ghostly white face split into a grin. The vampire's fangs looked particularly ghoulish in the fire's glow.

Too late, the clink of metal against metal reached my ears. My heart leapt into my throat.

Vampires were fast—so extremely fast. But Sienna was no slouch either. Even as the vampire's chain-link rope swung toward us, she unleashed a gust of wind so powerful that only she was left standing. The metal rope missed my friends and me, but the vampire was back on his feet in no time.

"Ahhh!" Sienna shouted as she unleashed another powerful blast of air.

This time the vampire was ready. He stumbled but didn't fall. And when he struck out, the chain-link rope found its mark: me.

My knees nearly buckled from the impact. Gregory was on his feet, charging the vampire. The fanged cowboy laughed as he backhanded Gregory so hard, he flew into the cave wall.

"No!" I screamed as his body crumpled to the ground.

Sienna gasped as she hurried to Gregory's side.

Fight. You must fight.

Two fireballs appeared in my palms.

"Fire fae," the creature sang, voice soft and seductive like the opening notes of a romantic ballad. "You will be worth all the rest combined. Fighting will be pointless, girl. Come now. It would be a shame to harm such a beautiful fae."

The vampire's unnaturally green eyes glowed expectantly, dimming slightly when his charms fell on deaf ears. As he realized that the vampiric ability to compel prey into submission wasn't working on me—thanks to Dad's potions—his grin turned to a snarl. One of my fireballs streaked toward him. My aim was dead on, but I was no match for vampire speed. Yanking the metal lasso, he dodged the assault gracefully. The ice was slippery from the water dripping off me, and his tug had the desired effect.

"Ahhh!" I cried out as I lost my footing.

I released the second fireball a split-second before my knees smacked the wet ground. Sharp rocks sliced my leggings.

The vampire gave the lasso another yank, dragging me toward him. The rocky terrain tore the exposed skin on my knees and calves. His pale nostrils flared. If there was any doubt whether I was bleeding, it vanished.

No. No. This can't be happening.

Gritting my teeth against the pain, I let the vampire reel me in like a fish. Bloodlust turned his eyes crimson. Like a teenager convinced he was about to get into his date's pants, the fanged creature was no longer thinking sensibly. The way he held my gaze made it obvious he'd already forgotten his first attempt at compulsion hadn't worked. I waited until he bent down and grabbed my arm, intending to pull me to my feet.

Flames erupted in my hand, and I slammed my palm into his stomach. Those crimson eyes flashed back to green an instant before the fire consumed him. Gasping for breath, I stumbled out of harm's way.

"Not so smug now are you, you fanged bastard?" I sneered.

The vampire twisted in agony as he retreated through the opening. I didn't follow. There was no need; he'd be a pile of ash before ever reaching shore.

Sienna choked on her tear-filled laugher. I wiggled out of the metal rope and rushed over to where she knelt next to Gregory.

"Is he alive?" I asked hurriedly.

She nodded. "He's got a pulse." She stroked his forehead softly.

Gregory stirred, eyelids fluttering open. "I'm alive," he croaked, trying to sit up but unable to manage the small movement. "Probably not for much longer."

"Don't say that," Sienna pleaded.

"My right leg is definitely broken," Gregory grunted. "Possibly the left, too. I'll only hold you back."

Tears still glistened in Sienna's eyes. She shook her head defiantly. "No. We're not leaving you."

Gregory met my gaze over her head. "Brie. Tell her. We have to split up."

"No. We can't. We're better together," Sienna insisted. She turned to look up at me, positive I'd side with her if she gave me her puppy-dog eyes.

One look at the bloody remains of my pants, and the flicker of hope on her face died a swift death.

"Are you bleeding anywhere?" I asked Gregory.

"Does internally count?" he tried to joke.

"I'll burn away my blood in here, and then run toward the shore. That should keep the others away from here until Sienna can get you help," I replied.

Honestly, I wasn't sure burning the blood would be enough. I could only hope that with my open wounds, my scent would lure other vampires astray before they entered the cave.

"Others?" Sienna asked, a fresh wave of tears falling down her red cheeks.

"Really? Promise me that you'll start taking school more seriously if we make it out of this," I said, this time with no teasing undertones. "Cowboys hunt in packs. Usually three or four of them. Our barbequed buddy has friends out there, and his bonfire is going to draw their attention."

Summoning my magic, I directed a spray of fire at the swatches of my blood on the ground. At the same time, Gregory sent a stream of water from the pool to douse the fire, something we probably should've done as soon as we sensed trouble.

"I'll go first, lead any other vampires away," I said without meeting my friends' eyes. "Sienna, wait a few minutes and then go. Run for the canyon. Don't stop for any reason."

"No." She shook her head. "I won't make it alone."

Spinning to face her, I placed my hands on her shoulders and stared into her eyes. "You will only make it alone. Gregory is too badly injured. I'm bleeding. You are the only chance we have. Promise me that you will not stop until you sound the alarm. Promise me. You have to get back and send help."

Sienna responded with several hiccupping sobs before gaining enough composure to say, "Okay. I promise."

"I love you both," I told them, hugging Sienna quickly. There was a lot more I'd have liked to say. No time for sentiment, though. So, turning my back on my friends, I shimmied through the narrow opening and out onto the ice. The small smear of my blood from the cut on my hand caught my eye.

You idiot, I chastised myself, burning away the lure that had hooked the vampire. *Speaking of the vampire....*

He must have been very old, because he'd managed to make it all the way to the sand before collapsing. His burning remains formed a magnificent bonfire.

Ice cracked beneath me.

Don't have to tell me twice.

I darted for the beach and headed left. My heart hammered against my ribcage as my sneakers beat a frantic rhythm on the frozen sand. My knees throbbed, and my breath was ragged. I didn't hear any telltale signs of a pursuer. Nonetheless, vampires were pure stealth. Between the wind and the pounding of my pulse in my ears, it was impossible to hear much of anything.

Forty yards down the beach, I chanced a glance over my shoulder and nearly wept when the coastline was still clear. "Oh, thank Gaia."

Well, sort of clear. Orange flames danced in the wind, a bizarrely beautiful ballet that seemed choreographed, like the vampire's death was destined for this moment and his pyre planned in advance. But it was the turquoise and amethyst smoke swirling like ribbons in the air around him that made me pause.

I crouched in a bed of seagrass and watched the fruits of my magic unfold. Soon, emerald and ruby wisps wafted up from the fire to join the production. The sight should've disturbed me. Vampires were evil, but they were living creatures—sort of—just like fae or shifters or casters. Still, I found myself unable to look away from the fascinating rainbow of smoke.

Children in the canyon whispered to one another at slumber parties that the color of smoke from a vampire fire was determined by his victims' auras. I didn't know if that was true, but the number of different colors of smoke would've suggested this vampire had claimed a lot of souls in his undead lifetime.

Off in the distance, I thought I saw a shadow moving on the frozen ocean. *Sienna,* I thought and said a prayer to the Goddess for my best friend.

The fire burned out moments later, the wind carrying the jewel-tone smoke out over the ocean. It was only then that I noticed the lights on the highway. I held my breath and tried to remain as still as possible, expecting the beams to grow larger as they neared. But they remained stationary.

It's his caravan, I realized.

Cowboys may not have ridden horses, but they did travel from area to area in large trucks. Once they trapped a fae or shifter in their lasso, they stuffed the victim in the container on the back for transport.

Stupid, Brie. Why did you stop moving? I chastised myself.

The other vampires were no doubt scouring the beach for the fire fae who'd killed their associate. Just because I couldn't see them didn't mean they couldn't see me. The cowboy's last words played in my mind: *You will be worth all the rest combined.*

"Stupid. Stupid. Stupid," I whispered.

Okay, think, Brie. Sienna and Gregory are counting on you. You need to distract the vampires, keep them away from Sienna.

I inhaled deeply and summoned my magic. Instead of calling forth flames, I simply heated my right palm and placed it on the ground long enough to melt the ice. Sand stung my cuts, but the pain was nothing compared to what would come next. Once I was satisfied the scrapes were clean enough, I bit down on my jacket sleeve and ran my hot hand first over one leg and then the other to cauterize the wounds.

Stars blotted my vision. Tears pooled in my eyes and froze on my cheeks. For several long moments, passing out seemed like a serious possibility. The sensation passed. I blew out a breath I didn't know I'd been holding.

Okay. That's over. What's your next move?

I squinted into the darkness, scanning the beach for signs of life. I didn't need to look far. In a blur of motion, a tall, slim figure sped from the highway to the pile of vampire ash on the beach.

Follow my scent. Follow my scent.

Crouching low, she—at least I thought the vampire was female—scooped a handful of ash in one gloved hand and sniffed.

What the hell?

I'd learned about vampires in school—their origins, diet, hunting patterns, tracking abilities, that sort of thing. None of the lessons included anything about one smelling the remains of another.

A second vampire, this one male, joined the first.

There were a lot of hand gestures exchanged, but I was too far away to hear the accompanying conversation. It seemed like they were bickering. Then again, maybe vampires always looked annoyed when they talked to one another. My knowledge of vampires was entirely from school, not experience.

The male raised his wrist to his mouth, presumably speaking into some sort of communication device. The woman's watchful gaze panned the beach. My breath caught in my throat when she stopped and narrowed her eyes in my direction. *Can she see me?* She sniffed the air. *That's right. Follow my scent. Away from the cave.*

"Faeling," she sang sweetly, the wind carrying her voice to my ears.

Not the wind. Too far, I decided, recalling Elder Gacey saying something about how some vampires were able to project their voices into the minds of their prey. *Is that what's happening?*

"Come out, sweet faeling. Don't make Auntie Liza come find you," continued the female vampire. Liza turned to face her male companion. He stroked her cheek with the back of one finger. The gesture was both intimate and nauseating. He leaned closer as if to kiss her.

Really? Right now? Just follow my scent already!

Then, in a blink-and-you'll-miss-it instant, Liza was pinned on her back. The other vampire's hands encircled her long, pale throat.

My hand wasn't fast enough to cover the gasp that escaped my lips. Terror held me captive. Neither vampire glanced in my direction. The male ran his fingertips across the ground and then brought them to his lips.

From such a distance, it was hard to know for sure, but I thought he might've tasted something. The ashes?

"That child," the male thundered. "She incinerated my brother. My *brother*, Liza."

His voice wasn't in my head, I was almost certain. It sounded as though he was right in front of me, yelling in my face instead of Liza's. I swore I could feel his cool breath wash over my cheek.

"Mat...please...." Her voice was strained, like her vocal chords were being crushed.

Still straddling Liza, the male straightened and shouted, managing to sound both furious and seductive at the same time. "Hear me, faeling! Hear me now! You murdered my brother. There is nowhere you can hide that I will not find you, nowhere you can run that I will not follow. Your blood is mine!" Mat's roar sent shockwaves rippling through the air. Even the ground seemed to tremble with his ire.

The male yanked Liza from the ground by her neck and shook her like a ragdoll. Either she was too scared, or he was too strong, because Liza didn't fight back. My throat felt tight, like his hand was crushing my windpipe instead of hers.

Is that possible? Is he using her as a proxy?

Vampires didn't wield magic, only fae and casters did. But I had heard tales of powerful casters who'd retained their magic even after their conversion to a vampire. Had the male been a warlock before turning vampire?

"Hear me, faeling! Your magic will be mine!" Mat screamed, slamming Liza against the frozen earth.

Air fled my lungs in a rush as though the wind had

been knocked out of me, yet I was still crouched in the same patch of seagrass. The male was definitely a warlock/vampire hybrid. That fact diminished my odds of survival significantly.

Just let it be worth it. If Sienna and Gregory live and remain free through the night, whatever happens to me will be worth it.

The male turned and started back toward the caravan as Liza struggled to sit up. Another set of headlights appeared around the bend behind the parked truck. The new vehicle stopped beside the first and two vampires emerged from the passenger side. One unhooked a metal lasso from his waist and with a flick of his wrist sent it arcing through the air. A clanging noise pierced the night.

"What's this 'bout a fire faeling?" he called. "Don't tell me y'all can't wrangle a child?"

"Be serious, Rican," Mat snapped. "I am in no mood for your jokes."

Rican laughed. "Don't sink your fangs into my ass just because your brother got himself crisped."

The hybrid ripped the metal lasso from Rican's hand. "This is not a toy." He threw the chain back at Rican. "You and your brother go north. Liza and I will take south. If you two morons find her first, give a shout."

They don't know about Sienna and Gregory, I thought with some relief. *Sienna must've gotten by the caravan.*

"I can handle a faeling," Rican replied, all traces of his earlier amusement gone.

"This one's different," Mat said grimly.

He and Liza began moving in my direction, their eyes sweeping the beach steadily. *Time's up. Act now, Brie.*

My hiding place was about to be exposed. I had one

more trick up my sleeve. Otherwise, there was no choice but to fight.

All fae had the ability to cast spells, just like witches and warlocks. The difference was in the source of our magic. Fae magic came from nature, from the elements. It was powerful but limited in many ways because we could only harness one of the elements. Caster magic came from within, giving them access to a much broader range of abilities. But their magic came at a price. Every time they cast a spell or brewed a potion, a piece of their magic, and themselves, was lost.

Taking a deep breath, I mouthed a quick prayer to Gaia, asking for strength and speed. Then, I scooped two handfuls of wet sand as I stood and summoned my magic.

With the power of all four fire moons aiding me, I was soon holding two perfect glass orbs with flames swirling inside. I murmured an incantation beneath my breath, "Sparkdium perpetual."

Please work.

I hurdled both balls at the same time. They exploded twenty yards to the south of me, thousands of shimmery pebbles hanging in midair like frozen raindrops.

Vampires were known for having notoriously short attention spans and a tendency toward distraction. Mat and Liza didn't debunk the stereotype. They sprinted toward the spectacle, gazes fixed on the beautiful lightshow.

As soon as they were past my hiding spot I bolted north. With their heightened senses, they must have heard the slap of rubber against hard ground, but they didn't give chase. I stuck close to the highway, as Rican and his brother zoomed past in the opposite direction, hurrying to join their associates at the fiery display.

Adrenaline masked the pain in my legs, but the frigid air felt like shards of glass in my throat and lungs as I ran for my life—or at least my freedom. Still, I didn't slow…until I reached the parked vehicles.

I'd made Sienna promise that she wouldn't stop for anything. Not until she rang the alarm bell. That alarm bell was still miles away, at the top of Fae Canyon. And yet, I couldn't tear my gaze from the trucks. Fae were inside. Fae who the vampires would sell into service. Fae who needed help.

Sienna and Gregory need your help.

But my friends were still free. They still had a chance of escape. The fae inside those trucks did not. I couldn't leave them.

Crouching beside one of the truck's enormous tires, I peered around the rear bumper. All four vampires were still standing in a semicircle around the suspended drops. Liza tapped one with her nail and watched as it shattered in a million more crystalline orbs.

"Spread out, fools," Mat bellowed, though he seemed just as transfixed as the others. "The child must be close."

My hands and feet had a mind of their own. I was standing on the back bumper of the truck, fingers fumbling with the door latch before I appreciated what I was doing. By then it was too late for second thoughts. The vampires must have been in a hurry because the lock was undone.

Why didn't the captives just push it open and run?

Once the heavy doors were open, I understood. Twenty fae, of varying ages and sexes, were chained together in the metal compartment. Thick lassos were cinched around each fae's waist. Some of the captives were bloody and bruised, while others appeared relatively unscathed. The sight made me heave.

"Do you have the keys?" a woman asked me, her voice high-pitched and tinged with panic.

With my hand pressed to my lips, as though that might help keep the bile down, I shook my head. I swallowed hard, and managed to say, "I can maybe melt the chains. I'm weak, but I'll give it a try."

"Won't work," croaked an elderly man near the back. Blood ran freely down his face from a gash in his forehead. "The chains are warded with strong caster spells. It's going to take more than one fire faeling to melt them."

Smooth metal brushed my cheek as the lasso slid over my head from behind. Pain shot from my navel through to my spine. I was jerked backward, my legs flipping up over my head as I somersaulted through the air. By some miracle, I landed on my feet and dropped immediately to a crouch, prepared to charge at the first vampire I saw.

I barreled into Liza, catching her in the stomach with my shoulder. She emitted a surprised gasp as we fell to the pavement, me on top. The punches weren't pretty or proper, but they were effective. I struck her over and over again, all the while thinking of Sienna sprinting for help. *Buy her time.* I thought of Gregory huddled in the cave where we'd enjoyed so many nights, with only the hope of help on the way keeping him from full-blown hysteria.

Don't let them find him.

I saw my brother's little face, his thumb between his lips. *He's just a child.* And my father, he was too proud to let any vampire take him anywhere. He would die before he gave his blood or his magic to anyone.

"You can't have them!" I screamed, the words clawing at my throat. And then, my blows were no longer connecting. I was suspended in midair, just like the drops I had conjured, and staring down at Liza's battered face.

"You are a fiery one, aren't you, faeling?" Mat said, sounding almost impressed.

Below me, Liza's split lip knitted back together, but blood continued to pour from her mouth. Mat bent low and stared back and forth between Liza and me. "You are the pointy-eared brat who killed my brother, yes? The fire faeling?"

I said nothing, afraid he might drain me right then and there, both as revenge for his brother and because drinking my blood would enhance his vampire abilities and his caster magic.

"I will take your silence as an admission." He grinned. "So young and so accomplished." He knelt so that we were at eye level. "In one night, you kill one vampire and render another impotent."

My glare faltered. Impotent? What did he mean? Liza's bruises and cuts were healed. All she'd truly lost was pride.

Mat's keen vampire eyes missed nothing. "Her fangs, faeling. You broke her fangs. A vampire is dead without her fangs and no one to hunt for her."

"Mat, no!" Liza wailed. Her long, pointy nails flashed

crimson in the moon's glow as she lashed up at me. I braced for a blow that never came.

Mat's fingers encircled her wrist, those razor-sharp nails millimeters from slicing open my cheek. "Sorry, love. The child is a precious commodity." He grinned at me again, exposing his fangs. Instinctively, I recoiled. "Ah, so you do know fear. You are smart as well as gifted." Shaking his head sadly, he added, "If Queen Lilli was not offering so much for one with your abilities, I would keep you for myself. The blood tribute will be a nice consolation prize."

Queen Lilli?

Her seat of power was an island in the Pacific Ocean, which was not the closest domed kingdom to Fae Canyon. That was Los Angeles. The realization brought on a fresh wave of fear. How would I ever make it back to my family with a frozen ocean between us?

Mat's long fingers transferred from Liza's wrist to my throat. I felt a stab of pressure but had no trouble breathing. And then, I felt nothing.

Sienna and Gregory are safe at least, I told myself as consciousness faded.

It didn't matter whether that was true. I needed to believe the lie if I was going to survive what came next.

CHAPTER ONE

Present Day Dome▪ Islan▪ of Oahu, King▪om of the Americas

"BRIE! BRIE! BRIE!"

Energy pulsed through the arena stands in the Royal Coliseum. Despite the hollowness in my gut, I flashed a toothy grin for the dozens of shutter pixies circling for the money shot as I prepared to claim my victory. My opponent, a male were-liger, limped toward me for what would no doubt be the final play of the match. Pain glistened in his dark eyes, and I felt a pang in my heart.

Forfeit, Rocko, I thought.

In that moment we were opponents, but outside the arena we were friends. To an outsider, the dynamic might have been confusing or nonsensical, but those friendships were our way of rebelling against the casters—against the royal family who used our blood for profit and sport.

Come on, Rocko. Forfeit.

Male pride, particularly among shifters, was a funny thing. Bloodied, bruised, and all but defeated, the were-liger preferred losing in battle over taking the—in his view—coward's way out. Cursing Rocko's ego, I crouched low and charged.

Maybe fae pride is a funny thing, too, I thought, because I preferred my victory pure, as opposed to finishing him off with magic. That would have been the easy way out.

"Brie! Brie! Brie!"

Rocko and I clashed in midair, a tangle of long limbs and matted fur. We crashed to the grassy earth. Rocko snarled and snapped, but his sharp incisors only grazed my flesh. He was weak and losing steam fast.

"Brie! Brie! Brie!"

We began to roll, tufts of dirt and grass and liger hair flying up around us. He was pure muscle, heavy. When Rocko pinned me beneath his weight, a collective "oooh" went up in the stands. It felt like a dragon had his foot on my chest—a sensation I knew firsthand since three of the fire breathers were regular fighters.

The odds on me just got shorter, I thought wryly, imagining all the money the gamblers would lose if Rocko won. For a second, the arm I had around the liger's throat loosened.

Are you crazy? There is honor in losing justly, but not in throwing a fight.

I wrapped my legs around Rocko's waist, my ankles

barely crisscrossing, and squeezed with both my thighs and my arm.

"Down but never out, folks," the announcer sang as Rocko's consciousness waned, and he slowly transformed in my steel embrace.

"Brie! Brie! Brie!"

Clinging to his last shreds of awareness, the were-liger batted the ground three times and then went limp in my arms.

I'm going to pass out, I thought. The edges of my vision darkened.

"It is official, ladies and gentlemen," the announcer declared. "Maybrie of the Fae has just won her one hundredth battle at the Royal Colosseum!"

One hundred? I thought with wonder. Though it sounded like so many, it felt like I'd fought even more.

With my victory official, two medics rushed from the sidelines to attend to Rocko. It took all three of us to roll him off me.

"Are you okay, Ms. Brie?" one of the medics asked. "Do you need an energy boost?"

I gulped air greedily but managed to shake my head. "No, thank you. I'm fine…." The girl's name was on the tip of my tongue, but my oxygen-deprived brain couldn't quite recall it. *Janis? Jenny? Jacqulyn?*

"Joanna, Ms. Brie. The name is Joanna," she supplied. I felt horrible for forgetting. Joanna knelt beside Rocko, a syringe in one hand, and injected him with a revival potion.

A tremor ran through Rocko's limbs. His eyes popped open, and he offered me a lazy smile. "Congrats, Brie," he mumbled as he began checking over his scrapes and bruises.

"Good match, Rocko. It was a tough win," I admitted and held out my hand.

Shutter pixies swarmed us, capturing the sports-womanly gesture and projecting the image onto the jumbotron floating overhead.

"In honor of her centennial win, His Royal Highness Prince Kai wishes to present Maybrie of the Fae with a special present," the announcer boomed.

At this declaration, the image on the jumbotron switched to the Royal Box. Prince Kai sat on his redwood throne. His sister, the princess Sarah, perched on her own throne beside him. Queen Lilli, I noted, was absent.

Smug, entitled, caster, prick, I thought.

Prince Kai was heir to the Kingdom's Throne of Winter. He acted as though his mother's crown was already atop his head, at least when it came to the perks of being a ruler. Politics? Responsibilities? Day-to-day squabbles between the races? Not so much.

"Would you like to see a healer for that?" Joanna asked, gesturing to the three gashes on my left forearm where Rocko's claws had penetrated the skin.

The wounds were deep and bleeding freely. Adrenaline masked the pain, but once it wore off…well, I would be waiting tables at Pele's with one arm. But the injury would heal quickly enough. The royal family regulated fighters' diets, which included pineapple shakes with a powdered infusion that sped the healing process. At first, I resented the mandated meals, but admittedly the free food was a major perk of the job.

"Nah, the cream you have should be good," I told Joanna.

She bit her lip. "Ms. Brie...." She began but was too nervous to voice her thought aloud.

"I'm fine." I gave her the same smile I always wore in the arena—the fake one that I'd practiced in the mirror every day since arriving in Hawaii.

Joanna returned the gesture with a genuine grin and removed a jar of green ointment from the belt at her waist. The cream stung as I dabbed it over the wound. I gritted my teeth and willed the sensation to pass.

"Congratulations on your centennial victory," a deep voice interrupted.

A shadow fell over me, and I looked up to find Prince Kai staring down at me. He offered me his hand. I pushed off the ground and stood on my own. The prince tried to hide a smile. Overhead, the jumbotron showed the entire scene for the spectators.

"Brie! Brie! Brie!"

"They adore you," Prince Kai said quietly. "You are a fan favorite."

I said nothing. My "fans" were fickle creatures. If I won, they adored me. But if I fell from the podium, they would shift their loyalties to the new champion before I hit the ground.

Five feet away, the male medic was helping Rocko to his feet. The were-liger's body was covered in a rainbow of ointments, all meant to numb the pain of his injuries. He limped over to where Prince Kai and I stood. The prince cleared his throat, and when he spoke next, his voice filled the colosseum.

"Maybrie of the Fae, it is my honor to present to you the orange hibiscus." The prince handed me a small, white box with the royal family's crest on top.

"Thank you, Your Highness," I said, lowering my eyes as I accepted the box.

I eased open the top and nearly gasped when I saw the blood-orange petals covered in a layer of frost. Absently, I stroked the frozen petals with my fingertips. *Home.* That was my first thought, but it was quickly overshadowed by the power radiating from the flower. It was imbued with a spell and…magic. Caster magic. And a lot of it.

"This is a very nice gift. You shouldn't have. Really," I muttered so low only the prince could hear me.

Prince Kai's dark eyes glanced passed me, and the image on the jumbotron switched to the crowd. When he spoke, his voice was no longer magnified. "The royal family likes to express their gratitude to those who have served us faithfully," he said quietly.

I gritted my teeth at "served us faithfully." It was meant as a compliment, but to me it was a reminder fae were considered lesser than casters. Oddly, I also felt a pang of guilt. I was not faithful to the royal family. I had never been faithful to the royal family. Originally, I fought because they made me. But I'd won more than enough fights, and more than enough prize money, to leave the pits in my past. I continued to fight because I was good. And the money—that was still a big motivator for me.

"And you, Brie," Prince Kai continued, oblivious to my inner musings, "have proven your loyalty."

"I do receive a percentage of the bets, in addition to the winner's purse," I replied.

The prince smiled. "I know, but…." He trailed off as though worried whatever he'd been about to say might come across as offensive.

"What?" I asked, shifting uncomfortably under his scrutinizing gaze.

Prince Kai gave an embarrassed little laugh. "Nothing. I apologize. It is just that from what I am told, I am surprised to hear that you fight for personal wealth."

I swallowed thickly and forced a tight smile. "No offense, Your Highness, but you don't know me. I happen to like my condo, which I own. I happen to enjoy the sushi at Taste of Tokyo and the wine at Vino Noir and clothes from the boutiques on Fae Avenue, none of which are cheap."

The prince's eyes narrowed suspiciously.

"Thank you again for the flower," I continued. "It's beautiful."

"You are very welcome." For another awkward moment, Prince Kai stared at me as though studying a plant he was having trouble classifying. "Would you have dinner at the palace tonight?" he blurted.

Five feet away, Rocko snorted but hid his laughter behind a large hand.

"My mother would love to honor you in person," the prince added. It sounded like an afterthought, an excuse.

Then she should have come to the fight, I thought wryly.

"I have to work but thank you for the invitation. Please pass my gratitude along to the queen."

"Work?" Prince Kai's eyes went wide. "You have another job?"

The question sounded like a polite inquiry, but it felt

personal, like he was prying into my private affairs.

"I do," I said simply. "Now, if you will excuse me, I would really like to shower." Dried blood had crusted on my arm, blades of grass clung to my hair like green extensions, and dirt mixed with sweat on my clothes and face. I'd seen my image on the jumbotron, and it wasn't pretty.

"Of course, of course. How rude of me." Prince Kai smiled that winning smile that enthralled so many of his subjects. "I am sure we will see each other again soon, Maybrie. Until then, be well."

The saying was customary, a phrase uttered by the baristas who mixed my morning latte and one I said to my patrons after they paid the check. But coming from Prince Kai's lips, it sounded…different. Intimate. It sounded intimate, I decided. I didn't like it.

According to the rumor mill, Queen Lilli wanted her son and heir to marry sooner rather than later. And, if the gossip columns were to be believed, she wanted him to marry a fae. Which made a certain amount of sense. Casters could take magic from fae, but only if we shared it freely. There were loopholes, spells that could get around that pesky requirement, but then the magic was tainted, ugly. Any fae who married the prince and became his princess would share her magic willingly with him. And if they fell in love, the magical bond between them would be that much stronger.

I felt a jab in my lower back. Rocko had moved to stand behind me. He nodded pointedly at the prince, who was staring at me expectantly. "Um, you as well, Your Highness," I managed.

The prince took my hand and bowed low, brushing a kiss over my dirt-streaked knuckles. For some reason, I shivered. When Prince Kai released me, I turned and followed Rocko out of the main arena to the locker rooms.

"Better be careful, B," Rocko teased. "That royal warlock has his eye on you now."

I rolled my eyes. "Don't even joke. Besides, even if he does marry a fae, he won't choose a fighter. I mean, come on." I gestured to my torn tank and ruined shorts. "This doesn't quite stack up to the gowns worn by the girls at Madame Noelani's."

Madame Noelani's Academy touted itself as a finishing school for exceptional fae. But the students weren't taught to use their magic or spell work—only witches and warlocks learned spell casting in the kingdoms. Instead, Madame Noelani's fae were taught elaborate dances, to play an instrument, a variety of languages spoken around the world, and the art of romance. All of these lessons served to make them suitable companions for wealthy casters.

"I don't know," Rocko said, expression serious. "Prince Love 'Em and Leave 'Em can have any female he wants—witch, fae, vampire—"

"And he has," I interjected.

"—shifter, whatever," Rocko finished as though I hadn't said anything. "If I were him, I'd want my wife to be…fiery."

My hand was on the door to the female locker room. "Pun intended?" I deadpanned.

Rocko laughed. "Yeah. I mean, he does need someone

to keep him warm when he travels outside the dome."

I pushed the door open and put one foot inside. "And on that note, I'm leaving now."

"See you tonight at Hideout?" he called after me.

"Yeah, I'll swing by after my shift," I said right before the door swung shut.

Mine was the last fight of the day, and because female fighters were less common than males, the locker room was blissfully quiet. After the noise of the arena, and the eyes of the spectators, solitude was welcome.

I found my locker and muttered, "Reserasseum." The door sprang open, and I reached for my towel. I was just about to tuck the box with the hibiscus on the top shelf when I noticed another box in the locker.

"What the hell?" I muttered.

Using a locking spell instead of a physical lock should've kept most anyone out. The only exceptions were possibly another fire fae or a very good caster. Few witches and warlocks would waste power breaking into a locker, particularly since nothing appeared to have been taken.

This box was bright blue with a silver ribbon tied in a neat bow. A small, white card hung from a thin string. I ripped it off and read the one line: "Champions deserve gold." That was it. No names, not even mine. I gripped the box between both hands and concentrated. There were no spells or enchantments within it—that was a relief.

Tentatively, I fingered the silky ribbon. *Do it. Just like ripping off a bandage.* When I flipped open the lid, I held my breath and flinched, still half-expecting the contents to explode in my face. Inside, nestled in a bed of white silk, was a delicate white-gold bangle. Upon closer inspection, I noticed tiny rose-gold hibiscuses along either side. With that, I knew who'd sent the gift.

"Prince Kai," I whispered. "You presumptuous ass."

I shook my head and returned the bangle to the box. *First thing tomorrow, that is going back,* I thought. Putting the box back on the shelf, I slammed the door shut. Annoyed, I ran one finger down the cool metal of the locker and muttered, "Claudere."

A gold bangle? Do I look like the gold bangle type? Is it the dirt beneath my nails or the grass stains on my knees that he finds so alluring? And seriously, breaking into my locker? Am I supposed to find that sweet? Because minor criminal acts are definitely not sweet.

I ranted to myself, mumbling aloud occasionally, as I stomped to the showers. I was not the first female fighter to catch the prince's eye. In the five years I'd lived beneath the dome and fought in the arena, the heir apparent had wooed an overwhelming majority of us. I probably should've been less surprised by the overture itself and more surprised that it'd taken Prince Kai so long to turn his affections my way.

Lost in my own head, it wasn't until I turned off the water that I heard the sobs. "Hello?" I called loudly. "Who's here?"

A loud hiccup preceded more sobs, muffled this time as though the crier was holding something over her mouth. I wrapped a robe around myself and followed the sounds, as well as the trail of towels and random articles of clothing flying around the locker room. The commotion was coming from the back corner, near the saunas and whirlpools. Unsecured locker doors banged open and shut as the sobs grew louder again.

I had a feeling I knew who was behind the windstorm, even before I found her curled into a small ball in the back row of lockers.

"Sumi?" I said her name quietly, not wanting to startle her.

The air fae had a hand towel pressed against her lips, and she rocked back and forth. Blue-black hair hung around her face, and one hand cupped the side of her neck, kneading the skin like dough. Her bright-green eyes flitted in my direction.

"Maybrie!" Sumi's delicate features screwed into a grimace. "I'm so sorry to have bothered you."

"You didn't," I promised, easing down on the bench in front of her. "I know how hard it can be to control the magic when you're upset." I was big on personal space, so I didn't touch the young fae. "Do you want to talk about it?" I asked softly.

Sumi's pale face still bore signs from her early morning fight. A bruise had formed around her right eye, and through a rip in her shirt I saw stitches along her ribcage. But something told me that her tears had nothing to do with her injuries.

Sumi wiped her runny nose with the back of one hand. "I'm being dramatic," she said, not meeting my gaze. "I am fine. It's sweet of you to ask, but there is really nothing to discuss." She pulled harder at the soft skin on her throat.

"I was taken by vampires, too," I admitted.

That fateful night was not something I talked about. Ever. After a few beers at Hideout, my friends swapped stories about their captures, about how they'd come to live beneath the dome. Not me. Never me. The night Mat and his crew stole me away from Fae Canyon, from my family and friends, was one I would carry with me always. But the story, *my* story, was personal. I didn't know precisely why I was willing to share part of it with Sumi. Maybe because, like me, she'd been taken as a teen. Maybe because the way she rubbed the spot where she'd been bitten, even though the marks were long since gone, was a familiar gesture—one I still performed on sleepless nights when I was alone in my bed.

"How did you know?" she asked, those green irises shimmering with unshed tears.

I touched my own neck, two inches below my ear where Mat had bitten me and taken his payment from my blood. "I would like to tell you that the memory fades just like the marks, but I'm not in the habit of lying. It does get easier, though." I paused, not sure how much to pry. Wounded fae, just like wounded animals, needed time and patience before letting their guard down. Press them too hard too soon, and they could lash out. When Sumi didn't respond, I changed the subject. "But hey, I saw your fight today. You were amazing."

The younger girl gave me a small smile, and I noticed her bottom lip was swollen and starting to bruise. "Thank you. That means a great deal from someone like you."

"I'm meeting up with a couple of the other fighters at this placed called Hideout tonight. Maybe you'd wanna

SOPHIE DAVIS

come?"

Hope filled the young teen's face, but then her expression fell. "I live at the commune," she said, plucking at a loose thread on the hand towel. "We have a curfew."

Those recently transported to the domed island were housed in the commune, where guards and house mothers and fathers watched their charges' every move. Log records monitored entry and exit times, and the rooms were equipped with audio listening devices to check for whispered talk of rebellion. Only after a transplant to the dome had proved they weren't a threat and had no plans for escape was the individual allowed to move to a private dwelling. Even still, the illusion of freedom was not true freedom.

"Maybe next time," Sumi was saying.

"Not so fast." I grinned at the young fae. "Can you be ready at ten?"

"But, how?" Sumi asked, a delicate wrinkle appearing between her brows.

"Let's just say I know a guy...."

50

CHAPTER TWO

PELE'S PIT WAS one of the few fae owned and oper-ated businesses under the dome. Located on the outskirts of the city, it catered to an eclectic clientele from all walks of life. It was one of the few places where shifters ate alongside vampires, and casters shared booths with fae. I had started out busing tables there at sixteen to fill my down time between fights. Pele's owner, an earth fae named Jon, had promoted me to a waitress not long after.

"You sure you don't want to leave the pits and come manage this hole?" Jon grumbled for the thousandth time as he peered through the pass-through window at me.

I grabbed two tuna steak dinners. "You couldn't

afford me, old man."

"Ain't that the truth," he called in a gravelly voice. "But you don't fool me, Brie. You don't fight in the pits for the paycheck, and we both know it."

I bumped the swinging kitchen door with my hip and stuck my tongue out at Jon. "You're right, I do it for the clothes."

It was an old joke. Jon had never understood why I'd never traded bruises for ball gowns and accepted Madame Noelani's offer of enrollment at her finishing school. When I was nursing broken ribs or covered in a full body bruise, I sometimes wondered the same thing. Then I remembered—the idea of an arranged marriage of magical convenience made me queasy.

"One tuna steak, rare, with pineapple fries," I said, placing the plate before a were-bear who worked construction outside the dome. "And one tuna steak, well-done, with broccoli casserole," I added, setting the second dish in front of the petite fae across from him. "Anything else I can get for you two?"

"No thanks, Brie. This looks great," the were-bear said, his voice deep with a thick southern accent. He was older and had been a patron of Pele's longer than I'd been working there, but that accent was as constant as his long, black beard. Though there was quite a bit more white hair threaded through it now than when I'd first met him.

"Hey! You!" A pretty blonde fae in the next booth over snapped her fingers at me. "We need refills. Your tip is so seriously going to suffer."

"Give 'em hell, girl," the were-bear chuckled, noticing

the way my fists clenched at my sides.

"Enjoy, guys," I said to my current table, and headed over to the blonde and her friends. "Sorry about that. Busy night," I told them, trying to sound at least a little apologetic. I gathered up their glasses and started to turn.

"Don't mix those up," said one of the girls, her nostrils flaring as though the idea of inadvertently sharing a glass with one of her friends was more disgusting than toe fungus.

"Yeah," added the blonde. "I mean, hello, *germs*."

"I have a good memory," I replied.

"Doubtful," the blonde snickered under her breath.

"Excuse me?" I rounded on the table of catty girls, remembering another reason I'd never become one of Madame Noelani's students.

The blonde snapped her gum, and I started wondering when the finishing school had gone downhill. Much as I disagreed with the premise, Madame Noelani's pupils were taught to be ladies and gentlemen, to become a part of high society. These fae were something but definitely not ladies.

"If you had any brains, you wouldn't be serving fried grease to freaks," the gum-snapper said, enunciating each word as though I was hard of hearing, as well as stupid.

"Kaleen," hissed the girl beside her. "Don't you know who that is?"

Kaleen—definitely not her given name, but the one assigned to her at the finishing school as part of assimilation training—rolled her big, blue eyes. "Nobody, that's who."

"I apologize for my friend," said the other girl, a soft-spoken brunette. "She's had a trying day."

At least one of you pays attention in etiquette class, I thought.

"You never apologize to servants, Lani," Kaleen chastised.

Her friend ignored her and focused on me. "I attended the fights today. Your performance was unequalled. And I thought the prince's gift very thoughtful." She lowered her gaze. "Few would think of giving one of us a small piece of home in such a beautiful way. Or at all," she added quietly.

Beside her, Kaleen paled. "You're Maybrie? But you're, like, one of the wealthiest fighters in the kingdom. Why are you serving like a common fae?"

Girls like Kaleen, those desperate for acceptance into a society that was not ours, often said fae like it was a dirty word or an insult. I was proud to be fae, and I didn't have the patience for stuck up self-haters.

Around us, Pele's had gone quiet and still. Jon appeared beside me, four takeout containers piled in his large hands and his cooking apron still tied around his waist. "Ladies, it's your lucky night. Meals are on the house." He set the stack on the table. "Just do me a favor and don't come back."

Kaleen looked as though she wanted to argue, but between the face tattoos and his icy glare, she didn't dare cross Jon.

Lani shoved Kaleen out of the booth. "My apologies, sir," she said. Then, in a much louder voice, "And to the rest of you, I do hope this scene has not ruined your meals." She tried to hand me a tip, but I waved it off.

"No need. Just get your friend home safely." One

whiff of Kaleen as she passed, and I had smelled the alcohol. The brunette's gaze widened as she collected the takeout containers. "I have no interest in reporting you." Recreational drinking was strictly forbidden at Madame Noelani's Academy.

"Thank you," the girl whispered, and the foursome hurried out the front door.

"You okay?" Jon asked once they were gone.

I rolled my eyes. "Sticks and stones."

His large hand came to rest on my shoulder. "Sometimes I think it's backward for you, Brie."

The rest of my shift was uneventful. Three were-lions who trained fighters for the pits stopped in and left me a big tip, which was nice. A vampire sat in my section for two hours sipping bloody cocktails and staring out the window, which was normal. And quite a few patrons made a point to congratulate me on my big win. It was nice, if not a little embarrassing; of all my reasons for fighting, glory had never been one of them.

Once off the clock, I changed in Jon's office, swapping my khaki shorts and Pele's Pit t-shirt with the erupting volcano on the back, for a pair of dark skinny jeans and a white halter top. I hollered goodbye to Jon and the kitchen staff and caught a cab to meet my friends at Hideout.

I'd forgotten my phone at home, but I knew the gang would already be at the bar. It was fight night, after all. We always went to Hideout on fight nights. Of course, I hadn't counted on everyone else under the dome being there, too. Hideout was popular, but not usually packed to capacity.

The line was around the corner when I arrived just before ten. Fae, shifters, vampires, and a few of the more adventurous casters waited as the bouncer strictly enforced the one-out, one-in rule, only implemented on particularly busy weekend nights. An alarming number of the females wore slinky dresses—Hideout was more shorts and tanks than silks and ties. Suddenly, I felt underdressed in my jeans.

Who're you trying to impress? I walked to the front of the velvet rope and flashed a smile.

"Hey, Brie. Great fight today," said one of the bouncers, an-ex fighter named Falcon. "Rocko's already inside trying to forget his loss."

I laughed. "Sounds about right. Look, I hate to ask this…." I glanced at the long line of eager partiers. "But I have a friend coming soon. She'll be with Kenoa. He's helping me—"

"Already on the list," Falcon said, cutting me off with a wave. "Name's Sumi, right?" he added, noticing my confused expression.

"Yeah, that's right. How did you know?" I hadn't thought to call ahead, and Kenoa wouldn't have either. There was no need, since we both knew all the bouncer and never waited in line.

"Prince Kai put them on when he arrived," Falcon told me.

Realization dawned. The extremely long line and the over-the-top outfits instantly made sense. The prince didn't frequent Hideout, but when he decided to put in an appearance, the magical community came out in full force to bear witness. I hated those nights.

"Why, Gaia? Why?" I said, eyes rolling toward the sky—or, well, the top of the dome where millions of stars twinkled like the night sky.

Falcon laughed. "Come on, Brie. He's good for business." He unhooked the rope and gestured me through. "Rocko and the gang are on the second level, usual table. Drink one for me."

The first floor of Hideout was packed with sweaty bodies gyrating in time to the beat. Despite the clearly posted signs that warned all magic use and enchantments were prohibited, glasses floated freely beside their drinkers and more than a handful of dancers were sporting actual beer goggles. Laughing at their stilted movements, I shook my head and squeezed through the sea of hormones and body odor to the staircase.

As promised, Rocko and my other friends were at our usual spot, a curved booth overlooking the dance floor. I was still two tables away when the group of fighters stood and started clapping. Heads turned in their direction.

Cala, a were-jag and one of the few female fighters in our group of regulars, gestured toward me. "Give our girl Brie a hand, folks!" she cried.

By the time I reached our table, the entire second floor was standing and applauding. "I really hate you guys," I grumbled as I slid in beside Cala.

She laughed and plopped down on the cushioned bench. "It's a big achievement, Brie."

"Yeah, B," chimed in a were-bear named Rudy as he handed me a glass across the table. "Not many fae live long enough to compete in one hundred matches, let alone *win* a hundred matches." He winked and raised his drink in cheers.

Just when I'd resigned myself to toasting with the beer, an auburn-haired cocktail waitress appeared. "For Luck's Sake for our champion," Everly said, placing the glass in my hand.

"You're the best," I told her.

"Tell that to the losers at the corner booth." She rolled her caramel-colored eyes. "They keep spilling their drinks and blaming me."

"Want me to rough them up?" I offered, only half kidding.

She shook her head. "Nah. They're friends with Clive. He might dock my pay to cover their hospital bills." Clive was the were-lion owner of Hideout. "I'll be back by in a little while to chat. You guys have fun." She blew a kiss toward the right corner of the booth, where Rocko caught it and pressed his hand to his heart.

"Too precious," Cala drawled.

"Hey, guys," I said loudly so the whole table would hear me. "No jokes about fae dying in the pits once Sumi arrives, okay?"

"Sumi?" Rudy reached for a handful of dill popcorn from the bowl in the center of the table. "She the new girl? The air fae from Japan?"

I nodded, taking a sip through the cocktail straw in my drink.

"Poor thing," Cala said. "She's only been here, what? Two weeks?"

"Something like that," I agreed.

I was glad I'd spoken up when I did. A second later,

Kenoa and Sumi appeared on the second-floor landing. Kenoa was a water fae and a native islander. As a former fighter, his shoulders were as wide as Sumi was tall. Standing together, they looked like the odd couple. He pointed a meaty finger in our direction and rested his fingertips lightly on the small girl's back as he guided her our way.

"Night off, Ken?" Rudy asked the obvious. "What's the royal warlock gonna do without you?"

"Settle for his second favorite bodyguard," Kenoa replied dryly. Most of the fighters weren't huge fans of the royal family, or casters in general, so Kenoa's chosen profession wasn't one we normally discussed.

"He's here tonight," Rocko interjected, giving me a meaningful look that I ignored. "Rare for the pampered warlock to venture to these parts."

Kenoa's dark eyes landed on me, too. "The prince has his reasons," he said mildly.

Please don't be implying I'm a reason, I thought.

Cala and I scooted over, and I patted the bench for Sumi to sit. She waved shyly to the table as Kenoa pulled over a chair. The other guys were all shifters, and therefore the size of refrigerators, and only so many of us could fit in one booth.

"What's your poison?" Rocko asked Sumi as Kenoa grabbed a beer from the ice bucket closest to him.

"Poison?" Sumi glanced at me as though maybe she'd misheard him.

"What would you like to drink?" I clarified.

"Oh." She laughed, her pale cheeks turning bright red. "I am sorry. My English is not very good."

Rudy snorted. "You speak English better than anyone at this table, sweetheart. Don't apologize."

This only made the teenager blush harder. "Um, maybe a rum and coke? I do not drink. In my village…I saw that ordered once in a movie."

"Here, try this." I offered her my glass, and she took a tentative sip. "Oh, my. That is not," she shook her head as though to erase the taste from her memory, "to my liking. Not at all."

Rudy threw his head back and laughed. "Told you that girly nonsense you drink is awful."

"Just because it's pretty to look at, doesn't make the drink girly," I shot back.

Cala reached across me and handed Sumi her drink. "Here. This might be more for you."

Sumi was even more hesitant when she tried Cala's beverage, nervous after mine proved so unsatisfying. But she took a second sip and smacked her lips together lightly. "This is good."

My best friend smiled smugly. "See? Can't go wrong with the classics." No matter the bar, occasion, or time of day, Cala always drank champagne. She smiled at Sumi. "Want a glass of your own?"

"Please."

The night passed in a blur of okay music, good conversation, and bad jokes. Just like they did when I'd first arrived to the domed island, the shifters welcomed Sumi with open arms. I could tell she was surprised by the comradery within our group. It had been strange for me at first, too, the idea that in the arena we ripped each other to shreds—in some cases literally—but maintained friendships in the outside world. As late night dwindled into early morning, the petite teenager let down her guard and seemed to enjoy herself.

"You did a nice thing." Kenoa's deep voice in my ear caught me by surprise. Cala and Rudy had taken Sumi downstairs to dance. Rocko was outside spending Everly's break with her, and the other three—Lenny, Dylan, and Jefferey—were off looking for late-night companions. So, for the moment, it was just the two of us.

I nudged him playfully in the ribs. "I seem to recall once upon a time someone did the same for me, when I was new and spending my nights crying for home. Besides, she's so young."

"You were younger," Kenoa reminded me.

At fifteen, I'd been one of the younger fighters to enter the pits. Kenoa was the youngest. He'd been thirteen. For nearly a decade, he had reigned as King of the Ring. Just two years prior, Kenoa had finally retired and gone to work as Prince Kai's personal bodyguard. He certainly didn't need the income, though. In fact, the whole situation was something of a mystery. No one understood why the champion fighter had accepted the position.

"She'll be okay. Sumi's strong," I said with more confidence than I felt.

"She is," Kenoa agreed, nodding his giant head. "Only strong fae choose the fighting pits." He nudged my shoulder. "That's how I knew you'd be okay."

On the dance floor, a tall, well-dressed caster made his way to where Sumi and Cala jumped up and down offbeat to the music. Three men the size of Kenoa and one woman, who was easily over 6'3", trailed the warlock at a respectful distance. I shook my head when Prince Kai tilted his dark head of hair and, presumably, asked Sumi to dance. The tiny air fae's face flushed, and she giggled at the formality. But, instead of accepting the invitation as most girls would have, Sumi shook her head and refused.

I smiled. "Yeah, she made the right choice. There's no way Sumi would've made it at Madame Noelani's."

Calling it a "choice" was generous, laughable even. When I'd arrived on the island, the Director of Fae Relations, a caster named Akoni Akana, gave me several options of ways I could serve the kingdom. Not one of the options was to return home to Fae Canyon.

Madame Noelani deemed me pretty enough for her academy, so that was my first option. I turned down the offer immediately. Option two was House of Mana, where fae were well-compensated for sharing magic with the establishment's wealthy clientele. When I said *hell no*, Akoni Akana came at me with option three: house fae. A house fae shared their magic with an entire family, like a well that could be pumped whenever one of the members got a dry mouth. It was even less appealing than the previous two options. That left me with options four and five: hard labor on one of the non-domed islands or toilet duty at the palace.

None of those options seemed tolerable.

So, I had asked about the fighting pits. Akoni Akana had tried to warn me away, telling me all the dangers of the pits and predicting that I wouldn't last one fight. She said that shifters and vampires were too much for a little faeling like me to fight. But I'd made my choice, given the limited options. I'd never once regretted it.

"He's not so bad, you know," Kenoa said softly.

"Who?" I asked absently. My gaze was still on Sumi, and my mind still half in the past.

Some upbeat, fast-paced song came on, and Rudy grabbed Sumi's arm and started swinging her around wildly.

"Really, Brie? We're going to play this game?"

I turned to face Kenoa. "What game?"

The water fae snorted. "Whatever, Brie. Just keep an open mind." Sipping his beer, he kept his dark eyes on my lighter ones.

"Hey, there's no seriousness on celebration night." Kenoa and I both turned to find Rocko at the head of the table, hands on hips. "And you two are entirely too serious. You know what the penalty for that is, don't you?" He started imitating dances moves from the disco era. "Shots. Shots. Shots. Shots."

"Oh, Rocko, no," I groaned. "I'm beat. I was just—"

"No." He wiggled a finger in front of my face. "I'm the one who got beat today. Badly. So, you're buying. Fire & Ice shots all around."

I couldn't help it, I laughed. "Okay. But just one," I warned.

One turned into three. Naturally, our friends returned to the table for toasting the rounds. Even Everly snuck a shot when no one was looking, which probably meant the same table from earlier was still giving her trouble.

When Rocko tried to talk me into a Penicillin shot, I

took a stand for what was left of my sobriety. I shook my head firmly and regretted it immediately.

"I'm leaving," I announced.

"No," Rocko whined. "Just one more."

I placed a hand on his shoulder. "I fought today. Then, I worked a shift at Pele's. Now, I can barely keep my eyes open."

"Let her go." Everly stood over her boyfriend and swatted his head playfully. She smiled down at me. "Go. Be safe. Let me know when you get home."

"Thanks, Everly." I stood and hugged her carefully around the tray of empty glasses in her hand.

The corner table of assholes started shouting "Waitress!" through cupped hands.

"Duty calls." Everly rolled her eyes and went to attend to her customers.

I looked around the table. Only Rocko and Kenoa were present.

"Kenoa, could you—?"

I didn't even finish asking the question when Kenoa said, "I'll make sure Sumi gets back into the commune without any problems."

"You're the best."

Everly was standing next to the table of assholes. One made a comment about the length of her shorts. The pyramid of beer cans that spread across the entire table suddenly toppled. Before my best friend could do something that would surely get her fired, I summoned my magic and heated the metal cans, which were now littered across the assholes' laps.

Maybe a few holes in their clothes will teach them manners.

Their yelps were music to my ears as I exited Hideout.

There were many advantages to living beneath the dome, obviously. For most people, the consistently warm temperature was one of the biggest benefits. Not for me. Stepping out into the night air should give you goosebumps—something to indicate the temperature has dropped. It didn't. Not usually anyway. Maybe it was because I'd just used magic, or maybe Hideout was warmer than normal because of all the bodies inside, but I swore I felt a slight chill in the outside air. *Or maybe the Director of Dome Functions finally took all your comment cards to heart and programmed lower temperatures for late night.*

"Finally," I muttered when I saw headlights and the telltale taxi light in the distance.

The car slowed to a stop, and the driver rolled down the passenger window. "Where to?" His words cut off abruptly as he appraised me. "Never mind, fae."

The driver didn't even bother rolling up the window before speeding away, as if he couldn't wait to put miles of pavement between us.

"Jerk," I grumbled.

Behind me, loud laughter dwarfed the muffled music from Hideout. I spun to find a group of very drunk individuals stumbling my way. *Great,* I thought.

"What?" cackled a female caster. She eyed me through narrowed lids. "Stay among your own kind, and that wouldn't happen."

Still fired up from the jerks inside Hideout, I snapped back without thinking. "This is where 'my kind' congregate. You're the ones out of place."

The laugher died and the female caster took a step

toward me. "We are never out of place, *fae*." She jabbed a finger in my face. "You need to remember your place."

Suddenly feeling completely sober, I clenched my hands into fists. *Don't break her finger. Don't break her finger.*

Fae were only allowed to fight in the pits. Little squabbles and a few punches between fae or fae and shifters were tolerated. But a fae assaulting a caster outside of a bar? That would have consequences.

"It's too bad we can't go back to the days when all establishments were separate," her friend lamented. With the amount of product in his hair, he probably could've made his own weatherproof dome.

Walk away. Go home. I turned back around and searched in vain for another taxi.

"Yeah. At least fae knew their place then," one of them called, purposely pitching her voice so I had no choice but to hear.

Ignore them. Ignore them. Ignore them.

"Yeah, their place beneath us," said one of the guys. "Right, babe?"

Something about the way he said it gave me pause. I glanced over my shoulder and looked at the lone female who had yet to speak. My heart sank. She wasn't a caster. More than likely, she was one of Madame Noelani's graduates; the warlock with his arm around her shoulders reeked of wealth and privilege. I glanced at their hands, each wore a traditional wedding ring.

Poor girl, I thought. Once a fae agreed to marry a caster, there was no going back, not for Madame Noelani's students.

The girl said nothing in response to her husband's

asinine comment. More than anything, her silence set my teeth on edge. It wasn't that she couldn't speak her mind, but she would've been taught not to.

"Because you did such a bang-up job of taking care of your world without our help," I said.

"Look around you, fae," said the guy with too much hair gel. "Our world is just fine."

"Having to erect a dome is not 'just fine,'" I shot back.

One of the other guys snickered. "She just said 'erect.'"

The warlock with his arm around the fae removed it and walked toward me with slow, menacing steps. He pushed the female caster with the jabbing finger aside. "You have an awfully big mouth for a fae," he sneered. "You really should be more careful who you run it off to."

"You aren't the first jackass to make that suggestion," I volleyed.

Casters like this guy assumed they could say whatever they wanted to fae without consequence. Legally, that was true. But I was dangerously close to risking legal woes and handing out a little vigilante justice.

"Careful, fae," the caster warned. "You don't want to tango with me."

"Not if you were the last dance partner on this frozen planet," I replied cheekily.

"Watch yourself." The caster stepped even closer, until we were nearly nose-to-nose. "You obviously aren't aware of who I am. If so, you'd be a lot more respectful."

Doubtful, I thought. For better or worse, I never got the chance to say that aloud, because someone intervened.

"But you are not, clearly, aware of who she is," called

SOPHIE DAVIS

a deep voice from the shadows.

I knew even before he stepped into the light: Prince Kai.

Because another narcissistic warlock is just what this confrontation needs.

68

CHAPTER THREE

"YOUR HIGHNESS," said the over-gelled caster, bowing deeply to his prince.

"Oh, Prince Kai we heard you were—," the female caster began. The prince cut her off with the slight raise of his hand.

"Good evening, Your Highness," the fae's husband started. When the prince didn't interrupt, he pressed on, emboldened. "I don't know if you recall, but we met at the Sugarcane Ball last year. My name is Akamail Palakiko, and my parents are—"

"I know your parents well," the prince said flatly. "In fact, your mother recently performed an everlasting spell for me." His dark gaze landed on me. "It was quite impressive, at least in my humble opinion. Brie, what did you think of his mother's spell?"

The hibiscus. It had been enchanted, imbued with magic so that it would remain frozen in perpetuity. The spell was simple but impressive.

"I'm pleased with the results," I said.

Akamail paled. His skin took on an eerie glow in the manufactured moonlight. Bloodshot eyes looked from me to the prince and back again. "You're Maybrie of the Fae?" he stammered.

"Just Maybrie," I replied dryly.

"If I'd known…," he began.

"Ignorance is an excuse of the uneducated," Prince Kai said. "I'd venture to guess that you are extremely well educated."

I didn't bother hiding the snort of laughter. Prince Kai flashed me a smile. For that brief moment, we were coconspirators, and I despised him a little less.

"Your Highness, we were only—"

"Leaving," the prince interrupted. "You were only just leaving."

As if conjured by magic, a taxi appeared. The prince gestured to the vehicle. "I suggest you all depart before you say something else that you cannot take back."

The other casters hurried over to the taxi, but Akamail remained where he was for a moment longer. He bowed again to his prince and mumbled, "My apologies for my inexcusable behavior, Your Highness."

The prince laughed, though it was clear he found nothing about the situation amusing. "I am not the one you should be apologizing to." His eyes didn't stray from me. "Though, something tells me your words will fall on deaf ears."

Akamail turned to me, pride evident in his gaze. "My apologies, Maybrie."

Without waiting for a response—he wasn't going to get one out of me and he knew it—he pushed his wife toward the waiting vehicle. As they passed, I reached for the girl's arm. She was young and pretty, probably a recent graduate. Her hazel eyes flicked up to meet mine before returning to her expensive shoes.

"You deserve better," I told her.

As expected, she said nothing in reply.

"Honestly, you don't need to put up with that," I pressed, releasing her arm. As an afterthought, I called, "What's your name?"

"Honie," she said softly. The single word carried on the light breeze.

"You deserve better, Honie," I repeated.

With a final furtive glance over her shoulder, the fae climbed inside the taxi with her jerk of a husband.

Neither the prince nor I spoke until the taxi's taillights were a distant memory. In those moments, a thousand thoughts flitted through my mind. I wondered if he'd chastise me for inciting a fae wife to rebel against her caster husband. I sort of hoped he would; I was itching to unleash some unspent aggression. I also hoped he wouldn't, so my mouth didn't get me in anymore trouble.

I also wondered why the heir to the Throne of Winter was alone outside a bar lurking in the shadows and why he chose to intervene. Where were his bodyguards? I'd spotted four of them inside Hideout. Had Prince Kai purposely given them the slip? Or were they too lurking in the shadows, just not seen yet?

His perfect features and obsidian gaze were hard to ignore in the moonlight. His broad shoulders and trim waist were a silhouette of strength and poise. *Ugh. Why is my brain betraying me in such a heinous way?*

"Are you okay?" He spoke so softly, for a moment I thought that I'd imagined his question. The way he stared at me indicated he was waiting on a response, though.

"I'm not a damsel in distress," I snapped. The words came out harsher than I meant.

Kai laughed. He *laughed*. Like I was cute or funny.

Crossing my arms over my chest, I shot him an icy, defiant glare.

All traces of humor fled his expression. "Oh, I know you are not a girl who needs saving," he said quickly. "At least, not from a physical altercation. But sometimes words cut deeper than swords."

Hadn't Jon said something similar earlier in the night? His words had been less poetic, but the sentiment was the same.

"May I give you a ride home?" Prince Kai offered.

"I'll find a taxi," I replied stiffly. "But thank you."

The prince held up a hand. "It is late. Please, allow me to do this." A mischievous twinkle appeared in his eye. "I would never forgive myself if one of my subjects was injured, or worse."

"I can take care of myself," I insisted.

"I was not speaking of you," he said knowingly. "Hideout is full of drunk idiots. It is only a matter of time before another of them stumbles outside, quite possibly before you find a taxi. So, please, allow me to sleep tonight with peace of mind."

That was how I ended up in the back of a royal limo with Prince Kai. I'd never been in such a luxurious vehicle before. Hell, I'd barely been in any vehicles at all. My eyes widened even farther when he handed me a crystal goblet of water.

Soft ukulele music played through unseen speakers as I sipped the cold water. Dark tint on the windows made the fact that I stared at the glass seem ridiculous. I felt, and saw in the reflective surface, the prince watching me. Several times, his lips parted as though to ask a question. Each time, he thought better of it.

After I'd watched Prince Kai do this several times, he finally gave voice to the thought on his mind. "Where are you from, originally?"

In my five years beneath the dome, only two individuals had ever asked me those words. Not even Cala and Everly knew about Fae Canyon. Like with Sumi, I didn't know why I shared a part of myself with Prince Kai.

"California," I said into the darkness. "Fae Canyon." I didn't look at him when I answered, but I saw his nod of recognition in the window.

"I have heard of it. The canyon was supposed to have been beautiful before the Freeze," he offered.

Finally, I turned to face him. "It's still beautiful," I said.

"Yes, forgive me. You are correct. There are many places where the frozen landscape is a sight to behold." Pausing, he studied me. Those dark eyes felt like they were boring holes in my soul, but I refused to lower my gaze.

"Have you ever seen the frozen islands of our kingdom?" he asked.

I didn't know why the question surprised me. Maybe because he should have known that I was not permitted to leave the confines of the dome. Fae like me weren't allowed field trips. I wasn't one of Madame Noelani's girls; I wasn't whisked away on romantic getaways to the frozen black sands or ice volcanoes by eligible warlocks hoping to woo me for my magic.

Instead of reminding Prince Kai of these facts, I simply said, "No."

"The frozen waterfalls are my favorite," he admitted. "Kenoa and I went ice climbing last weekend. Did he tell you?" The prince laughed. "For such a big man, he moves so fast."

"You climbed icefalls?" I asked doubtfully. "I thought casters can't survive outside the domes?"

"I'm young and healthy," Prince Kai replied in a light tone. "I can usually do a day in the cold and up to thirty-six hours if the sun is out during the day. I once remained outside the dome for two days." He shivered at the memory. "I would like very much never to do that again."

"What happened?" I asked, oddly intrigued.

"Kenoa and I went hiking on the Big Island," Prince Kai began in a soft voice. "We became lost," he chuckled, "which is not uncommon, sadly. A storm set in, though. We were not able to find our way to the pickup location for the helicopter. I am to understand the pilot waited as long as weather permitted. Search teams found us two days later, in a cave. I don't remember much of the second day. If not for Kenoa, I would be dead."

I'd seen press conferences royals gave when a bodyguard died in the line of duty. They always said things like, "If not for my bodyguard, I would be dead." But no queen or king ever expressed a fraction of the genuine affection for those who'd given their life in service as Prince Kai did for Kenoa.

What a strange bromance, I thought.

"Why did you ask him to come work for you?"

It was hard to say which of us was more surprised by the question.

"Kenoa protects me. He does not work for me," the prince said carefully. "There is a difference."

I had no response that wasn't likely to start a fight, so I remained silent.

"But I suppose I asked him to take the position because we have known one another a very long time. I trust and admire Kenoa," continued the prince thoughtfully.

"Okay, but then why did he accept the offer?" I countered.

Prince Kai furrowed his brow. "I suppose because we have known one another a very long time. He trusts me and I would like to think admires something about me."

Fae and casters weren't friends. They didn't trust one another. If they were a married couple, maybe. But the way the prince spoke about Kenoa made it sound as though the caster believed they were friends.

No, I thought. *The prince isn't telling me the whole story.*

The limo slowed as we finally reached my building. It took until that instant to realize that no one had ever asked my address—neither the driver nor Prince Kai.

Nonetheless, we'd arrived.

"Thank you for the ride, even if your motives were purely selfish," I said, reaching for the door handle.

He seemed to understand I was teasing. Well, sort of.

"They were," he said with a shrug. "You are welcome all the same."

The door opened from the outside. Prince Kai's driver, a large caster whose chest rivaled Rocko's in girth, stood outside the limo. Smiling at the large man, I climbed out.

"Brie?" the prince called after me.

"Yes?"

He gave that same embarrassed half-laugh he had in the arena. "I never asked—is it okay if I call you Brie? Do you prefer Maybrie?"

He's nervous, I realized. *Why is he nervous?*

"Brie is fine," I said slowly.

"Brie." Though he'd said my name numerous times, it sounded like he was trying it on for size. "Brie, will you call me Kai? Just...Kai?"

"Um, sure. I guess. If you want," I replied. I had no intention of speaking to him again, though it seemed rude to point that out.

The driver placed his hands behind his back and stared toward the sky. The gesture was symbolic as he only pretended he couldn't overhear our conversation.

Kai licked his lips. "Will you have dinner with me, Brie? Just me. Nothing formal. We could eat at the palace if you prefer a private setting. Or even your apartment." Kai's eyes grew as wide as dinner plates. "Is that as presumptuous as it sounded? I apologize. Of course, we can go out. I just imagine you are not the type of girl who would appreciate her picture alongside mine in the tabloids." This time, his nervous laughter sounded self-deprecating. "I do not think I have ever muddled an invitation so thoroughly. I am usually good at this. I mean, at…will you have dinner with me?"

No. That was the response that popped into my head. I had no interest in the caster prince. Yes, he was good looking. But he represented all that I hated. He was the epitome of a caster jerk.

His mother wants him to marry a fae, I reminded myself. That thought was almost even less appealing than being just another of Kai's one-time dates. I didn't want to audition for the role of fae wife.

Instead of saying no and getting on with my night, I was surprised to hear myself ask, "Why?"

"Why?" he repeated, taken aback. "Well, I guess because I find you fascinating. A female fae fighter? That is rare. You could have left the pits years ago. You could have enrolled at Madame Noelani's. You chose not to, and I find that intriguing. I find *you* intriguing."

"How did you know…?"

He kept talking as though I hadn't spoken. "And now that I have bared my soul and admitted to all of these things, will you *please* do me the honor of having dinner with me? One dinner. That is all I ask."

No. "Can I sleep on it?" I asked. *Sleep on it? Just say no.*

He smiled. "Of course. Good night, Brie."

No. I won't go out with you. "Good night…Kai."

An arctic blast met me as I entered my penthouse condo. *Home.* It was a good thing air conditioning was included in the monthly fees; I loved the frigid air but would've hated to pay the bill. I shed my jeans and top in the foyer and threw them down the laundry chute. The building was overwhelmingly casters, but when my clothes came back clean and folded, it wasn't so hard to overlook the bother.

My cellphone was right where I'd left it, on the charging station next to my bed. I slipped on flannel pajamas and faux-fur lined slippers, grabbed my phone, and headed back downstairs. In the kitchen, I programmed a cup of cinnamon tea in the QuickDrip machine. While it brewed, I scrolled through a string of texts.

CALA (2:43 A.M.): *Get home okay? Hit me back so I don't have to worry.*

EVERLY (2:31 A.M.): *Congrats again on the big 100. U rock!*

ROCKO (2:20 A.M.): *2nd place is first loser, except when it's to you. Congrats again, B.*

KENOA (2:19 A.M.): *Sumi is safe at the commune. You're a goddess, B. Night, luv.*

JUNO (1:08 A.M.): *Hey, B! Heard about the 100th. You are my hero. We're at Sweet & Salty, come by if you're out celebrating.*

TENLEY (12:49 A.M.): *Congrats, B! Come have a drink at Spellcaster.*

JUAN (12:10 A.M.): *Just heard. Congratulations, Brie.*

ANTONIO (11:29 P.M.): *Rocko went down! Hard. You and me next Arena Day. Rematch from last year.*

CHRIS (11:03 P.M.): *Great seeing you at Pele's tonight. Let's have dinner soon.*

I didn't read any farther. The text from Chris, or rather Christina, hadn't included any questions, but she would be expecting a response. Pronto.

Leaving my cell in the kitchen, I carried the steaming mug of tea to my wraparound patio with a three-hundred-sixty-five-degree view of the city. There, buried inside the cushion of my favorite lounge chair, was another cell. This one was special and wouldn't work for anyone besides me.

"Infusium," I whispered, pressing my thumb to the round indent at the bottom.

My skin glowed orange as the sensor read my magical fingerprint, and the phone came to life. Instead of numerals, a rune keypad of symbols appeared on the display. Typing in the proper sequence, I then hit the center symbol to place the call. She answered on the first ring.

"I see you received my text," Christina answered.

"I did. What's up? Do you need to change the meeting time?" It was one of the few reasons Christina dared to contact me on my regular cell.

"No. Everything's a go." She hesitated, which was unusual. Christina was the most assured fae I had ever met; she never worried that her words might offend or upset.

"Christina?" I pressed. "You're scaring me."

She laughed. "Sorry. I just…I have an assignment for you. You're not going to like it, I can already tell you that."

"Anything," I said automatically. Sipping my tea, I

waited out the pregnant pause.

"I understand that Prince Kai invited you to the palace for a celebratory dinner," she said finally.

I nearly spit hot tea all over myself. "How do you know that? That is…only his driver…. I know you wouldn't ever trust a caster so—"

"Brie, what are you talking about?" Christina cut me off.

"What are *you* talking about?" I countered.

She sighed, annoyed. "At the little ceremony after your match, Prince Kai asked you to have dinner at the palace with the queen. Except that's obviously not what *you* were talking about. So, tell me about the incident where his driver was present."

"It's a long story," I began. I took another sip of tea as though it might give me courage.

Telling Christina about Kai's offer wasn't the hard part. That was simple, in fact—it was standard operating procedure for my role. No, I was more concerned about admitting that I hadn't outright refused him. But Christina and I had no secrets. At least, not when it came to the important stuff. And this was definitely important.

"The prince gave me a ride home from Hideout, and he asked me to have dinner. Like a date, I guess. I don't know. He said it would just be the two of us. Queen Lilli wouldn't be there."

"You said no?" Christina asked.

I hesitated before reluctantly admitting, "Not exactly. I mean, I'm going to turn him down. Obviously. He was just being sort of pathetic, and I—"

"Pathetic?" Christina scoffed. "Prince Kai? Did you

sustain a head injury during your fight?" She sounded truly concerned, not sarcastic.

"No," I replied, drawing out the word into several syllables. "I'm serious. The point is, I'm going to refuse him. Tomorrow. Well, later today. I'm going to tell him no," I promised. "Oh, and I'm going to send his gold bangle back, too. He needs to know my magic isn't for sale." There, I'd told the truth.

"A gold bangle?" Christina repeated. "Interesting. Diamonds? Or rubies since you're a fire fae?"

"Huh? What do you mean? It's a simple gold bangle. Nothing flashy."

Why did she want a physical description of the bangle? The bangle had nothing to do with anything. I'd only mentioned it because I was positive Christina already knew about the present. Where was the lecture on standing firm in the face of the prince and his gifts?

"Interesting," she repeated.

"Whatever." I sipped my tea. "Interesting or not, later today, the bangle and my polite refusal to his date offer will be on their way to the palace."

"No," Christina said firmly.

"No?" I repeated, positive I'd misheard.

"This is even better than I'd hoped for." She sounded giddy. "You're going to go on that date, Brie."

"Excuse me?" Dread filled my gut like molten lead. "Why? What possible good would come of it?"

"Don't play stupid, Brie. This opportunity is just what the rebellion needs. You have been instrumental in advancing our cause. The money you've donated...there wouldn't be a rebellion without you."

Christina wasn't usually so forthcoming with the gratitude.

"Are you buttering me up?" I asked. "If so, you're being extremely transparent."

"We need eyes and ears inside the palace, Brie," she said, ignoring my question completely. "We need to know what, if anything, the royals know of our activities. Our last three cargo runs have been delayed because the exit port was discovered ahead of time. There's a source of information, a leak, within the palace, and I want to know who it is. Your money has really driven the cause, but inside information would be invaluable."

"I know," I said, rubbing my temples warily. "But Christina, this is…I am not the right fae for the job. We have members among Madame Noelani's recent grads. One of those girls is—"

"They're not the ones that the prince asked on a date, Brie," Christina snapped. "All I'm asking is for you to go, look, and listen. Pay attention, notice things, and report back to me. Directly to me, and only to me. You just won your one hundredth match; a little spy work should be easy for you."

"They're not the same," I grumbled.

"It's one date, Brie." Christina's patience had worn thin. "You can do this."

Could I really? I was a crap liar and had never tried to infiltrate a book club, let alone somewhere with as much security as the royal palace. I thought of Sumi sobbing in the locker room, of Honie at the mercy of her caster husband, of the fifteen-year-old fire fae who'd been so scared all those years ago and who'd cried herself to sleep too many times to remember. Those were the people the rebellion fought to save, to protect. They were the number one reason I still fought in the pits. I used my prize money to help fund the rebellion because I believed in our cause.

"You owe me," I told Christina finally.

"Take a number." A soft click was the only indication that our call was complete.

Replacing the phone in its hiding place, I didn't move from the patio. Even with the slight chill in the air, I started to sweat in my flannel jammies, but I remained on the lounge chair. The artificial sky eventually began to lighten, turning from black, to blue, to pink, and then to blue again. The temperature increased as the sun made its ascent. My tea was cold, and I was hot. Still, I didn't budge from the patio.

I'd joined the rebellion because I wanted to help those who couldn't help themselves. The name-calling and taunting I endured daily were nothing compared to what many fae and shifters endured hourly. At least I enjoyed a semblance of freedom in everyday life. That wasn't the case for all of us.

In the early days, my involvement had been mostly monetary. Over time, I'd grown close with Christina, among other members of the rebellion, and started taking a more active role. But I was too well-known to take part in much of the dirty work.

Until now, I thought. *Now, my notoriety is the only reason I'm in this mess.*

Spying on the royal family was dangerous. If caught, they'd hand me over to the vampires to be drained of both my blood and my magic.

Don't get caught.

Easier said than done, of course. But honestly, it wasn't the consequences of being caught that frightened me most. Sacrifice was something I was all too familiar with. It was the date part of the assignment that scared me. I had only marginally more dating experience than spying experience. The last time I'd been on a first date was ages ago. Not since... *Tanner.*

CHAPTER FOUR

"KAI? HI, IT'S Brie," I said, pacing back and forth in front of my bed.

"Brie?" he said as though my name was unfamiliar. Ever the politician, Kai recovered quickly. "Brie, hello. How are you? Forgive me, I did not expect to hear from you so soon."

"Kenoa gave me your number," I explained. "I hope that's okay?"

"Of course. I guess I could have given it to you last night when I asked you to dinner. That would have been helpful." He laughed softly. "I wasn't eager to be turned down, so I suppose I might have overlooked that detail."

"Um, right," I said, hesitating. "Well, is the offer still

on the table? Or…?" I trailed off, giving him the opportunity to make life easier on both of us. Part of me hoped that he'd simply admit he was drunk when extending a dinner invitation to a lowly fighter fae. When he didn't answer immediately, I pulled the phone away from my ear and looked at the screen to ensure we he was on the line. We were still connected.

"Um, Kai?" I finally ventured.

"Yes, sorry. I am here. Are you…do we have a date?"

Closing my eyes, I exhaled slowly. *Christina is right. We need to know what, if anything, the royal family knows of the rebellion.* "We do," I confirmed. "But…having dinner at the palace would be better. I'm private, you know? It's just one date, and I don't want to cause—"

"No need to explain," Kai assured me. "How is tomorrow evening?"

So soon? I bit my lip. *At least it will be over with.* "Tomorrow works."

"Shall I send a car for you around seven?"

"I'll be ready," I said.

It sounded like Kai was smiling. "I am looking forward to it, Brie."

"Cool. See you tomorrow." Without waiting for him to say anything further, I disconnected the call.

Tossing the phone on my unmade bed, I ran my hands through my hair. Was this really happening? Was I really going on a date with Prince Kai? Back up—was I really going on a date? It had been over a year since my last relationship ended, and the desire to date again just hadn't been there since.

It's not a real date, I reminded myself. *No. But he thinks it*

is. You have to pretend you're on a real date while really snooping—
also something you don't know how to do.

I flopped on the bed and asked the vaulted ceiling,
"What could possibly go wrong?" After several moments
of contemplation, I decided the best way to pretend this
was a real date was to treat it like a real date. If some cute
fae guy asked me out, what would I do?

Probably turn him down.

Absently, I made a baseball-sized fireball in one palm
and began tossing it back and forth between my hands.
"But if you didn't? If you said yes, what would you do
next?" I asked myself as the fireball flew toward the
ceiling. "Probably call Cala or Everly."

No. Not Everly. Not for a first date.

I reached for my phone with one hand and caught the
fireball in the other. I hit number two on my speed dial.

"You didn't text me back last night," Cala accused.
Her voice was scratchy, like she'd just woken up.

"It doesn't sound like you lost any sleep over it," I
replied dryly.

Cala yawned. "We went for pancakes after Hideout.
What are you doing for the rest of the day? Wanna hit the
beach?"

"Can you come over?" I asked.

"Is everything okay?" Cala suddenly sounded more
awake.

"I'll explain when you get here."

The contents of my closet were strewn across my bed
by the time Cala arrived with takeout from Pele's. Her
chestnut curls were messy and piled in a high ponytail
atop her head. Still, she looked chic in designer cutoffs

and a graphic tee.

"Donation time?" she asked between sips from her malt shake.

"I wish." I glanced back and forth between a pair of dark jeans and a black cocktail dress I'd worn to the royal family's annual reception for the fighters. "I have a date."

Cala nearly spit her shake on the hardwood. "Oh, sweetie. This is so good!" she exclaimed. "It's about time. But why haven't you said anything before now? Where did you meet him?"

Slumping onto my bed, I rested my head in my hands and massaged my temples. "It's Prince Kai," I admitted, staring at my chipped toenail polish instead of my best friend.

Cala laughed uneasily. "I have were-senses, but I couldn't have heard you correctly."

When I didn't join her in giggling, Cala's eyes widened. "B, surely you aren't serious?" she finally asked. My silence must have told her that I was indeed quite serious. "Oh, Brie. This is…well I don't know what this is."

"Christina," I said simply. It was explanation enough.

"Brie, this is dangerous. That's what this is." Cala set down the bag of food and came to sit beside me. "Whatever her plan is, it can't be good."

I sighed. "She says she just wants me to keep my eyes and ears open."

"Look, you know I am one hundred percent behind the cause," my best friend started. "But we have trained professionals for these types of assignments." Cala took my hand and squeezed. "Why you?"

"Because I'm the one he asked out," I admitted.

"What does that matter?" Cala raised an eyebrow in challenge. "He's mercurial. He'll have his eye on someone else next week. He hit on Sumi last night. Well, he asked her to dance. I kinda think he was just trying to be nice, but still."

"Will the girl he asks out next week be part of the rebellion?" I asked softly.

Cala sighed. "Maybe not."

"I have to do this. The opportunity is too good to pass up," I said, sounding eerily like Christina had earlier.

"Right. Okay, well then what do you need from me?"

I smiled at my best friend. "Thank you, Cala." I explained the whole needing-to-pretend-it-was-a-real-date thing, "So, my first thought was that I'd call you. Now, you tell me, what would you do next?"

Cala tapped her chin thoughtfully. "Shopping," she said finally. "I'd say we need to go shopping."

Next thing I knew, we were in a taxi on our way to the Fashion District. Cala dragged me from one boutique to the next, hurdling slinky dresses, low-cut tops, and tight pants over the top of fitting room doors for me to try on. My protests about the extravagant prices didn't dissuade my best friend from her mission. Once we'd purchased not one, not two, but *four* potential date outfits, it was off to House of Locks. As the premiere salon beneath the dome, even the junior stylists were booked for months in advance. Nevertheless, when the top two female fighters showed up without appointments, only a princess was exempt from rescheduling.

"Admit it, Brie, today was fun." Cala smiled at me in the mirror as Niall, her go-to stylist, put the finishing touches on her new lob.

I studied the new bright-crimson highlights in my dark hair. It had been a long, long time since I'd indulged in a day of pampering. My nails were filed into points and shimmered with shiny black lacquer.

"It was," I agreed.

"Yeah, that sounded convincing," Cala snorted.

I blew out a long breath. "I did have fun. Honestly. That's sort of the problem, I guess."

"Niall, would you mind wrapping up a bottle of that coconut oil you used?" Cala asked her stylist. "And Kalmi, Brie hasn't had color in a while. She'll need new shampoo and conditioner." She waited until we were alone before turning back to me. "It's been over a year, Brie," Cala said gently. "Tanner would want you to live. To enjoy life."

"I know." I bit my lip as I considered how to phrase my next words. "He would want me to enjoy my life with a fae, though. Not with a caster…especially *that* caster."

There was a strange spark in Cala's dark eyes. I didn't like it.

"Good thing this isn't a date then," she said evenly.

"Exactly." I chewed on my lip some more. "But I still need to tell Everly."

"Right, Everly." Admiring her new lob in the mirror, Cala tapped the curled ends to test the bounce. "She'll understand. It's for the cause, right?"

"Yeah, I guess. I just don't want her to think I'm betraying her brother's memory, you know?"

Tanner and Everly had been as close as any two siblings I'd ever met. She'd always been nice to me, but once I started dating Tanner, Everly had welcomed me like a sister. After his death, she had been the only one who understood my loss. Would she feel differently toward me if I entered a new relationship?

Cala squeezed my hand. "You don't have to tell her. It's one date. One *fake* date."

"I'd rather she hears the truth from me before she reads the story in the tabloids," I replied. Having a private dinner at the palace reduced the risk of someone snapping a picture of Kai and me together, but overzealous photographers had been known to bribe palace guards for access to the grounds.

"Everly will understand," Cala said again, squeezing my hand one more time before releasing it.

"I hope so," I muttered as I saw Niall and Kalmi approaching in the mirror.

⬤ ◆ ⬤

That evening I worked the dinner rush at Pele's, hocking salmon melts and tuna steaks to a busier than normal restaurant.

"Are you offering free shakes in here or something?" Rocko asked when I stopped at his table.

"It's Brie. They're all here to see the famous fire fae fighter," Juno, another waitress, teased as she breezed by, two plates of pineapple fries in her hands.

"That true?" Rocko asked.

I shrugged. "Every time I hit a milestone win business

picks up. Just you tonight?"

"Yeah, Everly's working," Rocko replied. He hadn't bothered to open his menu, since he always ordered the same thing.

Everly. You have to call her tonight, I thought. Then reconsidered. *Or tomorrow. Before the date.*

"I owe her a phone call," I muttered.

"She gets off at ten," Rocko said helpfully.

I gave him a tight smile. "Good. I'll call her then." *Or tomorrow.* "I'll have your steak wrap out soon."

The rush didn't die down until well after nine. I stayed to help Jon clean the kitchen. Then, I decided it would be poor form to leave the dish room in such a chaotic state and donned a pair of rubber gloves to help the dishwasher. When there wasn't a dirty plate, cup, or utensil left in Pele's, I offered to mop the floor for Juno, since she was the closing waitress.

"Is your water out or something?" Juno asked.

"Huh?"

The older fae laughed. "You sure don't seem like you want to go home. Uninvited houseguest?"

No, just a phone call I don't want to make, I thought.

"Go home, Brie," Jon called from the kitchen. "Get some sleep. You look awful."

"Thanks, old man," I called back dryly.

Though, when I finally went home and looked at my reflection in the bathroom mirror, I had to agree. I looked awful. Probably because I hadn't slept the night before. The prospect of fake dating a prince had my stomach in knots and my head on overdrive.

I knew I should call Everly. I'd procrastinated long

enough at work that the clock read 12:14 a.m. She would be awake, though. Most nights she closed Hideout and didn't get home until three or four in the morning. Everly was definitely a night owl.

And yet, I didn't call. I couldn't bring myself to dial her number. Everly would say she understood, say that she was cool with anything that supported the cause. But I didn't want to hear the twinge of sadness in her voice.

So, to avoid an uncomfortable confrontation with my friend, I confronted my own painful past. Boxes of pictures and press clippings from Tanner's fights were tucked in the back of a dresser drawer in one of my guest rooms. Every so often, when I was feeling particularly nostalgic, I dug out the box and went through the contents.

I smiled as I relived memories with Tanner—some of the happiest of my life since leaving the canyon. We'd spent days at the beach, splashing in the waves. Once, I'd let Tanner and Kenoa take me to the North Shore to surf. I took one look at the size of the waves and made the firm decision to stay on the beach.

Hours passed as I looked at the photographic evidence of my only romantic relationship. Tanner had looked so handsome in a tux for the Sugarcane Ball. He'd hated dressing up and fancy parties; hated the casters pretending they weren't all stuck up jerks; hated the fae who stroked the casters' egos in the hope of making a match with a wealthy companion; hated the vampires who lurked in the corners to remind us all to be on our best behavior or risk draining.

Really, Tanner had hated just about everything

beneath the dome. But he'd loved me. *And the rebellion,* I thought. Tanner *had* loved the rebellion. He was the reason I became involved with the cause. He would've understood my fake date with Kai, just like Everly would. I knew that. Why, then, couldn't I stop obsessing? Why was I driving myself crazy with worry over their feelings?

Because you like Kai. At least, you don't hate him as much as you thought you would. Yes, that was the problem. The prince was different than I'd expected. *Give him time. He'll show his true colors,* I thought.

But Kenoa had known Kai for ages and seemed to like the prince. What did that mean? I didn't know, but it was time for a shower. The sun was on the rise, and if I wasn't going to sleep, I needed to start my day.

By the time I'd showered and made my morning coffee, I had a missed call from Everly. It was like the universe reminding me of my promise to be an adult and tell my friend the truth.

"You're up early," I said when Everly answered her cell.

"I actually got to bed at a decent time," she laughed. "I figured maybe we could grab breakfast? I feel like I've barely seen you lately."

I had been sort of MIA lately. Training for my last fight and waiting tables took up a lot of time. "I was going to ask you the same thing." It wasn't a lie, but I still felt guilty. "Um, maybe I could bring over pancakes from Hot Off the Grid?"

"Why don't we meet at Hot Off the Grid? I haven't been out to eat in ages," Everly replied.

I hesitated. Privacy seemed best, but she was less likely

to cause a scene in public. "How's an hour sound?" I asked.

"See you soon," Everly sang and disconnected.

I arrived at Hot Off the Grid twenty minutes early. The fae hostess offered to let me skip the line and go straight to a table. Perks of the job. I politely refused since I had time to kill anyway.

Everly ended up being twenty minutes late, which worked out perfectly with the wait for a table.

"Sorry. Sorry. Sorry," she apologized profusely as she slid into the booth across from me. "The bus schedule is all messed up for some reason."

"You didn't have to take the bus," I said quickly, feeling like a real ass for not having offered to pick her up in the taxi.

House fae didn't make enough money to take taxis or buy new clothes or even eat out in restaurants. They were only provided a small apartment and a food allowance. That was why they had second jobs and finances were still tight for most of them.

Everly waved me off. "I don't mind, usually. It's actually sort of fun. You never know who you'll meet."

The shifter waitress came over, and Everly and I both ordered cinnamon pancakes and pineapple juice.

"So, what's new with you?" Everly asked once the girl had left with our menus.

Tell her now. I cleared my throat. "Well, um, I have sort of a...thing."

"A thing?" Everly laughed. "Tell me more."

"It's a thing set up by Christina."

Had we been alone, I wouldn't have bothered being

cryptic. The rebellion was serious, though; I wasn't about to run the risk someone at a nearby table would overhear our conversation and report it to the Director of Dome Security.

"Oh, I see. Are you looking forward to it?" Everly asked tightly.

Though not an active member of the rebellion, my best friend knew Christina well.

"No. I can honestly say I'm not." That was true. I was not looking forward to spying on the prince, which was technically my assignment from Christina.

"Oh." Everly furrowed her brow, clearly unsure what she could say that wouldn't send up red flags.

"Christina has decided to play matchmaker," I said carefully.

"Oh," Everly said for a third time. "Who's the lucky warlock?"

Good, I thought. *She gets what I'm not saying.* I lowered my voice, scanning the pancake house for eavesdroppers. "Prince Kai," I said when I was satisfied no one was listening.

To say Everly was shocked would've been an understatement.

"It's a long story how this all came about," I added.

The waitress returned with our drinks. Clearly sensing the tension, she left promptly.

"I just wanted you to hear it from me. So you'd know the truth," I tried when Everly still didn't respond.

She sipped her pineapple juice thoughtfully. "I understand. And Christina wouldn't have arranged this date if it weren't," she paused to search for the right word, "a good fit."

It sounded as though my friend was justifying the situation to herself more than to me. Still, she was taking the news way better than I'd anticipated.

And you were worried, I thought. "Exactly. I'm the right fit. Right now, anyway," I agreed with Everly.

The earth fae forced a smile. "Just don't go trying on crowns or anything," she teased.

At least, I thought she was teasing.

CHAPTER FIVE

THAT EVENING, DRESSED in white, silk pants and a pale-blue halter top, I sat in the back of a limo as it sped toward Iolani Palace, home of the royal family. My leg shook as my foot bobbed up and down. I crossed and uncrossed my legs repeatedly. The entire situation was so far outside of my comfort zone that I didn't even know which part of the night I worried about the most.

The limo pulled to a stop, too soon for my nerves to have settled. Instead of waiting for Kai's driver, I opened the door myself and climbed out. I quickly realized we were not at the palace but rather a small cottage on a lagoon.

"Is this…?" Before I could ask the driver if he'd taken

me into the woods to murder me, Kai emerged from the cottage.

He wore a perfectly tailored navy suit, a button-down shirt, and a tie swung over one shoulder.

I laughed uneasily. "I hope I'm not underdressed?"

"Not at all." He gestured to his outfit. "I had a meeting that ran long. This string of disappearances that has been in the news is…never mind, you don't want to hear about business. Come in." He held the door open wide for me. "Dinner is in the oven. It shouldn't be too long. You look amazing."

"Thank you," I said, though the compliment barely registered.

The entire situation was too surreal for my brain to process much of anything. I'd expected the palace, though the quaint cottage was a welcome surprise. The interior was furnished with hand-carved tables and chairs. Plush rugs covered the floor, along with fluffy pillows stacked in front of a hearth that seemed to invite a person to stretch out. Rich aromas drifted from the kitchen. A bottle of wine and two glasses were already set out in front of the roaring fire.

Fire? Interesting choice, I thought. Then again, the temperature had been abnormally cool today.

"What is this place?" I asked.

"The gardeners' cottage." Kai walked over to the oven and peeked at the contents without opening the door completely. "Or should I say, it used to be where the gardener lived. I use it as an office now. I thought the palace might be a little formal for you." He gave me a lopsided grin. "Is this okay?"

"It's perfect," I said honestly. "Dinner smells great."

"Kalua pork." The prince beamed. "It is one of the few dishes I make. Though it's obviously not a whole pig cooked in a pit in the sand, it is still pretty damn good. Wine?"

"Sure. Thanks." *So far, so good.* We carried our glasses onto the lanai, the screened-in porch that overlooked the lagoon.

The sun was just setting. In perfectly timed intervals, the sky transitioned through shades of blue. There was a breeze coming off the water, blowing cool air on my flushed cheeks. It was nowhere near as cold as I preferred but still a nice change from the usual nights that were too warm.

"Do you normally attend meetings all day?" I asked. "I've always wondered how you spend your time."

Kai chuckled. Raising one eyebrow, he sipped his wine and watched me backtrack in embarrassment.

"Woah," I said quickly. "I'm sorry, I didn't mean to imply that you don't do anything with your time. That was really rude." Clamping my lips shut, I bit the inside of my cheek to keep from saying anything else. Honestly, I didn't believe he did much *real* work, but I still felt like a jerk for saying so.

"Not at all. I am sure most wonder how I spend my days," he admitted. "After all, I am the party boy heir."

"Your words, not mine." Shooting him a mischievous grin, I tried the wine. It was fruity and absolutely delicious. A little of the tension in my muscles eased. I could do this.

"To answer your question, yes, it seems all I do is

attend meetings. There has been a lot happening lately, and it is my duty to represent the palace."

"The missing casters?" I guessed, taking another small sip of wine.

"Missing fae, too. Both are of deep concern to my family."

"Because you need the fae for their powers?" I blurted. There was more of an edge to the question than I'd intended, a sharp defensiveness that I should've kept hidden. *Stop running your mouth, Brie,* I lectured myself. *You're not supposed to be antagonizing this guy.*

"Yes, frankly," Kai said with a shrug. "In the beginning, that was our primary concern with regard to the missing fae. But now...." He ran one finger around the rim of his wine glass. "The numbers are startling, Brie. There is worry that we might have a killer on the loose."

"A killer?" I parroted. "That seems like a leap. I mean, the news hasn't mentioned bodies being found or anything like that."

"None of the missing have been found—neither fae nor casters—but that does not mean there is *not* a killer," Kai countered.

"True."

From inside the cottage, a timer dinged. Kai set his glass down and headed for the open lanai door. "If you will excuse me, I should check on dinner."

This isn't going so bad, I thought to myself. *He seems to find my bluntness tolerable. And there haven't been any awkward lapses in conversation.*

When he returned several minutes later, Kai carried

two plates of food that smelled as good as anything Jon whipped up at Pele's. One bite confirmed that the flavor was the perfect blend of salt and smoke. The guy could cook.

Interesting.

"My turn," Kai declared, setting his fork down. "We both know you don't need the money, so why do you work as a waitress?"

Prepared to fire off a snippy reply, I rested my fork against the plate. To my surprise, when I met his eyes, the prince seemed genuinely curious and not at all snarky.

Relax. It's just small talk. "Boredom," I admitted after a beat. "At most, I fight every few weeks. Less frequently now that I'm a veteran. My apartment gets lonely and sort of claustrophobic. Working at Pele's gets me out of the house and you never know who you'll meet."

That was all true enough. I made good tip money at Pele's and I liked being busy, it kept my mind off all the loss in my life. Of course, the amount of money I gave the rebellion was so great, it was only possible because I fought, not because I was a waitress.

I picked my fork up again and used it to point to the shredded meat on my plate. "This is excellent, by the way."

"I will let Sarah know. It is her recipe," Kai admitted sheepishly. "My sister is the chef in the family. I wouldn't know anything about cooking without her."

"Really?" I didn't bother hiding my surprise. Sarah wasn't the heir to the throne, but she was a princess. She didn't need to cook for herself. Chefs the world over would line up just to prepare a single dish for Queen

Lilli's only daughter.

"Yes, she is quite talented," the prince replied proudly. "In fact, she has been accepted to Chef Bourdain's Culinary Institute of Manhattan."

"That's amazing. Will she be able to go?"

Kai finished his wine and held up the bottle, silently asking if I wanted a refill before adding more to his own glass.

"Yes, please," I said with a nod. Drinking wasn't going to help me be a better spy, but it would likely help me be a better date.

"Security is indeed a concern for Sarah going so far from home," Kai answered. "If we are able to work out a plan with local authorities and the school, my sister will be able to attend. For her sake, I have been working on pulling it all together. Of course, that simply means more of those dreaded meetings."

"That's wonderful," I said honestly. "Not the meetings, obviously. But it's really nice of you to help your sister." My throat felt like sandpaper, and I had trouble swallowing the bite of jasmine rice in my mouth.

The royal family had always felt like dolls to me, not like real people. I'd never considered that they had hopes and dreams of their own. Or that those hopes and dreams might not be possible because of their birthright. To me, it had always seemed that the royals had everything handed to them. That they were spoiled and bored.

Those ideas suddenly felt naïve and foolish. Just because they were rich didn't mean they couldn't have passion and desire, too. *Am I just as nearsighted as I always accuse the casters of being?* I wondered.

"So, you fight in the pits for the money and wait tables to keep busy," Kai said as we sipped more wine.

"Yep," I agreed smoothly.

Or maybe not so smoothly, because Kai didn't appear to believe me. "I would bet there is more to it than that. I'll learn your secret one day."

I laughed uncomfortably. Both because it was a cheesy line, and because I hoped the prince would never learn my secrets. Plural. I had a lot of them.

"Will you tell me about Fae Canyon?" Kai asked, sensing it was time for a topic change.

I paused, noticeably startled. I didn't know what to say. He'd phrased it as a question, giving me a choice to answer, which was probably the only reason I didn't say no immediately.

"If that is private...."

"No." I shook my head. "I mean, it is. But you're not, like, overstepping or anything." He was definitely overstepping, but I found I didn't mind. Much.

"As you can imagine, I do not spend much time outside the domes. I am very curious about life in the Freelands," Kai added quickly.

"It's gorgeous," I said honestly. "It's pretty beneath the dome, don't get me wrong. It's just different. The frozen ocean is a sight for sure. I used to love to ice skate on a pond near my family's house. And there were these caves..." *Wait, why did you just say that?*

Thoughts of the caves, my last happy memories of home, were not something I wanted to share with Kai. He sensed my mood shift and jumped in.

"I have never been ice skating, but Sarah and I do enjoy surfing," the prince said.

I laughed, relaxing a little now that we were on to safer subjects. "They're not really the same thing."

"No, I suppose they are not." He laughed, too. "Have you tried water skiing? Or are you too busy with your many jobs?"

The conversation flowed easily from there. And I was surprised to find that I enjoyed talking to Kai. He was funny and interesting and thoughtful. A homecooked meal in the gardener's cottage was way more my style than a stuffy seven-course feast at the palace or a fancy meal at some high-end restaurant. I appreciated that he'd taken the time to plan something he thought I'd like.

That was the problem, though. I didn't want to have a good time. I wanted to hate him just as much as I had when he was more of an abstract concept than a flesh-and-blood person. Liking the prince, even a little, made me feel like a traitor to the rebellion. To Christina. To Tanner and Everly.

But even more unsettling was that I also felt like I was betraying Kai. I shouldn't have cared about betraying him, but the prince was only trying to get to know me, while I was waiting on an opportunity to snoop. The guilt grew more intense when I realized a part of me hoped I wouldn't get the chance.

"Tell me something," I said around a yawn several hours later. "Why did you ask Sumi to dance the other night at Hideout?" It was late, and I'd consumed just enough wine to ask the question.

"I would not have pegged you as the jealous type," Kai

teased.

I laughed. "Oh, I'm not. If I'm not enough for a guy, he is welcome to go somewhere else."

Kai grinned. "Then why do you ask?"

"Professional curiosity?" I ventured.

We both snickered, since the answer really didn't make sense.

"Her first fight was earlier that day, if I am not mistaken?" His voice rose like it was a question, but I had no doubt that he already knew he was correct.

I nodded. "It was."

"I hear the first fight is always the hardest. And I am told Sumi has had a hard time adjusting to life beneath the dome. I thought...." He trailed off and gave that embarrassed laugh of his. "I just played out what I was about to say in my head, and no matter how I phrase it, I will sound arrogant."

"What?" I fought another yawn and teased, "Were you going to say you thought if the prince asked her to dance, she might die happy?"

"Not in those words." He grinned. "Though no matter what words I chose, the inference would have been the same." His expression turned stern. "You are exhausted. Allow me to get a car to take you home."

"I'm sorry. It's been a long few days," I said sheepishly.

"It is after midnight. There's no need to apologize. Wait right here. I will be back in a few minutes."

"Um, sure." I smiled. "Thanks."

I expected him to call or text his driver, but Kai left the little cottage through the front door and disappeared into the night. My heart began thumping in my chest.

This was it, the opportunity I'd been not-so-anxiously waiting for.

Watching him through a window, I waited until Kai was out of sight. Then I dashed for one of the open doors off the living room—his office.

His desk took up an entire wall. Papers were scattered across the surface, as though he'd been working right up until the moment I'd arrived. Christina had said to keep my eyes and ears open, but she hadn't given me any specific instructions. Aside from finding a folder labeled "Rebellion," I wasn't sure what I was supposed to be seeing, hearing, or noticing.

Everything, I heard Christina's voice inside my head.

Whipping out my phone, I snapped birds-eye-view photos of the papers on Kai's desk. There were too many to photograph individually, and Christina could blow them up later. Then, I rifled through the files in the drawers. One labeled "Disappearances" caught my eye.

Bingo.

Flipping the folder open, I found a list of names— every known missing fae and caster. I snapped a picture of those pages, as well as the police reports filed in several cases. Kai also had interview summaries with the detectives assigned to Missing Individuals. As I fanned them out and snapped another shot, I heard the roar of an engine outside the cottage. Stuffing the pages back into the folder, I replaced the file with a slam of Kai's desk drawer. I hurried into the main room and leapt into a seat.

"Ready?" Kai asked, poking his head through the front door.

My heart was pounding with the rhythm of a thousand-horse stampede. Standing, I mustered a smile. "Yep." Adrenaline made my hands tremble, and I clasped them behind my back so he wouldn't notice.

To my surprise, there was no limo in front of the cottage. Instead, a restored roadster idled there. The dark-green paint was shiny in the moonlight, and the chrome rims were pristine. When I slid into the passenger seat, the leather was soft and smooth. For a guy who'd probably had a chauffeur his entire life, Kai navigated through the gears like a professional racer. With the convertible top down, the wind made conversation impossible. Instead of trying to shout over it, I closed my eyes and enjoyed the fresh, cold air against my cheeks.

All too soon, Kai slid the vehicle to a stop in front of my building. He put the car in park and turned to face me. With an amused smile, he reached over and tucked windblown strands of hair behind my ears. "So, what is the verdict?" he asked.

I wrinkled my nose and laughed uneasily. "What do you mean?"

"Come on, Brie. You were reluctant to go out with me. In fact, Kenoa bet me that you would cancel." Kai rested his head back against the seat. The moonlight added highlights to his chiseled features, giving me a weird fluttery feeling in my chest. "I don't know why you changed your mind, and I don't expect you will tell me. But at least tell me if you're glad that you did."

I squirmed in my seat, suddenly too hot despite the cooler-than-normal temperature. What was I supposed to say? What would Christina want me to say? What would I say if this was a real date?

"I am, actually," I laughed nervously. "Glad, that is. I had a good time." *And hopefully got useful information for Christina so I never have to play spy again,* I added silently.

"Good. Me, too." His grin was lazy, his dark eyes sparkling like black diamonds. "Does this mean you will go out with me again? Maybe dinner the day after tomorrow?"

A second date? That wasn't part of the deal! I thought frantically.

"You can sleep on it again, if you like," Kai added when I didn't respond right away.

"No. I mean, yes. A second date sounds…fun," I finished lamely, figuring it was best to consult Christina before refusing. I could always cancel later if she thought my first foray into the world of espionage was successful enough.

Let it be enough.

"Really?" Kai perked right up. "I had assumed you would say no."

"Why? Did it seem like I was having a bad time?" I asked awkwardly. Maybe the wine had clouded my perception because I thought I'd been a pretty good date.

"No, not at all. Quite the opposite." Kai's dark eyes grew thoughtful. "But I sense you are a very complicated person, Brie."

"That might be the nicest thing a caster has said to me today," I tried to joke as Kai scooted closer. *He's going to kiss me,* I thought a split second before it happened.

Except, *he* didn't kiss me. *We* kissed one another. Kai

tasted like wine and the fudge cake we'd eaten for dessert. His hand slid into my tangled hair. My arm looped around his neck. The prince slowly deepened the kiss, as though worried I might push him away. But I didn't, because I wanted to kiss Kai.

For those precious minutes, I forgot that he was a prince. I forgot that he was a caster. I forgot that I despised the royal family and all they represented. I didn't wonder if his attraction was based solely on my magical prowess. I didn't think about the pictures on my phone. I didn't think about what Tanner or Everly would say, or what Christina or Cala might think. Those were worries for later.

When Kai pulled away, I immediately missed his warmth against me. Still leaning in, he pressed his forehead to mine. My breaths were ragged, my head fuzzy. The drunk feeling wasn't from the wine, though I wished I could've blamed the alcohol. Instead, I was forced to face the truth: I was attracted to Kai.

His lips brushed my cheek and then moved to just below my ear. "I cannot wait," he murmured, "to see you again."

"Just tell me one thing first," I said, fighting the urge to kiss him again. "How much does Kenoa owe you for a second date? And when do I get my cut?"

CHAPTER SIX

ONCE I WAS alone in my condo, reality sunk in. I slumped into an armchair and let my head fall into my hands. *What have I done? He's a caster! And not just any caster, but the prince of all the casters.* The *prince. The heir to the throne. His family subjugates fae. And I just made out with him. Sweet move, Brie.*

I paced my living room, oblivious to the frigid temperature even though I hadn't changed out of my lightweight date clothes. Kai had left me so rattled. I was walking around my condo in a haze of confused and troubled thoughts. Should I call Cala? Would she make me feel better or worse? Should I call Christina? She would definitely make me feel worse.

You might not want to mention the kiss to Christina, I thought.

The phone felt heavy in my hand, the gravity of the pictures weighing it down. I needed to get the photos to Christina as soon as possible. Hopefully she'd analyze them and declare that it was more than enough intel for the time being.

Then you'll have no excuse to go on a second date, I reminded myself.

"Which is a good thing," I said aloud, because I needed to hear the words spoken. I ran my finger across my cell's screen. *Call Christina. Get this over with.*

"Tea first," I said to the empty condo. Dad always said a cup calmed the nerves, and I needed to chill out before I called my friend. Otherwise, she'd end up asking questions I didn't want to answer.

Thoughts of my family quadrupled my feelings of guilt over kissing Kai. The casters were to blame for everything. They were the reason I was ripped from my family without so much as a goodbye. The casters were the reason vampires like Mat hunted fae, even in the Freelands.

My hand flew to my neck automatically, to the spot where the vampire had sunk his fangs and taken his payment in my blood. I hated vampires even more than I hated casters.

The QuickDrip finished brewing my tea. Slipping my phone in my pocket, I folded both hands around the mug and headed for the patio. The ceramic was suddenly too hot to hold. I swore loudly as the mug clattered to the floor, boiling liquid searing my bare feet.

"What the...?" I looked down at my hands. Orange flames danced across my palms and threatened to climb up my arms. *Breathe, Brie. In and out. In and out. You control the magic, it doesn't control you.*

The flames slowly ebbed until they extinguished altogether. I leaned against the counter to steady myself. It had been a long time since my fire magic manifested on its own. In my pocket, the phone buzzed. I jumped as though it had shocked me. Even before I pulled the device out, I knew the sender: Christina. Sure enough, "Chris" flashed on the screen.

CHRIS (1:34 A.M.): *Still need to catch up. Let's do that soon.*

Sighing, I put the phone away without responding; I never answered on my everyday phone. That was the way it worked. Instead, I left the mess in the kitchen and trudged out to the porch.

As usual, Christina answered her own unregistered cell on the first ring. "How did it go? Did you learn anything?" she asked in lieu of a greeting.

I cleared my throat and spoke in my most business-like tone. "The royal family is looking into the disappearances."

Christina laughed bitterly. "Of course they are. Now that their kind are going missing, they're suddenly worried?" The question was rhetorical, and she didn't wait for an answer before pressing on. "I'm not surprised, but that's good intel. What else?"

"That's all, really. We met at a cottage, so I didn't see

the queen." I said. As soon as the words left my mouth, I realized how bad they sounded—like I'd had a lovers' tryst with Kai instead of a simple dinner date. "I mean, it's his office. I took photos of the files the prince has on the missing fae and casters."

"That's good, Brie. Well done. Put them on a clean chip, and I will have someone meet you for the hand off."

The glee in Christina's voice was unmistakable, and I felt sick to my stomach. Her praise was undeserved. Sure, I might have obtained useful information. But I'd also kissed the enemy. And I'd enjoyed it.

Christina's words finally wove their way through my muddled thoughts. "Wait. Why can't I just give you the chip directly? I'll see you tomorrow."

"No," she said flatly. "I don't want you near an extraction. Now that you're dating the prince—"

"Hold on," I cut her off. "We aren't dating. We went on *one* date. Singular." My heart was beating too fast, and I worried my magic would shoot out and melt the phone.

"He didn't ask you for a second date?" Christina pressed. She didn't bother hiding her annoyance.

I wasn't sure whether it was because she thought I'd blown my chance with him, or because we were spending precious minutes talking about the mundane details of my life love. Either way, it was obvious that she was only concerned with how I could use Kai's interest to further her agenda.

"He did," I admitted. "He asked me to have dinner the day after tomorrow."

"That's perfect," she said, more to herself than me.

"Perfect? Um, you said one date, Christina. I went on

my one date," I shot back.

"Yes, but he asked you on a second. He likes you, Brie. For now, anyway. We need to press that advantage as long as we can."

"Christina," I groaned. "I'm not good at this subterfuge crap."

"You must be *okay* at this subterfuge crap. Otherwise, he wouldn't have asked you out again," she countered. I groaned as she pressed forward. "Brie, the royal family will start looking into you soon. They will learn everything about you—your past, your current life, and your prospects for the future. You absolutely *must* pass muster. You have to be above reproach."

I rolled my eyes. "First of all, I think you're getting ahead of yourself. A second date is a little early for a background check. But also, I can't exactly change my past or my present. I've been careful to keep my ties to the rebellion completely off the radar. Other than that, I fight and wait tables. It's not like there's much to look into."

"There's a second date. Make sure there is a third," she replied, bypassing my concerns. "Remain close to the prince as long as you can manage. Whatever it takes, Brie."

I blew out a long, unsteady breath. "Christina…I can't do this. I can't make him fall in love with me."

"He doesn't need to fall in love with you, Brie. Now who's getting ahead of herself?" Christina laughed humorlessly. "Just keep him interested long enough to suit our purposes." Her voiced softened when she added, "You can do this, Brie. Tanner would—"

"Don't," I snapped. My tone was as fiery as the flame that appeared on my hand. "Don't you dare." Bringing up Tanner was a low, even for Christina. It took several long moments and several deep breaths before I dared to say anything else.

"I will spy for you, because I believe in our cause," I finally added, my teeth clenched together. "But I can't promise how long his interest will last."

"I understand," Christina said, a note of triumph in her voice.

"Where and when am I supposed to make the handoff?" I asked, ready to end the conversation.

"I'll text you the time and place once I have all the details."

"Okay."

"I'll be in touch," Christina said right before she disconnected.

I stayed awhile on the patio after our conversation, staring off into space and thinking. The wine might not have left me drunk, but it did leave me drowsy. Normally, I would've found the outside temperature too warm to sleep in the fresh air.

Not tonight, I thought as I curled into a ball and covered my legs with a light blanket. *Tonight is perfect.*

"Did you have rabbit for breakfast, Brie?" asked my trainer Botto. He was a mixed were-bear/air fae, who'd been working with me for years.

Hands on my hips, I paced in small circles as my

heartrate slowed. Once a week, we started practice with a timed mile. At best, I would shave around ten seconds off my previous time.

"Gross. How'd I do?" I panted.

Botto fiddled with the buttons on his stopwatch. "Five minutes, forty-three seconds," he said finally. "So, what *did* you eat for breakfast?"

That's thirty-three seconds faster than my record. "You sure that thing's accurate?" I nodded toward his stopwatch. "I had the same kale, pineapple, and banana smoothie as always."

"Well, something's different," he replied.

What's different? Oh, I'm just pretending to date a prince while spying on the royal family. Then I remembered the kiss. *Really, Brie? It didn't give you super powers.*

"Nothing I can think of," I told Botto, shrugging as though it would make the lie more believable.

"When you figure out what it is, make sure you keep doing it." He looped the string of the stopwatch around his thick neck. "I want to work on your offensive magic. I know, I know." He held up a hand to halt my protests. "You don't like to fight with your fire power. But Brie, you could have finished off Rocko ten minutes earlier than you did. Because you didn't, in those ten minutes, he nearly took you down a couple times. So, today, is all magic."

Throwing my hands up in mock exasperation, I sighed dramatically. "You're the boss, Botto."

I'd made it a point to practice magic every day since arriving on the island. But it was small acts—from simple locking spells to the occasional summoning spell when I was feeling lazy. It wasn't illegal for fae to cast, it was that most in the kingdoms never learned how.

But simple spells weren't what Botto had in mind. He wanted me to cast complex, offensive magic spells, which were extremely exhausting to perform. Particularly for a fae so out of practice with such powerful magic.

"I wish you could see yourself right now," Botto called from the opposite end of the target range two hours later. "You're sweating worse than a middle-aged father on his first session. And I'm not talking about a professional athlete." I gave him the finger, but Botto continued with his lecture. "Your heartrate is higher now than it was when you ran earlier."

Not for the first time, I cursed his ability to track my vitals. I thought the trainer's superior hearing came from his were-bear genes. But Botto swore it was his air magic that allowed him to calculate an opponent's vitals from half a football field away. Either way, before Kenoa, Botto had been the fighter to beat.

"Do you have a point?" I demanded, wiping the traitorous sweat from my face with the singed corner of my shirt. Botto had sent several fireballs boomeranging back with his air magic, and I'd missed a few.

"That you need to practice more, Brie. Magic needs to be a daily, not monthly, exercise. You are *so* powerful. Do you even realize how strong you are? And with such a useful element."

Did I know how strong my fire abilities were? Yes. Yes, I did. That knowledge was the reason I didn't use those powers while fighting. If the casters started to guess just how much power I really had, it wouldn't be long before I was forced to retire and share my magic with a nice caster guy.

"I do use magic every day," I insisted.

"Real magic, Brie. Not parlor tricks any tiny faeling can perform. All in all, you did good, though," Botto continued, jogging toward me. "Next time, I won't go so easy on you."

Despite the sweat and soot coating my skin, Botto clamped a large hand on my neck and squeezed. Hard. My teeth rattled as he shook me. The guy really didn't know his own strength.

"I'm proud of you, Brie. You're my first female fighter to break one hundred rounds in the pit."

"I'm your only female fighter. Period," I said dryly. Slinging his arm around my neck, Botto steered me toward the locker rooms. "And how many of your male fighters have broken one hundred?"

"Two." He grabbed a water bottle from the cooler and handed it to me. "For tomorrow, work on arms and cardio. You have the new training plan I sent you?"

"I do."

"Good." Despite this, he pressed on and reiterated the details. "Five miles—just a jog, nothing too intense. Then free weights—"

"I know, Botto," I assured him. Then I grinned up at him. "What? Don't you trust me?"

I trained five to six days a week, only three of those were with Botto. The other days, I was on my own with his carefully crafted workout plan. Even though I pretended otherwise to mess with him, I followed Botto's instructions to the letter. The easiest way to avoid using my fire magic was to keep my body in peak fighting form.

Botto ruffled my hair. Well, he tried to. The strands were tangled and matted, and his large fingers snagged. "Good practice, Brie." He gently unwound my hair. "I know you think I'm being hard on you about the magic, but there's a real chance you could make it to the next level."

I drained my water bottle. "I don't know, Botto. I feel like I have a lot of work to do before we take this show international."

"You do," my trainer agreed. "But I think we could start applying for some of the competitions in the other domed kingdoms."

Prior to my date with Kai, this was the opportunity Christina and the rebellion had been waiting for. If Queen Lilli agreed to let me enter inter-kingdom fights, I could act as a messenger between Christina and the other branches of the rebellion.

Would she still want me to pursue this avenue? I wondered. Probably not. At least, not until Kai's interest in me waned. Which, I told myself, would happen soon enough.

"Yeah, okay. Fill out the paperwork." I smiled at Botto. "At least we can see what the queen says, right?"

Running a hand through his hair, Botto glanced around the sports complex. Weights clanged, people grunted, treadmill belts whirred, and upbeat music set the mood. Still, he leaned down, ensuring there was no chance of someone eavesdropping.

"Even low-level inter-kingdom fights have big purses. *Huge* purses. It would be enough for you to buy your way off this island. You could buy your freedom. For real."

More importantly, I could buy the freedom of many fae. For real.

CHAPTER SEVEN

SUMI AND CALA finished with their trainers as I was pulling on fresh clothes after my shower. The teenage air fae was in better spirits than when I'd found her sobbing in the arena locker rooms, but she still looked bummed.

"Hey, Sumi, want to grab lunch at Pork Bellies with Cala and me?" I called as she headed toward the showers.

Her green eyes brightened visibly. "I would like that very much."

"Good." I smiled at Sumi and reached for a folded hand towel on the top shelf of my locker. The blue box with the bangle from Kai fell to the ground. "Take your time, we'll be here whenever you're ready."

As I bent to retrieve the box, a shadow fell over me.

"Whatcha got?" Cala drawled.

"Nothing," I muttered.

"Is that from," Cala looked around at the empty locker room, "Kai? Did the date go that well?"

I rolled my eyes and started towel drying my hair. "He gave it to me after the match the other day. It's a congratulations gift, not a because-we-went-on-a-date gift," I replied.

Cala shrugged out of her robe and shimmied into a metallic skirt that seemed way too dressy for pulled-pork sandwiches and corn on the cob. "How did the date go?"

"Well," I admitted. "I was, um, able to find common ground, just like Chris thought I might," I added cryptically.

"Really?" Cala's eyebrows shot up. "Will there be more dates?"

"Yes, because there's more common ground to find," I said carefully.

She pulled a see-through tank over her head. "Is that the only reason?"

I could've lied, and Cala would've smirked and pretended that I'd fooled her. But that just seemed silly. "The only one that matters," I replied firmly.

My best friend looked as though she felt sorry for me. It was worse than her all-knowing smirk.

"I am ready," Sumi announced.

She was so small and quiet that I hadn't heard her approach. Cala and I exchanged glances, and no more was said about the prince.

I dropped the blue box inside my workout bag, along with dirty, burnt clothes. "Let's go. I'm starving."

After eating way too much coleslaw at Pork Bellies, not to mention a pound of ribs, we decided to continue the girls' day and go dress shopping. The premiere social event of the season, the royal family's annual luau, was just two weeks away. It was one of the few parties open to all. On the surface, it was touted as a night of comradery among the factions. But really, the luau was Madame Noelani's night—it was when she introduced her most recent graduates to their potential partners.

"Attendance is mandatory for fighters," Cala explained to Sumi. "But it's actually sorta fun."

The younger girl was modeling an emerald silk gown that made her eyes pop and her exotic beauty even more pronounced.

Cala selected a crystal medallion on a long, thin rope of gold from the accessories tray and looped it over Sumi's head. "Watching the Noelites try to impress the delinquent future leaders of the kingdom makes it totally worth it," she added. "And there are always a lot of good looking fae and shifters, guys and girls—whatever you're into."

The caster saleswoman managed to look both amused and disgusted. The fact that so many wealthy families encouraged their children to marry a fae to bolster the family coffers did not sit well with the lower socioeconomic caster population beneath the dome. It was just another swing of the axe driving a wedge between our races.

"Noelites?" Sumi asked.

"The fae who attend Madame Noelani's Academy," I clarified. "It's a finishing school that prepares young fae for marriage to casters." I was a little surprised she hadn't heard of it. Surely Madame Noelani would've found Sumi attractive enough to offer the air fae a spot.

Sumi seemed more confused. "Why does one need to prepare for marriage?"

Smirking, I shook my head. "Good question."

"This is definitely the dress," Cala said, studying Sumi with a critical eye. "And the necklace. We'll keep looking for shoes."

"It is very beautiful," Sumi began softly. "But I am afraid I do not have the funds for such items."

"You're a fighter, right?" interrupted the salesgirl. "We're always happy to extend credit to fighters."

"Thank you, but that won't be necessary," I said. Turning to Sumi, I smiled. "Please, allow me to buy these as welcome gifts."

"Oh, no, I could not...." Sumi began.

"It's tradition," Cala insisted, quickly catching on. "There are so few of us. We female fighters need to stick together." She smiled at the salesgirl. "We'll take the dress and the necklace. Oh, and if you have a pair of earrings that match, that would be great, too."

"I believe we do have several pairs. How about a long, dangly pair?" the salesgirl asked.

"Perfect." Cala clapped her hands together and squealed. "You are going to turn heads, Sumi."

Sumi smiled shyly and hurried into the dressing room to change.

"What are you going to wear?" The grin Cala flashed made me uneasy. "Maybe something in *royal* blue?"

I rolled my eyes, but the ribs I'd eaten for lunch felt

like lead in my gut. My budding relationship with Kai put a whole new spin on...well, everything. The luau was still two weeks away. A lot could change in two weeks. Maybe the photos from the cottage would be enough for Christina. Maybe Kai would lose interest. Maybe the queen would deem me an unsuitable companion for her son. *That's an awful lot of 'maybes.'*

My pocket buzzed with an incoming text. I'd been waiting all day for Christina to send the time and location for the meet, but the name on the display wasn't Chris.

KAI (2:10 P.M.): *Hope your day is going well. Cannot wait for tomorrow.*

I smiled as I read the words. My fingers typed out a reply, and I hit send before I lost my nerve.

BRIE (2:11 P.M.): *Me neither.*
KAI (2:12 P.M.): *How is seven at the cottage? I will send a car.*
BRIE (2:12 P.M.): *Great on both accounts.*
KAI (2:13 P.M.): *Until tomorrow.*

When I looked up, Cala was watching me with a knowing smile. She didn't ask. She didn't need to. We'd been friends long enough that she could read my facial expressions with startling accuracy. I was just as good at interpreting hers, and I didn't like the smirk on my best friend's lips.

"What?" I demanded.

Cala shrugged as Sumi emerged from the dressing

room in jean shorts and a white tee.

Thank Gaia, I thought. At least for the time being, I was off the hook. Eventually, Cala would bring up our conversation from earlier in the locker room, but not in front of Sumi.

With Sumi's packages in tow, we left the shop. Once we'd found her car and loaded the dress in the trunk, I said goodbye to my friends and hailed my own taxi. The text from Christina came on the taxi ride home.

CHRIS (2:24 P.M.): *Hey, want to grab drinks at Pier? I'm dying for a pineapple margarita. How's ten?*

As per protocol, I didn't respond on my regular cell. Actually, I didn't respond at all. Not even on my unregistered phone once I was back in my condo. There was no need. Christina expected me at Pier at ten, come hell or fall of the dome.

At 9:45 p.m., I was sitting at the back bar of Pier, sipping soda water with lemon. The chip with the pictures of Kai's files burned a hole in the pocket of my shorts. Tapping my foot on the bottom rung of the barstool, I tried to remain inconspicuous as my gaze darted to the door for the hundredth time. Christina wouldn't come herself, and I wasn't likely to recognize the person I was meeting. *I should've brought a book or something.*

"Blind date?"

I looked up to find the bartender grinning down at me. "Excuse me?"

He poured a healthy amount of rum into a shaker,

then filled it with ice. "The soda water. The nervous fidgeting. Glancing at the entrance every five seconds." He capped the shaker and shook the cup with both hands. "I've been doing this for a while, and you're exhibiting all the classic blind date signs."

I glared at him.

"So, am I right?" The bartender poured his concoction into a glass, added a handful of cherries, and smiled smugly.

"No. I'm meeting a friend."

The bartender quirked an eyebrow as he walked to the end of the bar and set the drink in the service area for a waiter to deliver. Grabbing a rag from a bucket, he started wiping down the counter. "Is this friend male?" he asked me.

"Why do you care?"

The bartender spread his arms wide. "Look around. It's not exactly a hopping crowd." Narrowing his eyes, the guy resumed cleaning. "You're the most interesting person in here, Brie."

Reaching for my glass, I let my hand fall when I really processed his words. "How do you know my name?"

The look he gave me implied that I was a moron. "The first female to reach one hundred matches? And you're fae? Come on. You're famous."

"Famous might be a stretch."

My gaze flitted to the entrance again. A young caster stood at the hostess stand with his arm around a fae. Her long, blonde tresses were in perfect barrel curls, and her white, lace dress showed off long legs.

Definitely not my contact, I thought. The fae was one of

Madame Noelani's girls. Her demure demeanor and air of perfection left no doubt. With a pang, I remembered Honie, the fae with the jerk caster husband outside of Hideout. *That poor girl,* I thought again.

"Well, famous or not, you have one of the most recognizable faces beneath the dome," the bartender was saying. "Between you and the prince, I'm not sure who is more popular these days." He moved closer to me and lowered his voice. "Does the royal warlock know you're out here tonight? Does he know you're supposed to be having pineapple margaritas with Chris?"

I blew out a long breath, some of the tension leaving my muscles. *The bartender...really? He's my contact?* But I didn't respond right away. Just in case.

My cell buzzed on the bar in front of me.

CHRIS (10:04 P.M.): *Sorry. Got held up at work. Raincheck? Have a drink with the bartender for me.*

Yep, definitely my contact. I slid my phone into my pocket, simultaneously retrieving the chip.

"You know my name, but you haven't told me yours," I said to the bartender, extending my hand with the chip cupped in my palm.

"Elton."

We shook hands, and the small chip transferred effortlessly from my palm to his. The pass was clean, and I was pretty proud of myself. Elton smiled and slipped his hand into the pocket of his khakis.

"So, pineapple margarita?" he asked. "Or do you have somewhere else to be?"

CHAPTER EIGHT

MY HANDS WERE still trembling when I crawled into bed an hour later, and I regretted not taking Elton up on the offer of a margarita. The tequila would've done wonders for my nerves. Still, I had a long day ahead of me, and hard liquor on a training night was never a good idea.

This spying stuff is for the birds, I thought. It was weird to get such an adrenaline rush outside the arena. Handing off the chip was small, courier work. But it was a lot more active than most of the work I'd done for the rebellion. I'd have thought I would enjoy getting my hands dirty, but I didn't. Not really. Not like this. Not when it meant deceiving Kai.

It will be over soon, the spying and the tryst with Kai. "It's for the best," I mumbled.

Once this mission was behind me, I could move on to the inter-kingdom fights and acting as go-between for the different factions of the rebellion. That work, I was positive, would prove much more rewarding. That was the type of assignment Tanner would have been proud of. *Don't go there.*

But laying there alone, beneath my heavy down comforter, my first and only love's face invaded my mind. Tanner hadn't just been one of Christina's soldiers, he'd been her right hand. He and I had met during my second year on the island and became fast friends, before finally dating until his death.

Like me, Tanner's original contribution to the rebellion was money. He had been a great fighter with a lot of face recognition, and Christina had worried about him being on the frontlines. But Tanner was one stubborn fae, with a very useful type of elemental power: dimensional magic.

Tanner was the first and only dimensional fae I had ever met. In the canyon, I'd heard the myths and legends about fae with the power to manipulate space and time. Many elders believed the ability was a part of earth magic. My father believed it was the result of harnessing all four elements while casting a very powerful spell. From witnessing Tanner use his ability, I knew dimensional magic was all its own.

I smiled in the dark, recalling the way Tanner would teleport around the arena during a fight. One second, he would be across from his opponent. The next, he was behind them, ready to deliver the finishing blow. My boyfriend had been nearly impossible to beat.

But Tanner's magic didn't just allow him to teleport. He also had the ability to create a portal that others could use—a tunnel that ran from his physical location to any other physical location of his choosing, like the Freelands. That ability was the reason he'd been so pivotal to the rebellion. Before Tanner, they'd smuggled fae and shifters off the island on cargo planes bound for the mainland, which had resulted in a lot of failed shipments. Those caught trying to escape had been forcibly drained of their magic, and then handed over to the vampires like blood bags.

Tanner had saved a lot of lives by allowing fae to escape via his portals. And it had cost him his own.

Using magic didn't cost fae a part of themselves, not like it did casters. Not usually, anyway. But the amount of power Tanner had needed to create a portal was more than I'd ever witnessed another single fae use. Over time, using his magic began to take a toll on him.

At first, the lethargy would only last a few hours. Eventually, though, he would be bedridden and moody for days after each extraction. Tanner's performance in the arena began to suffer, and the large purses no longer came. He became frustrated over losing the fights, not because he cared about winning, but because it meant less money for the rebellion. Instead of stepping back from the magic, Tanner insisted on doing more and more extractions. He was determined to help the cause, determined to give them everything he had.

The exhaustion became worse, eventually followed by random, angry outbursts. Our fights over his excessive use of magic became fierce and ugly. Then came the memory lapses. Tanner started to skip his training sessions, simply forgetting to go, and he began losing more and more matches as a result. His trainer tried to cover for him—our trainers were required by law to report absences to the Pit Masters immediately—but others began to notice that Tanner wasn't around the gym much.

I begged him to stop the extractions. Or at least to allow more time between them.

"The cause is more important than one person," he would say.

The Pit Masters didn't care much about whether we won or lost our fights. They made money either way, and the less matches any one fighter won meant the longer it would be before we could buy out our contracts. But the Pit Masters did care if we didn't fight at all.

So, when Tanner stopped showing up for matches, the Pit Masters sent vampire enforcers to his condo. Since he no longer had his prize money stashed away, he couldn't pay out the remainder of his contract. The vampires took him to the cages beneath the arena and offered him two choices: fight or extinguishment.

Of course, before the vampires drained him, the casters had planned to take his magic by force. Tanner wasn't about to let that happen. He made the only move he could and created a portal. Too weak to use the necessary amount of magic to escape the dome completely, he only made a tunnel from the cages to his condo.

That was where I found him. He wasn't dead. At least,

not yet. But he was depleted, like a caster who'd used all his magic. No one had ever seen anything like it—a fae drained of magic and existing only in a coma-like state. The doctors didn't know what to do. Had Tanner been caster instead of fae, they would've attempted a revival— a sort of blood transfusion but with magic.

Of course, Tanner had been fae, so the doctors wouldn't even attempt to revive him. Not ready to accept reality, I spent months seeking out the most powerful fae beneath the dome. My efforts were fruitless. Though, in hindsight, I should've known that would be the case; the most powerful fae weren't beneath any dome. They were in the Freelands, in places like Fae Canyon. Those were the fae who really knew about ancient magic, who were capable of drawing unfathomable amounts of power from the world and channeling it into a spell.

Out of deference for Tanner's position as a champion fighter, two of the long-term care facilities for depleted casters offered their services. For a price, of course. I could have afforded it, but I didn't want that for Tanner. He deserved better. Still, the decision of whether to cease all life-extending measures was for Everly to make.

Four months, six days, and nine hours after I found Tanner in a coma, he was dead. We held a small memorial at his favorite waterfall on the island. The following day, Christina had his ashes smuggled to the Freelands so that Tanner could be put to rest among others of our kind.

Tanner's death was hard on me, but it nearly killed Everly. Christina offered to have her extracted immediately. But Everly wasn't about to leave behind the cause and let all her brother's hard work go to waste. She did more counseling for fae on the extraction waitlist than anything else these days, but it seemed to help her just as much as it helped them.

I didn't know at what point my memories turned to dreams, but my eyelids didn't want to open when my alarm went off at 5:00 a.m. I hit snooze three times before Botto's prerecorded voice started screaming through a speaker mounted beside my bed.

"Wake up, Brie! Wake up, Brie! Time to train, buttercup! Wake up, Brie! Lazy fae don't win matches!" And the recording got progressively more hostile from there.

I smacked the speaker several times before finally sitting up and yelling back, "I'm awake, you annoying ass!" Botto and his many colorful taunts disappeared.

Twenty minutes later, I had showered and was in the back of a taxi on my way to the gym. I had a change of clothes in my bag. After my workout, I had a shift at Pele's before my date with Kai.

Botto had said to make the cardio light, but I had too much nervous energy to take things slow. I practically sprinted the entire five miles, lapping Rocko several times.

"Your feet grow wings, B?" he called as I sped past him for a fourth time.

"Don't I wish," I called back without slowing.

Next, because I'd promised Botto, I spent an hour training with my magic. Hitting stationary targets with fireballs was easy. I'd been able to perform that sort of offensive magic for over a decade. I made a fire whip and practiced using it as a weapon but only managed to hurt myself.

I tried a few spells I remembered from my lessons back in the canyon. The first one, a fire ring meant to surround an adversary in flames, went pretty well. My second spell failed badly. When I muttered, "Scaldia," the flames in my hand should have shot into the sky and taken the shape of a dragon's head, which could then breathe fire from above. Instead, the flames leapt to my head and formed a crown of fire.

"Yeah, I'm totally ready to fight with magic," I muttered as I extinguished the flames.

Weights were my last rotation of the morning. Cala agreed to spot me and seemed a tad surprised when I busted out all my reps with little effort.

"Are you okay?" she asked as we switched positions so that I could spot her on the last exercise of our circuit.

"Yeah, why?" I replied innocently.

"Oh, I don't—shit! Brie, really?" Cala thrust her blistered palm in my face and pointed to the metal bar— the *glowing* metal bar—with her other. "Still want to tell me there's nothing wrong?"

"I'm so sorry!" I exclaimed and then laughed uncomfortably. "But nothing is wrong."

Cala sighed and arched an eyebrow. "You meant to heat the bar?"

"No, of course not. Magic just sort of happens sometimes, you know? Like when your adrenaline is going," I replied lamely. "And, I told you, I just spent an hour doing fire spell work."

She stared me straight in the eye. "No, sweetie. Magic doesn't just happen when your adrenaline is going unless you're prepubescent. It only 'just happens' to adults when we're upset. So, spill. Are you worried about," she looked around the gym, "tonight?"

"No," I lied. "And I'm not worried at all. The first date's always the worst, right?"

Cala rubbed the small, red mark on her palm. With her were-genes, the blister was already healed. "The first date is the get-to-know-you date. It's fun and easy and everyone laughs a lot. The second date—now that's the get-to-know-you, get-to-know-you date. You both let down your guard a little. You share seemingly intimate details about your life, but not like really intimate details, you know?"

I stared down at her, mouth agape. "No, I honestly don't have any idea what you're talking about."

Cala looked up at me like I was the most hopeless fae she'd ever met. "Okay, so tonight—where are you going? What're you doing?"

I did another check for eavesdroppers and then said, "Having dinner at his cottage."

"He's cooking again?" She sounded surprised.

Is that a good surprised or a bad surprised? I wondered. "Yeah, I guess. He didn't say specifically who was cooking. I don't know, maybe we're having takeout. Does it really matter?" I asked.

"Yes, it does," Cala said firmly. "He's sharing an intimate detail about his life with you: he likes to cook."

Are we really having this conversation? Girl talk wasn't exactly in my realm of comfort.

"He doesn't like to cook. I mean, he might. His sister is the chef in the family," I blurted out. "They're her recipes."

Cala leaned closer. "He told you that?" she whispered.

"No, I read it in her biography," I said sardonically.

"So, he's already telling you about his family. That's good," she said, sitting back on the bench and crossing her arms.

I couldn't help myself, but I regretted asking the question immediately. "Why is that good?"

"Means he likes you," Cala said simply.

"Okay, no more. I don't want to know the dating rules or whatever. It's stressing me out too much," I said, waving my hands.

"Dating rules? Who's got a date?" Rocko asked, appearing beside me.

I jumped. *You really need to worry more about the covert part of your assignment and less about the date part,* I thought.

Cala didn't point any fingers, but her smirk was answer enough.

Rocko turned to me. "Please tell me you're going on a date with the prince."

"Who me?" I asked in a voice that had never before come out of my mouth. "Why would you ask that?"

"Um, I don't know, because he's had his eye on you forever," Rocko laughed.

"Okay, but why do you want me to have a date with him?" I countered.

Casters didn't feed off the magic of the shifters like they did with the fae. The were-creatures were usually protectors, guards, soldiers, and fighters. They were free to do as they pleased once they'd completed their required service to the queen, as long as they remained in

Queen Lilli's territory. The animosity between shifters and casters was bad, but not nearly as bad as between casters and fae. Still, Rocko wasn't a fan of casters and hated the royal family on principle.

"Because then I can lay in bed at night and think about you giving that royal jackass the verbal tongue lashing of a lifetime." Rocko threw his hands up in the air. "It'll be epic."

"You should probably talk to someone about that fantasy. It sounds like you may have issues," Cala said, smiling sweetly.

"And I need to take a shower and get to Pele's before Jon gives away my job," I announced and turned to leave.

"Good luck tonight," Cala called after me.

Pele's was hopping when I arrived for my shift. Jon was both waiting tables and cooking. I jumped right in. For five blissful hours, all I cared about was remembering the napkins, the pineapple ketchup, and that the wear-dragon at table nine couldn't digest anything with so much as a single chili pepper next in it.

My shift ended during the lull between lunch and dinner, giving me plenty of time to get home, shower, and get ready for my date with Kai. And plenty of time to obsess over Cala's dating protocols.

I was in over my head.

CHAPTER NINE

"YOU LOOK GREAT," Kai greeted me at the cottage door. Wrapping an arm around my waist, he leaned down and kissed me softly on the cheek. "How was your day?"

"Not bad." A wonderful aroma surrounded me as we entered the cottage—a tangy blend of tomatoes, peppers, and cilantro. "Can I ask what we're eating, or is it a surprise?"

Kai grinned. "Lomi lomi salmon. The surprise is whether it turns out well."

His casual stance and easygoing smile lessened my tension, and I found myself relaxing just as I had on our first date.

He held up a bottle of white wine and raised his

eyebrows in question.

"Yes, thank you," I said politely.

Kai poured us each a glass, handed one to me, and then raised his own. "What should we toast to?"

"Another amazing homecooked meal?" I suggested.

A guilty expression passed across Kai's face. "I have an admission. Sarah prepared the meal. All I did was smoke the salmon. Do I lose points for wrangling my little sister into cooking dinner for you?"

Pursing my lips, I pretended to seriously consider his question. "Only a few."

"I will do my best to win them back before the night is over," Kai replied solemnly. "The salad needs to chill for a bit longer. Would you care to take a walk?"

"Yeah, okay."

Kai's office cottage was secluded, but apparently it was still on the same property as the palace. Plush gardens filled the expanse around the small house. Stone pathways wound through the fragrant array of hibiscus and plumeria flowers. I breathed in the scents as we strolled across the grounds.

"I never asked—how was your day?"

"Busy," Kai admitted, taking a sip of wine. "We had more meetings to discuss the disappearances. Every day we learn of at least a dozen more individuals who have gone missing in the past few years." He sighed wearily. "It is troubling."

Thinking of the extractions, both past and present, I gulped a healthy amount from my glass. "It's very troubling," I lied quietly.

Kai smiled and slid his hand into mine. "We will find

the missing," he assured me. "All of them." Squeezing my hand, Kai added, "You have my word."

And that's what I'm worried about, I thought. I didn't want him to find the non-casters who were missing. I drained my glass.

Christina would want me to press the issue. She'd want me to pump Kai for more information. How close was the palace to discovering what happened to the missing? Did they suspect there was an underground rebellion? I couldn't ask him outright, but there had to be a way to delicately gain intel.

With Kai's hand warm in mine and surrounded by so much beauty, I couldn't bring myself to do such an ugly thing. *This is why you're here,* a voice inside my head argued.

"Who lives in the other cottages?" I asked instead.

The sun began its descent with a full moon already visible in the darkening sky.

"Palace staff. We offer the cottages based on seniority," he told me.

"Just casters? Or fae and shifters, too?" I asked, trying not to sound overly argumentative.

"In the past, casters were given priority," Kai said carefully.

"And now?"

"Well, just this year, my mother agreed to invite one of my fae bodyguards to take up residence in the cottages," he replied.

"I thought Kenoa was your only fae bodyguard?"

Kai smiled. "He is. Kenoa turned down the invitation. A shifter gate guard and her family took the cottage instead. I hope to diversify the onsite staff housing much further as more caster families move out."

It was a very political response, even if it was just a vague promise of something that might happen in the future. Nonetheless, I could tell that he meant the words. He wanted them to be true. Whether he could get his mother to agree was another story.

In the distance, colored lights shone down on the white marble pillars of the palace. It was beautiful, ethereal even. From my own patio at home, I could see the royal residence in the distance. But up close, the view was more impressive.

Or maybe it was the fact I was with Kai, who would one day rule from that very structure. *That's a surreal thought.*

"Are you excited for the luau?" Kai asked as we started back for his cottage.

"Truthfully?" I wrinkled my nose. "I'm not big on social gatherings."

He pushed open the cottage door and gestured me inside. "Well, this year we booked Cauldron's Bottom for the featured entertainment."

My eyebrows shot upward. "Seriously? Aren't they on tour? The luau never has a fae band." I hadn't meant the comment as an accusation, but my tone was sharper than intended.

Kai shrugged, unbothered. "The luau date is between the band's Tokyo and New York show dates. It took some finagling, but I managed to make them an offer they could not refuse." He met my gaze, his expression unreadable. "Sarah and I were more active in the planning than we have been in years past, and we both thought it would be nice to have a wider variety." Kai grinned mischievously. "I am still working on the contract details, but the Hibernation Clan has also agreed to play."

Cala is going to die, I thought. She had the biggest crush on Van Deeds, Hibernation Clan's lead singer.

"That's amazing," I told Kai honestly. "Isn't Hibernation Clan a little…risqué, though?"

Kai grabbed bowls from a cabinet and began scooping the lomi lomi salmon into them. "Let's just say that my mother is not thrilled with our decision, and she has only heard their radio-friendly songs. But my sister is a big fan. When the band received a personal invitation from Princess Sarah to come to Iolani Palace, they were eager to accept."

"The palace? Isn't the luau usually held in North Shore, on the beach?" I asked, confused. The fact the luau was held on the beach made it my least hated mandatory social engagement of the year.

"Yes, well, this year we have more security concerns than in the past," he replied tightly.

"The missing casters?" I guessed, moving around the kitchen and opening random drawers until I found silverware.

Kai looked at me pointedly. "And the missing fae. The shifters, as well, for that matter."

"I get it. You care." I smiled so he wouldn't think I was being glib. Well, not too glib, anyhow.

"I do. But that is not our main concern with the luau. You see, we always receive a fair number of threats before any event. As I am sure you are aware, Madame

Noelani uses the luau as a way to introduce her most recent graduates to society. Many do not agree with the practice, so we expect a certain amount more of those threats. This year, for whatever reason, the increase is exponential." A tinge of color crept into his cheeks. "And I have said too much about work for the evening," he finished.

"I like hearing about it," I said quickly. *Idiot. You might as well have shouted that you're part of the rebellion that most likely sent those threats.* "It's interesting," I added, which didn't sound any less weird. "I just mean, I've never really thought about this stuff before."

"Attend one security briefing with me, and you will have had your fill of hearing about, thinking about, and discussing this stuff," he laughed.

Kai refilled our wine, and we took our bowls outside to eat on the lanai.

"So, what is it exactly that you dislike about social gatherings?" Kai asked.

I speared a piece of salmon with my fork. "The people, mostly."

He threw his head back and laughed. "You are refreshingly honest."

The food churned in my gut. *Honest? No, I was definitely not an honest person.* "It just all feels so fake, you know? Cas...*people* always ask the same questions, but they don't care about the answers. It's exhausting. And repetitive," I continued.

"I could not agree more." Kai grinned. "You might not believe it, but every caster asks me the same questions, too. They all want to know when I'm getting

SOPHIE DAVIS

married. But what they really want to know is not when, but to whom, and if I would possibly consider their daughter. Talk about exhausting."

I laughed. "Not quite the same, but I'll give it to you. Maybe if you brought a date, they'd ask you different questions." My laughter died. *Why did you just say that?* I thought frantically.

"Hmmm." Kai looked at me thoughtfully. "Too bad the only proper date I've had in ages is averse to public outings."

I swallowed hard. The luau was a big deal and very public. Going as Kai's date would open up the world of paparazzi and tabloids. Social media would go crazy. I wasn't ready for that.

"Tell Princess Sarah the salad is awesome," I blurted out in what had to have been the most awkward conversational lane change ever. But at least it worked.

We moved on to safer topics like music and television. I found we liked a lot of the same movies and bands, though our taste in comedians differed greatly. Kai told me about his last business trip to the domed city of Austin, where he was treated to a rodeo. I told him about the time Cala and I went snorkeling and ended up with burnt behinds because we hadn't thought to reapply sunscreen.

The air grew chilly the longer we stayed outside, and I actually shivered. "I swear it feels like it's getting colder," I told Kai.

"It does seem so," he agreed. "Why don't we go inside?"

I checked the time on my cell: 11:28 p.m. "I should

146

probably be getting back. I have training early tomorrow."

"Of course. Walk with me to get the car?"

I hated the wave of relief that washed over me. If I went with him, I could honestly tell Christina that I never got the chance to snoop, because how was I supposed to say: "No thanks, Kai. I'd rather sit on my lazy ass while you go get the car."

"Sure," I said finally.

Kai didn't put the top down this time, which my bare arms appreciated. In a sleeveless shirt and no jacket, I wasn't really prepared for the drop in temperature.

"I have all of Sunday free," he said as we drove through the nearly deserted streets. "I know that's your day off from training. I thought maybe we could do something?"

"How do you know my training schedule?" I asked, narrowing my eyes in mock suspicion. Even if we hadn't reached the background check of our courtship, I was positive Kai had read the file on me that I was sure the casters kept.

Kai laughed softly. "That did sound a little stalkerish."

"Um, a lot stalkerish," I teased.

"Brew Another One," the Cauldron Bottom's most recent hit song, played on the roadster's impressive sound system.

Kai cleared his throat. "Have you ever been to the Ice Zoo on Maui? It is pretty amazing."

No. Because I'm not allowed to leave the dome, I thought bitterly, my mood plummeting. He knew I was confined to our island alone.

"I'm sure it is," I said quietly.

Kai parallel parked on my block and turned off the engine. He unbuckled his seatbelt and turned to face me. "Brie? Are you okay?"

"Fine," I replied, offering him the same smile I did for the cameras during a fight.

He shook his head. "No, you are not. Did I say or do something—"

"I can't do this, Kai," I blurted, grabbing the door handle. "I'm sorry."

"Wait, Brie," he called after me as I exited the car. "Please, talk to me."

I spun on the top step of my building. "There's nothing to talk about. I had a great time with you. Thank you for dinner, but I don't think we should do this again," I said curtly.

Kai stood at the bottom of the steps, looking as though he wanted to come closer but afraid of crowding me. He shook his head. "No, Brie. It was something I said that offended you. Please, what did I say?"

Tears pricked my eyes. *Don't cry. Not in front of him,* I lectured myself. *Never show a caster weakness.* "It's the fact you don't know that's the problem," I replied sadly.

He placed one foot on the next step. When I didn't turn and flee, he kept coming toward me, stopping once we were eye level. "Tell me, please," Kai said softly.

"Do you know why I've never seen the Ice Zoo? Why I've never been to Maui, period?" I asked, voice colder than the air outside the dome.

Kai's dark eyes registered alarm. He knew there was no good way to answer my questions.

"It's fine. I'll just tell you," I continued in the same frosty tone. "I'm fae, Kai. A fae with a fighting contract. I'm not allowed to leave the dome. My movements are tracked. Even if I did buy out my contract, I still wouldn't be permitted off Oahu without a royal dispensation."

He looked as though I'd slapped him. "Brie, I am so sorry. I did not think—"

"Exactly. You didn't think," I snapped. It took me a minute to rein in my anger. "Look, Kai, I had fun with you." Christina was going to have to find another spy, I decided. Which was probably for the best because I wasn't very good at the job.

"This can't work," I pressed on. "We've only been out twice. It's better if we just call it quits now before one of us gets hurt."

"You will be allowed to leave the island with me," Kai insisted.

It was the wrong thing to say. And he knew it immediately.

"Yeah?" I shot back. "What about all the other fae? What about the shifters? I'm sure they'd love to see icefalls and woolly mammoths, or whatever animals you have in the zoo."

Kai's jaw tightened. "You are—"

I wasn't finished with my tirade. "Why do you want to pursue this anyway? Because your mother wants you to marry a powerful fae? So you can siphon off my powers to keep yourself strong?"

Anger sparked in Kai's obsidian eyes. *Good,* I thought. *One-sided fights were no fun.*

"The queen's wishes have no bearing on our

relationship," Kai snapped, sounding like a haughty caster. "I asked you out because I find you fascinating. I want to spend more time with you because you are one of the few people I have met who is not afraid to speak the truth to my face. I know the system is bent, Brie. I'm trying to prevent it from breaking."

"Too late," I said, one hand on the door sensor.

"Brie, please. I know you have enjoyed my company. Let me prove I am different than your preconceived notion. Let me prove it's not too late to repair the damage between our races."

I turned and pushed the door open.

"Goodbye, Kai," I whispered over my shoulder.

CHAPTER TEN

CHRISTINA HAD TEXTED at some point on my ride back from the cottage. *I can't deal with you right now,* I thought as I wiped tears from my eyes with the back of my hand. My stomach was sick over the fight with Kai. It wasn't that I didn't mean everything I'd said to him, because I most definitely did. In fact, in a do-over, I'd lay a lot more truth on him.

I wanted to talk to someone about the argument, but who? *Cala,* I thought. It was after midnight, though; she had an early morning session with her trainer.

Everly will be awake, I considered. However, venting to her wasn't optimal; crying to my deceased boyfriend's little sister about my dating life just felt wrong. Besides, she would think that I was so upset over the situation because I actually liked Kai. She would think that he'd disappointed me by turning out to be the narrow-minded caster I thought he was before our first date.

Then, an even better idea occurred to me: I could write a report about my fight with Kai—and all the other conversations from the evening—and send it on a chip to Christina. I wouldn't have to deal with her directly, at least right away, and she'd still get a run-down of my findings.

I typed furiously for over an hour, detailing my conversation with Kai about the increased security at this year's luau, including the location change from North Shore to Iolani Palace. I included a note about Botto submitting paperwork for me to fight in other kingdoms, hoping that knowledge would soften the blow when she inevitably found out Kai and I were finished.

The fight with Kai didn't make it into the final report. While cathartic to write, I deleted that confrontation after realizing how whiny I sounded. I could just hear Christina saying, "I don't see the problem. He's a caster. Of course he didn't consider that he might hurt your feelings by suggesting a trip off the island. What did you expect? He probably thought you'd be grateful for the opportunity."

Am I overreacting? I wondered as I loaded the final report onto the chip.

If I'd only gone on those dates with Kai for the rebellion, then the answer was yes. He'd made a poor choice of words that I should have overlooked in favor of furthering the cause. Staying close to him no matter what—that had been Christina's directive. My personal feelings wouldn't have been a consideration.

But I hadn't gone out with Kai strictly for the rebellion. I had gone out with him for me, which was why the comment got under my skin. It was the first time I'd admitted that to myself.

The following day, I spent all morning training with Botto on my offensive fire magic. We ended practice with a sparring match. He still won, but I held my own. At one point, I even managed to cast the fire-breathing dragon head I'd been attempting the previous day. Unfortunately, it spit flames at me instead of Botto. That was when he called it quits on the session.

"You just need to focus all that power," Botto said as he walked with me to the locker rooms.

"I'm trying," I told him.

"You're distracted," Botto shot back. "Distracted fighters die in the arena, Brie."

I rolled my eyes and pushed open the door to the female locker room. "I think I heard that somewhere before. Where was that? Oh, right. My alarm clock tells me every time I oversleep."

After showering, I headed to my shift at Pele's. Cala called several times and texted me while I was working.

CALA (3:46 P.M.): *How'd it go last night?*
CALA (5:02 P.M.): *I want details.*

CALA (6:36 P.M.): *B. Call me. I'm starting to worry.*

I considered reaching back out to her once I was home, but I didn't. I ate a late dinner alone on my patio, wrapped in a quilt due to the chill in the air, all the while staring at Iolani Palace in the distance.

I wonder what Kai's doing, I thought. *Don't go there.*

I woke up the next morning to over a dozen text messages from Christina. The last few messages were just rows upon rows of question marks. I didn't respond. Instead, after my morning workout, I took a taxi to Pier and sought out Elton.

"Awfully early for you to be drinking," he called when he saw me enter the bar.

I smiled thinly and slid onto a bar stool. "Just here for the view."

Elton placed a cocktail napkin on the bar in front of me and started filling a glass with ice and water. "Meeting another friend?" he asked evenly.

"Sort of." I reached into my pocket and retrieved the chip. "But, um, something came up, and I can't stay long. Would you be able to give my friend Chris something for me?"

Elton looked at me appraisingly before finally nodding slowly. "Sure." He held out his hand, and I placed the chip on top.

"Thanks. I appreciate it." I got up to leave.

"Want to stay for a drink? Bartenders are great listeners," he said.

I was going to say no. But I had no plans the rest of the day, unless you counted sitting alone in my condo and brooding.

"Pineapple margarita," I told Elton decisively.

A drink turned into two, which turned into three. There may have been a fourth, but I couldn't have said for certain. No one else came and sat at the bar, so I let myself babble at Elton about life. Just as promised, he was a great listener.

"I mean, Tanner was just so *me*. You know? He got me. Other guys don't get me," I rambled.

"All other guys or just one certain guy?" Elton asked knowingly.

"He should've known better," I replied nonsensically, since I hadn't actually told Elton about another guy or my issues with him. Though, had I been completely sober, I might've remembered that Elton knew about my mission involving Kai.

"People say stupid shit sometimes," Elton said easily, taking the abrupt segue in stride. "Maybe give him a chance to explain?"

I shook my head. "He tried. It only made it worse."

"Have you ever said or done something without thinking?" Elton tried.

"Story of my life," I hiccupped.

Elton rested his elbows on the bar across from me and bent down to meet my slightly unfocused gaze. "This guy important to you?"

"In a weird way," I mumbled.

"Then maybe you should think about giving him a second chance? Just because?" Elton shrugged and straightened to his full height. "Just an unbiased opinion."

"Am I biased?" I asked.

He laughed. "I'm not sure. But you do need another margarita."

"No." I shook my head, and the world spun a little. "I definitely don't. I need to go home."

"Want me to call someone?" Elton offered.

"Already on it," I replied, pulling out my phone.

Twenty minutes later, Kenoa arrived with Sumi. The three of us ended up staying for dinner. As Kenoa said, it wasn't like I had any real food at my house, and I needed to eat. It was nice sitting with friends who didn't ask pointed questions or give knowing looks. Sumi talked about the other fae and shifters she'd met at the commune, which made it sound as though she was making friends. Kenoa didn't talk much at all, but that was normal. He was the strong, silent type.

The sun had set by the time we dropped Sumi off at the commune. It was cold enough that I turned on the heater for the rest of the ride to my building.

"So, what's the deal with Sumi?" I asked Kenoa.

"What do you mean?" he replied without taking his eyes off the road.

"I mean, isn't she sort of young for you?"

The large fae snorted. "I was meeting with her when you called. I've been asked to train her."

"Really?" I arched an eyebrow. "You gonna do it?"

"I don't know yet." Kenoa sighed loudly. "It'd be a lot on top of my regular job."

"You could just be a trainer," I suggested.

"If I take the job, I'm not leaving my position at the palace," Kenoa said flatly, like the topic wasn't up for discussion.

But the topic was one I very much wanted to discuss. "Why are you so loyal to him?" I asked bluntly.

"Because I know him," Kenoa said simply.

"Then you know he's a pompous jerk," I snapped.

"You really want to have this conversation now?" Kenoa spared a glance at me.

"Yes, I do."

Did I, though? If I'd already made up my mind about ending my budding relationship with Kai, why did I want Kenoa to explain his friendship with him? Validation that I was right, and the prince was an ass? That wasn't what I would get, and a part of me must've known that.

Kenoa pulled to a stop by the curb in front of my building and put the car in park. He turned and gave me his full attention. "I've known Kai for over two decades. We played in a soccer league together when we were about eight. Kai was chosen as one of the captains, along with a handful of other casters. He picked me first. No other fae was selected until all the casters had been chosen."

"So you became friends because his mother taught him to be politically correct?" I asked, narrowing my gaze to the point my eyes crossed.

Kenoa laughed. "Kai didn't pick me because I'm fae. He picked me first because I was the best. We got to know each other and yes, we became friends. When I told Kai I was retiring from the arena, he asked if I'd consider taking a position as his bodyguard. Security has been an increasing issue around the palace. He wanted someone he trusted close to him."

I held his dark gaze. "Why did you accept, though?"

Kenoa rubbed a large hand across his face. "He's worth protecting, Brie. He's a good guy."

"Because he picked you first for soccer twenty years ago?" My brow furrowed. "I'm not buying it."

"He's a good guy because he's a good guy. Like I said, I know him. He's worth protecting generally because he's going to be king. When that happens, he wants to change the system. He's worth protecting personally because Kai has saved my life. More than once."

"Saved your life?" I crossed my arms over my chest. "How?"

"Not tonight, Brie. One day, maybe I'll tell you. That day is not today." Kenoa reached over and patted my knee. "Get some sleep. Think about what I said."

I did think about what Kenoa had said. A lot. I thought about it as I lay in bed, holding the frozen hibiscus Kai had given me in the arena. I thought about it during training the following morning. I thought about it as I blended milkshakes at Pele's during a double shift the next afternoon. I thought about it when I pointedly ignored more of Christina's texts and Cala's phone calls.

They weren't the only people I blew off either. Everly left several messages about grabbing lunch, but I couldn't bring myself to see her. My feelings were too conflicted and my guilt too strong. I needed more distance from the situation before I saw my friends, before they asked me about Kai and my mission.

Over the weekend, Rocko and Rudy joined the growing list of people I didn't answer. They wanted me to come to Hideout for drinks, which was typical. I chose to spend the night in with takeout from Taste of Tokyo and the latest action movie from were-panther director, Wesley Mosh. That was not typical.

On Sunday morning, I woke from a fitful sleep well before sunrise. Normally I spent my day off with Cala at the beach or having brunch with Everly or rock climbing with Rocko. Sometimes Kenoa and I would go for a hike. I didn't feel like doing any of that.

"Get it together, Brie," I grumbled as the QuickDrip brewed my morning latte. "You need to snap out of this funk."

As if in response, my phone buzzed. Chris came up on the display. When I didn't answer, she called back. Again. And again. And again.

This is not good, I thought as my finger danced over the accept button.

With a sigh, I finally answered. "Can I call you back in five?"

"Sure," a filtered voice replied.

Taking my latte to the patio, I retrieved the unregistered cell. The time on the display read 5:32 a.m. *Way too early for this conversation,* I thought. For several long moments I stared up at the night sky, at the manufactured stars, at the fake three-quarter moon. And at Iolani Palace looming in the distance.

A shiver ran down my spine. I checked the weather app on my phone: 25 degrees. *It almost never gets below sixty,* I marveled as I wrapped a quilt around my shoulders. Taking a deep breath, I finally dialed Christina's number.

"Oh good, you're alive," she greeted me. The words were anything but friendly. "Where have you been, Brie?"

"Did you get my present?" I answered her question

with a question.

"Yeah, I did. It doesn't explain why you've been dodging my calls," she snapped.

"I'm sorry," I said simply.

"You're sorry? I don't want apologies, I want progress. And real answers. What's up, Brie?" Christina managed to sound both annoyed and concerned.

"I can't do this, Christina." Before she could reply, I began to ramble. "I'm sorry. We got in a fight the other day, and it's over. Kai hasn't called me since then. I'm sorry. I know you were—"

"They're getting close, Brie. The authorities suspect the missing fae are being smuggled out of the kingdom," Christina interjected. "Those files you photographed? They show that the authorities have made connections between the disappearances."

"Okay," I said slowly, taking a long sip of my latte to clear the haze inside my head. "This is obviously bad."

"No shit, Brie." Christina was beyond pissed. She also sounded more than a little scared. I imagined her pacing back and forth in the stockroom of her boutique. "We need someone on the inside, someone who can steer the investigation in a different direction." Her words were measured, and it was clear she'd given this a great deal of thought.

"Use one of Madame Noelani's girls," I replied. "They are schooled in the fine art of persuasion."

"Fix things with the prince." She enunciated each word, like I was a toddler.

"I can't. We have irreconcilable differences," I said dryly.

For several long moments, there was a deafening

silence. If not for the clicking of Christina's heels on the concrete, I might have thought she'd hung up on me.

"What happened?" she asked finally.

I didn't want to tell her. I knew what she would say. "It's stupid," I admitted.

"Well if it's stupid, what's the problem? What, did he insult you? Offend you? He's a freakin' caster, Brie. What did you expect?"

Yep, that's the response I imagined she would give.

"You aren't really dating him. Suck it up, Brie. I need you. The rebellion needs you. Do you think Tanner would've curled up in his condo and sulked because some caster said something mean?" she continued.

"Don't bring him into this," I growled.

"Then do your job. You wanted an active role—this is it."

"What about the inter-kingdom fights?" I tried. "I could be a real asset as a messenger."

Christina sighed loudly and repeated, "Fix things with the prince." It wasn't a suggestion. It was a command.

I considered her words: *The rebellion needs you.*

I recalled the night outside Hideout and the fae girl, Honie, who was married to the caster asshole. Her situation wasn't nearly as dire as the fae and shifters the rebellion normally ferried to the Freelands—but that didn't mean she was in a good position. Evacuations were expensive. Even with wealthy donors like myself, the rebellion could only afford to bribe guards and cargo loaders and pilots and airport workers so often.

For that reason, the fae and shifters in the worst possible situations were given priority. Many had been torn from their homes in the Freelands. And every evacuee was someone who came to the rebellion for help.

Honie, and fae like her, never asked to be saved. Many didn't want to be. For them, life under the dome was sunshine and roses. Literally. They would endure a lot just to live under the dome's protection. But that didn't mean they wouldn't chose freedom if they knew it was truly possible, safe, and a better life awaited them.

The rebellion needs you. "Fine," I relented. "I'll see what I can do. But I make no promises."

"You're resourceful, Brie," Christina said. It didn't sound like a compliment. "I am sure you will find a way to mend fences."

Long after Christina disconnected, I sat on my patio with the phone in hand and stared at the cityscape. Spying on Kai and photographing files—that was one thing. Christina was asking me to go a step further. She wanted me to gain his confidence and use it to redirect a police investigation. I wasn't cut out for such trickery.

When I finally retrieved my everyday cell, the sun was high overhead, and my latte was cold. I stared at the phone, Kai's number on the screen. *Swallow your pride,* I thought. *The rebellion needs you.* To my relief, it went straight to voicemail. I hung up without leaving a message.

As I was heading upstairs to shower, someone knocked on my door. *Way too early for my crowd,* I thought. Saturday nights were always party nights since none of us trained on Sunday.

I peered through the peephole on my tiptoes and saw Kai standing outside my condo.

CHAPTER ELEVEN

CROUCHING DOWN LIKE he could see me, I leaned my back against the door. The prince knocked again. I couldn't answer it. I had yet to brush my teeth. My hair was matted on one side from all the tossing and turning, not to mention my puffy eyes and well-worn pajamas.

"Brie, please open the door," Kai called. "I know you are there. I can hear you moving around." When I didn't respond, he added, "Please, Brie. I just want to talk."

I ran my fingers through my hair, but it was no use. The knots had knots. I twisted the rat's nest into a messy bun. Deciding that coffee breath was better than morning breath, I downed the rest of my cold latte.

Finally, I took a deep breath and opened the door.

Despite his insistence, Kai seemed surprised. "Hi," he stammered, taking in everything from my sock monkey slippers to the pilled sweater that I'd purchased because it reminded me of one my father wore.

Gaia, he looks good, I thought traitorously. "Hey," I replied, drawing the two halves of the sweater closed over my flannel top.

Behind Kai, Kenoa stood with his hands behind his back. Staring off into space, he looked like he'd rather be anywhere else.

"I hate the way we left things the other night," Kai began. He shifted his weight from one foot to the other, looking more ill-at-ease than I'd ever seen the confident heir. "I cannot apologize enough."

The words pained me, but I said them anyway. "I'm sorry, too. I might have overreacted."

Kai chuckled softly. "We both know you do not believe that. You did not overreact. I…," he hesitated, searching for the right words. "I was insensitive. I do know the limitations placed on you and the rest of the fae. And I admire your resolve."

"My resolve?"

"I have dated fae before," he said carefully. "And they are always more than happy to take advantage of the privileges that my company affords."

"I'm not most fae," I said coolly.

Kai shook his head. "No, you are not. That is what first drew me to you, Brie. I should have known better. I *do* know better." He clasped his hands together in front of his chest. "Please give me a second chance."

I studied the prince. His dark eyes were fixed on my face. His hair was still damp from a recent shower, and his clothes were casual but neatly pressed. The soft lips that I couldn't forget fought a smirk.

"What's so funny?" I asked. My hand flew to my face, wondering what was causing his amusement.

"Sock monkeys?" Kai nodded toward my slippers. "I would have thought you more of a black, leather slippers girl."

"They were a gift," I retorted, smiling despite myself. Cala had given them to me for summer solstice. Taking a deep breath, I asked. "Do you want to come inside?"

Kai grinned. "I thought you would never...," he trailed off as he entered my foyer. Instantly, he began to shiver.

I smiled, taking perverse pleasure in his discomfort. The shoe was usually on the other foot, and I liked having the upper hand.

"I'll make some hot coffee. Regular or espresso?"

"Regular, please," Kai replied.

He started to close the door behind him, but I called over his shoulder. "You, Kenoa?"

"I'm fine out here, Brie," he said quickly.

I glanced between the prince and his bodyguard. "You're not standing outside my door. You're one of my best friends, and that would just be weird." Kenoa opened his mouth to protest, but I didn't give him the chance. "You know your way to the game room. Enjoy."

He flashed me a grin as he hurried inside. "Espresso, please."

Kai followed me into the kitchen and watched as I

programmed the QuickDrip.

"The game room is for my friend Rocko and the other guys. Mostly Rocko, though," I answered his unasked question. "Cream and sugar?" I handed Kai a mug of steaming black coffee.

Wrapping his hands around the cup, Kai looked like he was considering bathing in the contents. "No, thank you. Black is fine."

I led Kai out to the porch. "You can wait out here where it's warmer. I'll just be a minute."

Though I considered making the prince wait for an extended period of time—after all, he'd shown up unannounced—my father had raised me to be polite. Instead of dallying, I quickly slid on a pair of jeans and a tee, splashed water on my face, ran a brush through my hair, and gave my teeth a quick scrub. When I returned with a fresh mug for myself, Kai stood at the railing, surveying his kingdom.

"You have a wonderful view," he said as I joined him.

"That's why I bought this place," I admitted. Sipping my coffee, I rested the mug on the railing. "Do you have something against phones?"

Kai shifted, angling his body toward mine. "I did not think you would answer my calls."

"Maybe not," I retorted. I shrugged, as though I hadn't been checking my cell constantly for his missed calls.

"Brie," he began. "I really am sorry."

For a long moment, I stared at the blue-green water of the Pacific Ocean and its faux horizon. The image was a façade, of course—tropical waters didn't lay beyond the dome anymore. Frozen seas surrounded the island, complete with pale water and icebergs. The bright rays of sunshine that warmed our cheeks within the dome didn't shine on the other side of the barrier.

Kai reached over as though to brush his knuckles across my cheek. At the last minute, he thought better of it and let his hand fall back to his side.

"Brie," he started again.

"Do you really want a second chance?" I asked. My gaze never left the waves in the distance. They seemed to be a metaphor for my freedom: faux and altogether deceiving. "If so, no more apologies." Turning, I faced him fully. "Just don't make the same mistake again, okay?"

"You have my word."

Before our fight, the prince had wanted to whisk me away on a romantic day trip to the Ice Zoo. Instead, we spent that Sunday in my condo watching movies and talking. Kenoa remained in the game room, with the door open, playing Dome Raiders. Every so often, he'd grunt or yell. But like any good bodyguard, I knew he had one ear on our conversation. And he was positioned so that he had one eye watching the prince and the other on the television.

"Did you bring Kenoa as a peace offering?" I asked. We were sitting on the wraparound sofa in my living room, both curled in blankets.

Kai chuckled. "I am required to have at least one bodyguard with me whenever I leave the palace grounds. Kenoa graciously offered to come with me today."

I arched an eyebrow. "So it was his idea?"

The prince fixed me with his dark gaze. "Truthfully, I did not believe you would allow one of my caster guards into your home. Kenoa happened to agree with me. So, here we are."

He's trying to make amends, I thought.

My stomach growled audibly.

"How about some lunch?" Kai suggested. "We could order in, if you prefer?"

"How do you feel about burgers and fries?" I asked.

Kai smiled. "Perfect."

I called Jon directly to place an order for one salmon burger, one beef and mushroom burger, a tuna-steak burger with avocado, and three orders of pineapple fries. Thirty minutes later, Pele's delivery fae knocked on my door. I made Kai stay in the living room to avoid gossip.

Eating takeout in my dining room, which I almost never used, was a far cry from the homecooked meals Kai had prepared for our previous dates. At first, I worried it would be awkward with Kenoa there—the prince and I had never hung out together with another person. But the conversation flowed easily. Kai and Kenoa talked about their upcoming trip to the domed city of Manhattan. Apparently, King Steven was planning a parade in honor of Kai's visit, complete with giraffes, elephants, and acrobatic fae.

"That sounds like overkill," I commented, wiping my greasy hands on a napkin.

"Oh, I agree," Kai said. "King Steven is of the older generation. He abides custom. And, apparently, a parade is customary for visiting royals in his kingdom."

"Why are you going?" I asked.

Kai smiled. "For Sarah. I need to discuss the matter of her security with King Steven, so she can attend culinary school." Two red splotches appeared on his sharp cheekbones. "And because the king has asked me to meet his daughter, Princess Mia," the prince admitted.

"Oh, I see." I averted my gaze.

Kenoa cleared his throat. "I think I'll leave you two alone." He gathered his empty plate and takeout box and headed inside.

"I have no interest in Princess Mia," Kai said quietly.

Your feelings don't matter. Only the cause matters. "I understand." I shrugged like the prospect of him being introduced to a caster princess from another kingdom didn't bother me. "It's part of the job, right?"

Kai eyed me. "It is part of the job," he agreed. Then, in a much softer voice, he added, "For now."

What does that mean? I wondered. I didn't want to start a fight, so I didn't press the issue. *Let go of your feelings. You aren't really dating him.*

"How do you feel about a game of pool?" I asked, pointedly changing the subject.

"Pool? You have a pool table?"

"In the game room. Rocko is a pool shark. He's really the one who uses it," I replied.

Kai flashed a smile. "I can honestly say that I have never played, but I am always up for a challenge."

For some reason, I had a feeling the challenge he was referring to had nothing to do with billiards. I was his challenge. Did that make me a conquest? Did it matter? *Only the cause matters.*

Kai proved awful at eight ball. It was refreshing to see

him struggle, like he was a real person and not just this perfect caster prince. He was a good sport, though. He laughed when he hit the cue ball off the table and when he scratched the green felt because he missed his target entirely.

After three extremely long games of pool, we joined Kenoa playing Dome Raiders. Neither of us were very good at the videogame, either. Still, it was fun. Having the heir to the throne in my home should've been weird. But it wasn't. It was comfortable.

I studied Kai, the controller in his hand, eyes glued to the television. He grinned as his avatar set a vampire hive on fire.

"Yes! Finally, I can advance!" he yelled, pumping one fist in the air.

I smiled. *He's enjoying himself,* I thought. For a minute, I let myself believe that maybe our worlds weren't so different after all.

We ate sushi rolls from Taste of Tokyo for dinner. Watching Kenoa devour an entire sushi boat meant for five people was a sight to see. The guy was a bottomless pit.

"Did you decide if you'll take that trainer position?" I asked Kenoa as he licked spicy mayo off his finger.

Kenoa looked at Kai and several silent messages passed between them.

"I'm going to train Sumi," Kenoa said evenly. His eyes shifted to Kai again before he added, "She's very powerful, Brie. I believe she could be the next you, with proper practice."

"The next me?" I laughed. "That's a weird thought."

"You have won one hundred matches," Kai interjected. "You are the gold standard."

The way he looked at me gave me goosebumps. *Turn it off. Your feelings don't matter.*

After dinner, Kai and I sat on the patio and watched the artificial sun set, while Kenoa stretched out on the living room sofa to digest all the raw fish he'd consumed. By the time the stars appeared in the night sky, the temperature had plummeted. The prince and I layered on more blankets but still shivered.

Had I been alone, I would've summoned my magic and made a fire to keep warm. With Kai there, I felt weird using my powers. Instead, I did it the old-fashioned way—I used a lighter to ignite coals in the fire pit.

"May I ask a personal question?" Kai pulled the blankets tighter around his shoulders as I snuggled back into my lounge chair.

"You can ask a personal question. Not sure I'll answer, though." I forced a laugh. I didn't like personal questions, and I was certain I knew what he was going to ask.

"Why do you resist using your fire magic?"

It's none of your business, I thought. "It's complicated," I said instead. "I mean, I do use my magic. Just not that often. But my trainer has been making me practice with it. He thinks if I fight with fire, literally, that I could possibly qualify for inter-kingdom matches." *That's a good non-answer,* I thought.

Kai shifted uncomfortably in his chair. "I know. Botto came to see me personally. I have taken over the task of reviewing applications for anyone wishing time away from the dome."

Botto went to see him? I felt like my two worlds were mixing, and I wasn't sure I liked that.

"So then, what's the verdict?" I asked. "Are you going to let me go?"

The prince averted his gaze. "I would rather not start a fight," he said quietly.

"You aren't going to approve my application?" I demanded. *And the day was going so well.*

Kai cleared his throat, took a deep breath, and met my gaze. "Ordinarily, no. I am sorry, Brie, but you do not meet the requirements. However—"

"What requirements?" I snapped.

"Some of your past associations make you ineligible," he said carefully.

Tanner. He's talking about my relationship with Tanner, I thought, annoyed.

"However," Kai began again, "I have approved a specific fight, in the Domed City of Los Angeles, in four months."

So close to Fae Canyon, I thought, my heart pounding.

"I will be visiting the city on business, so technically you will have a royal escort. Traveling with me is a way to circumvent the eligibility requirements." He sighed, clearly wishing we were talking about anything else.

Your feelings don't matter, I told myself. Nonetheless, I was pissed. It wasn't right. It wasn't fair. Oahu wasn't my home. No one should be able to control or restrict my movements.

"I am sorry, Brie. My hands are tied." He reached for my hand. I let him take it. Intertwining our fingers, he added, "For now. When I become king, I plan to repeal some of the more restrictive mandates regarding travel outside the dome."

I thought about Kenoa's words: *He's a good guy. He wants to change the system.*

I took a deep breath and exhaled slowly to temper my anger. "I understand," I said tightly.

Kai laughed softly. "No, you don't. And I do not blame you. You should be upset. These laws," he shook his head, "they are old and outdated. When my ancestors and the other monarchs passed the mandates restricting fae and shifters from leaving the domes…it was a long time ago."

I stared at our joined hands. A part of me wanted to yell at him. Another part of me felt like an idiot for bringing up the topic in the first place. I'd only said something because I wanted to steer the conversation away from my magic.

Your feelings don't matter…. But he wants to change the system. I didn't know how I felt. About anything. Deep down, I did believe Kai wanted to revamp the system. But wanting to enact change and actually doing so were two very different things.

"Can we talk about something else?" I asked.

Kai smiled. "Of course. Could you tell me something first?"

"Maybe," I hedged. "What do you want to know?"

"Have I ruined our day together?" He sounded so despondent that my stomach clenched.

I shook my head. "No, you haven't. And, honestly, I do appreciate you telling me to my face. I would have been very upset to hear it from Botto that you were the one who rejected the application."

"I have wanted to tell you since Botto came to me," Kai admitted.

"I also appreciate that you have cleared me to fight in Los Angeles." That was true-*ish*. I was excited to visit a city so close to my home. And the rebellion had an active branch there. "I know you're doing this as a personal favor to me," I added.

"I am doing this as a favor to you," Kai agreed, running his fingers over my hand. "But I am also doing it because I believe the laws are too harsh." He offered me a tentative smile. "Can I ask you another question?"

My heart pounded in my chest. *What's he going to ask now?* In relationships, people shared their secrets with their partner, including their past indiscretions. I wasn't comfortable with that. My secrets were mine alone. They weren't up for discussion.

I pursed my lips. "Sure, I guess."

"I hear you enjoy the beach. Is that true?"

Relief washed over me. This was a softball question; I could handle this type of sharing. "I do," I said simply. "Did Kenoa tell you that?"

Color infused his cheeks. "He did. Please do not think I talk to him about you." He gave an embarrassed laugh. "Well, I suppose I have asked him some questions, but only because I want to make sure you are having a good time."

I averted my gaze and smiled. I knew I should be irritated that he talked to Kenoa about me. Or that Kenoa had told him anything. Yet, if he meant what he said, how could I be mad? Kai was being thoughtful. The girly part of me felt warm and tingly all over and not because I was sitting next to a fire.

"Well, you guys did bet on whether I'd take you up on that first date," I said after a long pause.

"You have me there." Kai squeezed my hand. "How would you like to have dinner at Lanikai Beach on Tuesday?"

A public outing? I thought, my mouth suddenly very dry. "Like at the Sand Dunes?" I asked uneasily, referring to the expensive restaurant I'd never ventured into.

Kai leaned closer so that our faces were only inches apart. "I was thinking something a little more low-key, like a picnic. Unless you would prefer a fancy restaurant on the water?"

"I'm not really a fancy kinda fae," I replied absently.

He was so close. All I could think about was our last kiss and how much I wanted an encore performance.

His mouth brushed across mine. *Why does this feel so right?* I wondered, as Kai reached across the chair and wrapped an arm around my waist. He gently pulled me closer.

"I don't know about that," he murmured, lips touching mine as he spoke.

His warm lips finally overtook mine. *I missed this,* I thought, surprised both that it was true and that I'd missed something I'd barely had. Kai's hands were in my hair, pulling my ponytail free. I wrapped my arms around his neck as I crawled over the chair arms, ditching my blanket. Fingers danced down my spine, over my shirt, and stopped at my waist. He pulled my hips toward his and sat up straighter. My hands ran over his well-muscled chest.

And that was when it happened.

Power surged inside of me. Kai jerked back as though I'd burned him. Within seconds, I realized that I *had* burned him. Liquid orange flames coated both of my hands like fiery gloves, and the faint smell of burnt cotton hung in the charged atmosphere.

"I'm so sorry," I gasped and jumped to my feet.

There were two singed patches on Kai's shirt, both in the shape of my hand.

"I am *so* sorry," I repeated. With the heat of his body no longer pressed against mine, the magic was easier to control. I extinguished the flames with a wave of my hands. "I swear that doesn't usually happen. Did I hurt you?"

Kai didn't respond. He was too busy staring at my hands. His dark eyes were wide with childlike wonder.

"Have you never seen a fire fae with flames on her hand?" I asked. "Can't casters do the same thing with a spell?"

"You are the only fire fae I have spent time with," Kai said, still looking at my hands.

"Do you want to see something else?" I asked. *This is a bad idea,* my inner voice said. *One kiss and you're putty in his hands.*

"Please," Kai replied.

I stepped closer so that I was standing beside the lounge chair. I extended one palm toward him and called the magic. This time, turquoise and amethyst flames twisted around my fingers. I nodded for him to raise his hand, too.

"Won't I get burned?" he asked cautiously.

I shrugged and hid a smile. "Only one way to find out."

Slowly, Kai climbed out of the chair and stood facing me. Taking a deep breath, he pressed his palm to mine. The flames leapt from my skin to his. The controlled blaze wrapped around our joined hands and formed a perfect bow. Mesmerized, Kai watched the fire binding us together.

I watched the prince. "It's not that impressive," I teased.

"It is," Kai protested. "You have exceptional control over your magic."

"Tell my trainer that. He says I lack focus and discipline, and I need to concentrate harder," I scoffed.

Kai smiled. "Quite frankly, Botto scares me."

I laughed softly and stretched on my tiptoes, catching his lips with mine. Suddenly, my fire magic stopped being the most fascinating thing about me. Kai spun me and slowly guided me backward until my spine was pressed against the patio doors. His mouth moved down my neck. I let my head fall back against the glass.

"Does this mean we have a date on Tuesday?" Kai asked as he kissed the soft spot behind my ear.

"Are you bringing dinner?" I breathed.

His hands were on my hips, and I couldn't seem to think straight.

"Only if you promise to bring a bathing suit," he countered, bringing his lips back to mine.

"Deal," I mumbled against his mouth.

A while later, I walked Kai to the front door. Kenoa

said a quick goodbye before running to get the car. Kai gave me a soft kiss, which turned hungrier.

"Brie. About that bathing suit," he began ten minutes later, one hand on the front doorknob. "It is entirely optional."

CHAPTER TWELVE

"HOW ABOUT SOMETHING in blue?" suggested the fae saleswoman, Cassie. "A nice jewel tone would complement your skin color."

She held up a one-shoulder, sapphire dress with a tutu skirt. It wasn't hideous. The color did look good on me. But the dress just wasn't *me*. She also held up a cornflower sheath that, while very pretty, was better suited for a daytime event.

Cassie's smile faltered when I didn't immediately jump on her latest choices. I didn't blame her; Cala and I had been in the store, Ivy of the Avenue, for over an hour. Cala's poor personal shopper was trying very hard not to get frustrated with us, but she grew visibly tenser by the second.

"Do you have something in a floral print?" Cala asked. She appraised me, starting at my hair and working her way down to my toes. "Nothing too low-cut. And we need straps. On both shoulders. Brie needs to stand out, but also look demure."

"Oh, I don't need to stand out," I protested. "I just need a dress that I won't look uncomfortable in."

Cala waved off my objections and stared pointedly at the polished and perfumed fae.

Cassie's smile was more genuine this time. "I believe I have just the thing, darling," she replied. Tossing the two selections she was holding to an assistant, Cassie rushed off.

"Want to talk about why you've been missing-in-action?" Cala asked me, staring expectantly over the rim of her champagne flute. "Or are we just going to pretend like last week didn't happen?"

I'd managed to avoid Cala until today. She'd cornered me in the gym and demanded we shop for luau dresses. It wasn't that I didn't want to talk to her, I just didn't know what to say; I'd put off the inevitable for as long as possible.

"Not here," I murmured, taking a small sip of my own bubbly. There were too many eyes around, and too many ears.

My best friend crossed her long, toned legs and sighed. "Fine. I'm just glad you agreed to get something new for the luau this year."

The saleswoman burst back into the room, trailed by an assistant with a rolling rack containing five floral dresses. She selected a white, knee-length dress with pale-pink and silver flowers embroidered on the bodice and a tulle skirt. It was beautiful. And the rebellious part of me liked the fact it was white. Most people under the domes shied away from white because it reminded everyone of snow, and subsequently, of life outside the domes. Casters would whisper about me and say I was inconsiderate—if they were polite—or possibly that I didn't know my place—if they were assholes.

"This Aikiohani design is from her spring collection. It's one-of-a-kind." The saleswoman flashed an I'm-buttering-you-up-so-you'll-spend-a-lot-of-money smile. "It is just perfect for a one-of-a-kind fae."

I looked at Cala. Her grinned stretched from ear to ear. "It's gorgeous. And you will *definitely* stand out."

That was the downside to wearing a white dress. Did I really care if I stood out because of this small act of defiance? No, no, I didn't.

"Let me guess," I began dryly, "it just happens to be in my size?"

Cassie laughed. "Maybrie, darling, you are tall and thin—of course the sample is in your size."

With a light touch, I ran a finger over the buttery silk bodice. Up close, the flowers had exquisite detail. I could tell each one was hand-sewn. The ribbon of white that separated the bodice from the tulle skirt would hit me at just the right place, and the tulle would give me the illusion of curves. Well, at least it would hide my narrow hips.

"Try it on, dear. See how it looks," Cassie coaxed.

I looked at the time on my cell. *Crap, I have to be at Pele's in ten minutes.* "I'm already going to be late for work. I don't have time to try it on right now," I told her.

The fae looked like she wanted to rip her hair out.

"Don't worry, I'll take it," I added before she went ballistic. "If it needs alterations…?"

A visibly happier Cassie finished my sentence, "Then you just call to schedule, darling. We will accommodate your very busy schedule, of course."

"Great. Thanks." I handed Cala the rest of my champagne and hugged her goodbye. "Gotta run."

"Call me later. I want an explanation for last week," she whispered in my ear.

When I reached the door, it occurred to me that a dress for the luau wasn't the only item of clothing I needed. "Do you carry bathing suits here?" I called to Cassie.

"One piece or two?" she replied.

"Um, one?" It sounded more like a question than an answer. "Actually, no. Two. It's for a date."

Both Cassie and Cala squealed, making it hard to judge who was more excited. Was I really so pathetic that even Cala's personal shopper thought my date was a big deal?

"Say no more, darling. When is the big occasion?"

I wrinkled my nose. "Tonight."

"The perfect swimsuit will be at your condo when you arrive home," she promised.

One problem solved, I thought. Sliding sunglasses over my eyes, I darted for the taxi idling in front of the boutique.

My shift was only four hours, but even between

traditional lunch and dinner hours, Pele's was busy. I had little downtime to think about how displeased Christina would be to learn that Kai had spent the day at my condo, and that we'd spent a significant part of the evening making out.

She doesn't expect you to blow him off when he tries to kiss you, I argued mentally as I mixed a pineapple shake.

Christina had said to keep him interested. Well, the only way to keep him interested was to let our fake relationship progress like a real relationship. Of course, Christina hadn't considered the fact that I might actually like the prince and enjoy our time together. Or that I might stop thinking of our relationship as fake.

You don't get that warm, gooey feeling when someone tries to kiss you unless you want them to kiss you, I thought while I loaded plates into the dishwasher. *How do spies do this?*

Christina would also be unhappy to learn that despite an entire day together, I hadn't learned anything new about the royal family's investigation into those who'd gone missing from beneath the dome. I felt guilty because I hadn't even *thought* about my undercover work or the cause. Instead, I'd spent the day talking about how some sci-fi movie didn't make logical sense and whether the lead actor in a biopic we watched had gotten some work done to his face.

You're laying the groundwork, I told myself. Christina wanted me to steer the investigation away from the truth. To do that, I needed to gain Kai's trust. That took time…and kissing, of course. *Tonight. Tonight, I'll work it into the conversation. Subtly, so he won't get suspicious,* I lectured myself as I rang in another order.

"Hey, Brie!" Jon poked his head out from the back office as I grabbed an order from the pass-through window. "Can you cover Juno's shift tonight? She's caught a cold or something."

A cold? People under the domes almost never came down with a common illness, like a cold or the flu. Although, the temperature had been dropping significantly at night, and in my short trips to and from taxis today, there had been a noticeable chill in the air. Then again, Juno may have just wanted the night off.

"I can stay for a little while," I called back. "Just as long as I'm out of here by six, six thirty at the latest."

Kai had texted me earlier in the day to say there would be a car outside my building at seven. I didn't need a lot of time to get ready, just a quick shower to wash off the grease smell.

"I'll take it," Jon responded, and then ducked back inside his office.

At five minutes to seven, I finally closed out my last table. Kai's driver was already waiting when my taxi pulled up to my building.

"Harton, right?" I asked when I saw the shifter in the driver's seat.

I didn't know him so much as knew *of* him. Kenoa mentioned the shifter's hiring to me a few weeks before I went on my first date with Kai. Apparently, Harton had been slated for the fighting pits but proved not a great contender once the Pit Masters saw him in action. So, the prince offered him a job as his driver.

"Yes, ma'am." Harton beamed, clearly pleased that I knew his name.

"I'm so sorry. Give me ten minutes, and I'll be back down," I said. Realizing how rude that sounded, I quickly backtracked. "Do you want to come up? I can make you a coffee while you wait. I won't be long at all."

Harton chuckled. "Thank you, Miss Maybrie, but I'm not sure Prince Kai would like that."

Though my feet were already headed toward my building's front door, and I was already on borrowed time, I stopped and turned around. "Do *you* want to come up, Harton?" I repeated. "You're more than welcome to have a cup of coffee upstairs instead of waiting down here on the street."

Harton was much younger and newer than most of Kai's personal staff. Because of that, he was more concerned with making a good impression and following the rules. But if the large, purple circles beneath his light eyes were any indication, the shifter needed some caffeine.

"It'll be our secret," I assured him.

As promised, a large box from Ivy's was waiting at the reception desk, complete with their signature gold bow. The card attached was handwritten in Cassie's loopy scrawl.

Maybrie,
Your date is one lucky guy.
Enjoy, Cassie.

"Allow me, Miss Maybrie." Picking up the box, Harton followed me to the elevator.

"Do you know how to use a QuickDrip?" I asked him once we were inside my condo.

"Yes, Miss."

I started up the stairs to my bedroom. "Help yourself, then. It's in the kitchen. There are pods for different drinks in the drawer beneath it. Feel free to use whatever you want."

"Thank you," Harton called after me.

Ten minutes later, freshly showered and changed, I found Harton checking out the video game collection in my game room. When I walked in, his cheeks turned red. He lowered his gaze, like he'd been caught with his hand in the cookie jar.

"I apologize, ma'am," he said quickly.

"Promise not to call me ma'am ever again, and we'll call it even. Cool?"

Harton's boyish smile tugged at my heartstrings. Memories flowed back and caused a stab of pain in my gut. With his light eyes and blonde hair, Harton could have passed for a grown-up version of Illion.

"Are you okay, ma—Miss Maybrie? I promise I didn't break anything," he said.

"I know you didn't. I'm glad you found your way in here," I managed to say. "I'm fine. It's just been a long day. Ready to go?"

The box from Ivy's was on the table in my foyer. Tearing off the bow, I reached between the neat folds of tissue paper and found the most impractical bathing suit ever designed. Harton's wide eyes and gaping mouth confirmed my thoughts. Before he could ask any questions, I stuffed the black scrap of fabric with its loops of delicate gold chain inside my tote bag. Shit, did he think it was lingerie?

Thanks to light traffic and Harton's impressive driving skills, we reached Lanikai Beach in much less time than expected. Passing a line of luxury sports cars and limos at the exclusive Sand Dunes restaurant, the driver stopped at a bend in the road that lead to a secluded stretch of beach. My phone buzzed just as we came to a halt.

"Hey, I'm so sorry. Work ran late," I began when I answered Kai's call.

He laughed, sounding a little out of breath. "It seems we have the same excuse for being late," he teased. "I was caught up as well, I'm sorry. I will be there shortly."

"I'm here now. Harton is a great driver with a real lead foot," I told him.

"He has been a wonderful addition to my personal staff," Kai agreed. "I'll be another twenty minutes or so."

"Oh, that's okay. Do you want to reschedule?" I asked, toying with the bathing suit inside my bag. My first thought had been that I might murder Cassie for selecting such a ridiculous swimsuit. At some point on the trip over, I'd started to wonder about Kai's reaction to me in such a skimpy outfit. Between my workouts and fighting, I knew that my body was in shape. Could I pull off this scantily-clad look, though?

"I don't want to reschedule," he said quickly. "Of course not. I want to see you. I will be there soon."

"Okay. See you then." I pressed the button to lower the partition between the driver and passenger compartments. "Um, Harton, is there somewhere I can change out here?" I asked. I realized what an oversight it had been to not slip on the bathing suit at my house.

"How about the Sand Dunes?" he replied. "I can call and ask them to clear the restrooms." His tone suggested that it was the most natural solution, that kicking everyone out of a busy restaurant bathroom wasn't a big deal.

"No," I said quickly. "That's too much trouble. I'll just…figure it out."

I opened the back door before Harton could get out of the front seat. He hurried around the car to me. *Does he double as a bodyguard?* I wondered but didn't have much time to contemplate the possibility that Kai had not only sent a driver for me but also, potentially, a babysitter.

"Harton, what time is it?" I asked.

The driver furrowed his brow, eyes shifting ever so slightly to the cell clutched in my hand. "7:20 p.m., ma'am—I mean, Miss Maybrie," he replied.

"That's what I thought."

He looked at me strangely but said nothing. The sun was still high in the sky, like it was midday. It should have been at least starting its descent. *Weird. Did Kai…no that's crazy. He knows I wouldn't approve of him altering the sun and moon cycles just so we could enjoy a date.*

"Miss Maybrie?" Harton asked, sounding as though he'd said my name several times.

"Hmmm?"

"The Sand Dunes will be more than happy to accommodate you," he informed me.

I glanced at the restaurant in the distance. As tempting as changing in a public bathroom stall sounded, I couldn't bring myself to use Kai's connections. I looked in the other direction and spotted a cluster of rocks a few yards down the beach.

"It's okay, really," I insisted, pointing toward the rocks. "That will do just fine."

"Prince Kai would definitely not approve of me allowing you to change in public," Harton said quickly, eyes wide.

"Yes, well, I do not work for Prince Kai, so he doesn't get to say what I'm allowed to do," I said with mock pleasantness.

Harton's eyes were wide. "No, no, of course not. It's just, I'll get in trouble if you…."

"Stand on the other side of the rocks, don't look, and keep an eye out for anyone approaching" I told him. "That will be sufficient."

Harton looked like he wanted to protest, but I had a feeling he was just as intimidated by me as by Kai. He didn't argue further.

Clutching my bag to my chest, I hurried across the sand, Harton close behind. The rocks I'd spotted were arranged in a circle, with an opening in the center where water collected during high tide. *Perfect.* Ducking inside, I stripped quickly and began to change into the suit. It had too many strings, and the metal loops didn't seem to lay right no matter how I arranged them.

"Next time I see you, Cassie, I will kill you for this," I muttered.

Snap.

My head popped up, and the top of the swimsuit fell from my fumbling fingers. "Harton?" I called.

No answer.

WTF. Where'd he go?

"Harton?" I tried again.

Nothing.

My heart rate increased, and my adrenaline began pumping. Both my hands glowed red, though I hadn't called my magic. I titled my head to one side and listened. There was laughter in the distance, from the Sand Dunes patio. Closer, I heard nothing but the crashing of the waves on the beach.

It's fine. You're fine, I told myself. Normally, I enjoyed the beach a great deal. Inside that rock enclosure, with even a small pool of water, it suddenly reminded me too much of the caves near Fae Canyon. Of the night I lost my family and friends.

Gregory. Sienna. I hadn't thought of their names in a long time.

A flicker of light drew my eyes downward. Flames shot from my palms, once again without me summoning my magic. *Does my body know something I don't? Is this some sort of fight or flight reaction?*

A light breeze carried the scent of saltwater and extremely expensive cologne. I released a breath I didn't know I'd been holding.

"Why would you do that?" I demanded as the prince appeared in the entrance to the rock enclosure. "Don't you know better than to sneak up on a fae?"

The sun-tinged bronze strands in Kai's dark hair glowed in the fading sun. A wide range of emotions played across his chiseled features in the span of an accelerated heartbeat. Finally, an amused smirk settled on his lips.

"It's not funny, Kai," I snapped, extinguishing the

flames that had started to travel up my arms. "I nearly incinerated you."

"There are worse ways to go." His dark, sultry gaze traveled south from my face. "I would have headed to the great beyond with your beautiful image in my head and a smile on my lips."

I looked down and realized that my chest was as bare as the day I was born. Jumping back into the shadows, my arms flew up to cover my nakedness. I overestimated the distance to the rock behind me, and my spine smacked against a particularly jagged section. Cheeks on fire with embarrassment and back smarting, I howled.

"Brie! Are you okay?" Kai rushed over to help.

"Fine," I said between gritted teeth. "Just please turn around. Or leave. Yeah, just leave. Let me fix my suit and…." I trailed off, mortified.

"Let me help. I promise I won't look." Kai covered his eyes with one hand and beckoned me over with the other. "Come on. I will tie it for you."

I sighed. "It's not that simple." Against my better judgment, I walked backward to stand in front of Kai, my back to his chest. "You can look now."

Gently, he took the straps in his hands. It only took a moment for him to realize that I hadn't been exaggerating.

"How does this work?" he asked. "Where does the big ring go?"

I shook my head. "I don't know. It's new. I was shopping with Cala earlier for luau dresses, so I just had the saleswoman throw a bathing suit into the box. If I'd known she would pick something so ridiculous, I would have spared the time to find one myself."

"And I thought my day was challenging," Kai teased.

While straightening the straps, he ran one finger along the nape of my neck. I shivered despite the warm night. *Did the temperature go up from earlier today?* Kai pressed his lips to the same spot and murmured against my skin.

"I think I got it. Turn around and let me see." He trailed kisses across my collarbone and down to my shoulder. Placing his hands lightly on my waist, Kai turned me to face him. Our eyes met, and he lowered his mouth to mine. My annoyance over him sneaking up on me was forgotten. He skimmed his knuckles along my ribs and deepened the kiss.

"The swimsuit looks great," he whispered when we finally broke apart.

I laughed. "You haven't actually looked yet." Stepping out of his embrace, I twirled. "Now what do you think?"

"Beautiful," he breathed, holding out a hand to me. "Are you hungry? Or do you want to go for a swim first?"

"Swim," I said decisively.

Kai grinned. "I had hoped you would say that."

That was when I noticed he was already wearing board shorts and a tee. The casual look suited him. The thin shirt hinted at the hard muscles underneath, and my stomach fluttered again.

We left the little rock enclosure, and Kai led me farther down the beach. Harton, Kenoa, and a caster I didn't know had just finished setting up a picnic—complete with a blanket, picnic basket, towels, and an ice bucket for the wine.

"Who's the other guy?" I asked.

"Makani," Kai answered. "He is one of my bodyguards."

"Two bodyguards tonight? Does your mother think I'm a threat to you?" I teased.

Kai laughed uncomfortably. "No. Nothing like that. My mother is very anxious to meet you, though."

My insides squirmed at the prospect. Technically, I'd met the queen several times. The first occasion was when I won my first fight. I'd just turned sixteen and was new to the dome. She'd come down from the Royal Box to congratulate me, and I'd wanted to slap her smug caster face. I met her a second time at the luau, the year I'd won my fiftieth fight. She shook my hand and spoke to me for exactly three seconds. I'd still wanted to slap her smug caster face. Our third encounter was at the first social gathering I'd been made to attend after Tanner's death, the Sugarcane Ball. Her Majesty had patted my hand and told me she was sorry for my loss. In hindsight, I saw her comment for the kindness it was. At the time, I'd wanted to slap her smug caster face even harder.

"I'm not sure that's such a great idea," I said.

"I told her that you might say that." He smiled down at me and reached for my hand.

I hesitated a moment. It wasn't that I didn't want to feel his long fingers between mine. I just wasn't sure about holding hands in front of Kenoa. Even when spending the entire day with both of them, I'd been careful not to show physical affection when Kenoa was in the same room.

Finally, I relented. If I was going to have any sort of relationship with the prince—fake or real—I had to get used to his bodyguards' eyes on me.

"You are all set, Your Highness," Makani called, standing up so straight it was a wonder he didn't have a metal rod for a spine.

"Wine is in the bucket with ice," Kenoa added. Then, with a wink, he said, "It'll stay chilled for a few hours."

I smiled. Like many strong water fae, Kenoa had the ability to manipulate the state of a liquid. He could turn a puddle to vapor or a block of ice with the snap of his fingers. And, using a small spell, he could make that liquid remain in the solid state for an extended period of time. Kenoa had always refused to tell me where he learned to cast, but he was much more adept than any other native fae I'd met.

"Thank you all," Kai said.

Kenoa gave me a nod. "Hey, Brie." Then he started up the beach.

I waved as he passed.

Harton and Makani didn't move. The latter glanced between Kai and his coworker.

"We have been instructed not to be more than three feet from your person at any time, Your Highness," Makani said stiffly, pointedly refusing to look at me.

For once, I didn't believe his behavior had anything to do with caster-fae relations. The bodyguard was trying very hard not to stare at my swimsuit. Or whatever this contraption was that Cassie had sent over.

I snorted. "Well that will make for an awkward date, now won't it?"

Kai laughed. "Yes, it most certainly will. Makani, I will be just fine alone with Brie if you wait at the cars."

"Sir," Makani began again. "This is not a closed environment. I cannot leave you alone."

Kai's eyes frosted over. I'd never seen him mad. It was oddly intriguing and quite a turn on. "You will wait at the cars. That is an order."

The prince wasn't even talking to me, and I felt the chill in his command. Harton flinched as though Kai's words had cut him.

Makani cleared his throat. "The recent changes to the Royal Protection Protocols state that I cannot leave you alone, Your Highness."

"I am not alone. Which is the point," Kai snapped.

"Makani, Harton—come here!" Kenoa barked from up the beach. He too had a bite in his tone.

To my surprise, Makani seemed to find Kenoa's authority above question, though he'd argued with the prince. With an overly formal bow to Kai, Makani started toward Kenoa, Harton loping after him like a lost puppy.

"I apologize," Kai said, turning to look at me once his guards were out of range. "These new damn protocols are a nightmare. I had to hire five new guards just to cover all the shifts. Makani is one of those recent hires. If you can't tell, he just completed his training."

"When did these new protocols go into effect?" I asked.

"Yesterday, formally. But I have known about them for weeks. My mother thought my sister and I needed more protection once we realized so many had gone missing beneath the dome. She proposed each of us have two bodyguards instead of one every time we leave the palace grounds. I resisted the change as long as possible."

"I see," I said.

The royals are nervous. That's a good piece of information to pass along to Christina, and I didn't have to do any digging. But the rebellion was bigger than Christina. It was bigger than me and even bigger than Kai.

"Is that why it's still light out? Does your mother think longer days and shorter nights might put a stop to the disappearances?" I pressed.

Kai laughed uneasily. "So, I guess you have noticed. To answer your question, no. With the recent cold nights, we decided to increase the energy we use to regulate the temperature. The artificial sun helps with that. Until we are able to return the dome to normal temperatures, the days will be longer."

He let go of my hand and stripped off his shirt. The sight could've registered as one of the natural wonders. Admittedly, I gawked. A lot.

"Enough business. How strong of a swimmer are you?" Kai changed the subject.

I tossed my bag with my clothes onto the blanket. "I can hold my own. Well," I looked down at the embarrassment that was my bathing suit, "I can normally hold my own. You might get another peep show if I'm not careful."

Kai beamed. "Sounds like a win-win for me." He sprinted for the surf. "Race you to the buoy and back!"

I darted after him. With Kai's long legs, I shouldn't have been able to catch him. Then again, I was in peak fighting condition. We reached the water at the same moment and dove into the waves. I was a good swimmer. Kai was a great swimmer. He reached the buoy several strokes before I did. But he must've been holding back, because I lost sight of him on the return trip.

Just as I reached chest-high waters, strong arms caught me around the waist. I flipped over and jerked my head out of the waves. Kai was grinning down at me.

"I think I won," he said.

I splashed water in his face. "No. This doesn't count. You haven't reached our starting line yet."

"There is still time," Kai assured me.

I put my feet on the ocean floor. Wet sand wedged between my toes and waves lapped my shoulders. Kai wrapped his arms around my waist and drew me closer.

His lips were just above mine when I replied. "You do know I almost never lose, right?"

His mouth brushed against mine. "Neither do I."

CHAPTER THIRTEEN

AN HOUR LATER we were drying off beneath the sun, which still shone in the bright-blue sky. We ate turkey sandwiches from A Broom with a View, Kai's favorite café.

"I figured that since you ordered takeout on Sunday, you wouldn't think too badly of me for doing the tonight," he said as he poured cold wine into my glass.

"I don't know." I narrowed my eyes and tapped my chin, pretending to consider this seriously. "You showed up unannounced. I had no time to prepare. You knew about this date for two days."

He laughed. "You make a valid point." Kai took a bite of his sandwich and chewed thoughtfully.

"What?" I asked, wiping my mouth with a napkin in case some mayo had smeared on my face.

"You mentioned shopping for luau dresses earlier?" He managed to make the statement sound more like a question.

"I did," I said cautiously. "Why?"

"That must mean you plan to attend." Kai's dark eyes went wide. He knew what he'd said wrong; my attendance was mandatory.

Let it go. Your feelings don't matter. Only the rebellion matters.

"It's fine. I know what you meant." Probably because it wasn't fine, and I was feeling a little catty, I added, "It'll take time for you to get used to a fae who isn't trained to be polite to casters no matter what asinine things they say."

Kai smiled tentatively. "I am not sure whether you are joking."

"I am. Doesn't mean it's not true."

"Well, I suppose it will take me time to get used to a girl who calls me on the asinine things I say."

I couldn't help myself, I laughed. "Okay then, honest mistake on your part. And yes, of course, I'm going to the luau."

"You may not currently have a choice about attending, but you do have a choice in who you bring as your date." Kai looked into his wine glass as he swirled the contents. "Would you consider being my date? Do not answer now." He glanced up. "Please. I know you will say 'no' if you answer now. Just think about my invitation. I will understand if you ultimately decide you are not ready for such exposure."

"Okay, I'll think about it," I agreed, downing the rest of my wine.

Christina would be over the moon that Kai asked me to the luau. It meant he planned to keep me around at least for another week or so. And, if he was willing to take our fledgling relationship public—well, I didn't know what that meant, except that Christina would like it.

The sun finally started to sink at 10:34 p.m. I knew because I rudely pulled out my phone to check. The sky didn't go through its normal range of colors, however. Blue turned to dark blue, which turned to black in under five minutes.

"Well, that needs some adjusting, doesn't it?" Kai joked as stars slowly peppered the artificial sky. "Any time we make alterations, there is an adjustment period."

"How does that all work, the dome and the sunset and sunrise?" I asked.

It was a topic I'd given very little thought to. I assumed the dome was some sort of forcefield or glass barrier. After all, I'd never seen it from the outside, and the armed guards that protected the interior boundaries made it nearly impossible to reach the edges.

"Magic," Kai replied.

"Magic? So, like, a strong witch cast a spell that made the dome?" I asked.

He laughed. "Honestly, I am not familiar with the ins and outs of dome construction or maintenance. I am only briefed on the very basic mechanics of it all."

Mechanics? So, was he kidding about the magic? Does it matter?

Actually, it did. If witches and warlocks had made the dome and were currently maintaining it, that would require a lot of magic; few casters could afford to use that much power without running the risk of depletion. Then again, rich caster families sometimes had three or four house fae that donated magic on a regular basis, so maybe depletion wasn't a concern after all. Either way, it was another tidbit of information to pass along to Christina.

As I was trying to think of a way to ask Kai whether magic or technology created the dome—that didn't sound like I was spying—the first moon popped into existence. Orange rays illuminated the sand. My throat constricted.

"Fire moon," I breathed, interrupting something Kai was saying about fruit. Or dessert. Dessert fruit? I didn't know or care.

A second orange moon joined the first.

"Night of Four Moons." I wanted to swallow the words as if that might keep them from coming true.

Kai was too excited to notice my sudden panic. "That is why I asked for a date tonight instead of last night." He gave an embarrassed laugh. "Well, that, and I didn't want to appear desperate."

A third orange moon appeared above.

"I'd like to go home," I blurted out. I grabbed my bag and began pulling my clothes over my bathing suit.

"Of course." Kai jumped to his feet and helped me when my head got stuck in an armhole. "Are you okay, Brie?"

My head popped through the correct shirt opening. I

looked up. *No. No, no, no, no.* The fourth moon had risen. And it was orange.

My mouth felt like I'd eaten actual sand for dinner. I smelled the iron scent of blood. In my periphery, shadows seemed to move with lightning speed.

"Brie?" Kai placed his hands on my shoulders. "Brie, look at me. Are you okay? What's wrong? Was the food bad?"

I started shivering. I swore I could see my breath. "They're really all fire moons? Like, outside the dome, too?"

It was a stupid question, since I knew the moon cycles inside the dome mirrored reality. Typically, I tracked those cycles very closely and would have avoided leaving my condo on Night of Four Moons. Of course, four fire moons hadn't graced the skies in five years. Since that night.

I heard the clink of a metal chain inside my head, but that didn't make it feel any less real. My breath caught. *No, no, no. This can't be happening.* Mat's cold voice sounded like silk as he told me that Queen Lilli was looking for a fire fae.

How did the fact that tonight was Night of Four Moons not occur to me?

"Brie?" Kai looked as though he was considering whether to shake me.

"Yeah, I just need a minute. Alone." I stumbled out of his grip and started toward the cars.

Cold sweat ran into my eyes and blurred my vision. I felt off balance, like the world was suddenly off-kilter. *Maybe it is. I am dating a prince,* I thought and giggled, though nothing was funny. Headlights appeared suddenly in the distance, blinding me momentarily. I swaggered sideways, right into a large, hard object. *The rock enclosure.* I sagged against one of the stones in the shadow of an overhang. It felt oddly cold to the touch,

A vampire's face flashed in my mind. *Or is he really here?* My gaze darted back and forth between the two possible entry and exit points of the beach. No bloodsuckers in sight. *You're okay.* Muffled voices filled the air. Whoever it was, they weren't trying to be sneaky; my hearing just suddenly sounded blocked with cotton. Fireballs appeared in my palms. The sight of all those fae in the back of Mat's caravan came into focus in my mind's eye.

"No. Don't think about it," I growled out loud.

I tried to take several steps forward and ended up crashing to my knees in the small puddle at the rock enclosure's entrance. Orange moonlight bathed my face in its fiery glow. I let my head fall backward and closed my eyes.

"Brie?" Kai called tentatively. "Brie!" This time he sounded scared. "Kenoa! Help me!"

Footsteps; someone running on the sand.

"Don't touch her," Kenoa snapped. "Get back. Let me handle this."

Kai must've done as asked and gotten out of Kenoa's way, because a moment later, I saw the big water fae's face above mine.

"You're going to be okay." His hands were like blocks of ice when he scooped me into his arms.

I heard the sizzle of water hitting fire. *Cause we're water and fire,* I thought and giggled. Kenoa looked down at me, eyes full of concern. We were moving fast. I was bumped and jostled in his arms. The smell of burnt hair filled my nose, and the arms beneath me again went suddenly very cold.

"Is she conscious?" Kai asked frantically as he ran beside us.

"Sort of," Kenoa grunted. "She can probably hear us, but she won't be responsive."

We stopped moving. I saw Harton out of the corner of my eye. He held the back door of the limo open. Kenoa lowered me onto the backseat and then got in and sat across from me. Kai slid onto my bench and gave Harton a nod to close the door.

"Don't touch her," Kenoa warned the prince.

Why is his shirt so wet? I'm not that heavy. Then I noticed some spots were singed, and I understood Kenoa's warning.

"The leather is not catching fire," Kai pointed out.

"Doesn't mean you won't. Neither did her clothes, but she burnt right through my shity." Kenoa reached into a compartment beside him and produced a fancy red vial. He knelt on the floorspace between us. Slowly, he reached out a large hand and touched one finger to my shoulder. When his skin didn't burn, he rested his entire hand on my arm. He glanced up at Kai and nodded. The prince took my limp hand in his.

"You need to drink this, Brie," Kenoa told me, speaking slowly. "It's going to suck. But you must drink all of it." He held up the vial for my inspection. I considered reaching for it, but my arm was too heavy to lift anything. Kenoa must've sensed this, because he brought the vial to my lips. "Ready?" he asked.

I managed to jerk my head back slightly, effectively agreeing to consume some unknown witch's brew that was probably going to make me vomit. *Is it too late to change my mind?* It was. Kenoa dumped the contents down my throat. The herbs tasted bitter, and the vial smelled sour. I wasn't very familiar with most potions, only the healing creams given to us in the arena. And I didn't buy tonics from the local apothecaries, as most were designed for casters anyway. Something told me this particular potion wasn't an over-the-counter product, though.

Whatever the case, I had no idea how long it would be before the potion started to take effect. Or what the effects would be. Apparently, neither did Kenoa or Kai.

"Will this work?" asked the prince, staring down at me and squeezing my hand tightly.

"It's what we give casters when this happens," Kenoa replied. "It definitely won't hurt her, but I can't say for sure if it will help either."

"Her eyelids are closing," Kai said softly, as I slid into darkness.

"Good. At least that part of the potion is working on her," Kenoa replied.

I felt weightless. And then, I felt nothing at all.

CHAPTER FOURTEEN

"I TRIED TO tell you Night of Four Moons wasn't a good idea," a deep voice said.

"You gave no explanation," a very annoyed voice answered.

"It's Brie's business. She agreed to go out with you, I just assumed she knew what tonight was."

"I guess we both screwed up," Kai snapped, sounding a lot like an entitled prince.

"Calm down. She's fine." Kenoa sounded more pissed off than I'd ever heard him, which was saying a lot since nothing riled him. "You don't get to act like a jerk to me after four dates with her. I've known Brie a long time, and I care about her, too."

Kai sighed. "I'm sorry, Ken. This is all a little unnerving. It was like the situation with my uncle all over again."

"She wasn't depleted. The opposite happened. I'm just glad the caster tonic worked on her," Kenoa admitted, all animosity gone from his voice.

"Yes, well, your kind cannot usually become overwhelmed with magic. Or, should I say, your kind does not usually allow that to happen?" Kai replied.

"Both," Kenoa answered.

There was a long pause. I sat up in my bed and squinted in the darkness at the wedge of light from the open door. Two tall shadows, one much leaner than the other, stood motionless in the hallway.

"She's awake," Kenoa said after several long moments. "You should go talk to her."

I cursed under my breath, hoping I'd be able to eavesdrop on the duo a little longer. They spoke like friends, like equals. Not that Kai was disrespectful to his other employees. Even before I realized that I didn't hate him, I couldn't say that I'd ever witnessed the prince being rude to his staff. But listening to him and Kenoa was different; I felt like I was learning more and more about their connection, one that nobody could figure out.

My bedroom door opened slowly, and Kai stepped inside. I caught the flash of white teeth and Kenoa's large hand waving before the water fae turned and started downstairs.

"How are you feeling?" Kai asked. He walked over and crouched beside my bed, apparently not even considering getting in next to me. Still dressed in his board shorts and tee, the prince shivered in the cold of my condo.

"Better." I managed a smile. "I'm sorry. I don't really understand what happened to me."

An almost violent tremor ran through Kai, and he crossed his arms over his chest. I reached up for the quilt folded over my headboard and wrapped it around his shoulders.

"Thank you," he said softly.

Flopping onto my back, I stared blankly at the ceiling. "I'm sorry," I said again.

"Do not apologize for something beyond your control." Kai wrapped his cold fingers around my hand.

"Kenoa's right. I should've known this night was coming. I usually track the moon cycles and the seasons more carefully."

"You could not have known there would be four fire moons," Kai offered. "The phenomenon is very rare. It has not occurred in years."

"Five years," I clarified. "The last time four fire moons shone at once was five years ago. And the time before that was the night before I was born."

He couldn't have realized the significance of the timing. Like me, Kai had been a teenager on the night I was taken. Nonetheless, he sensed there was more to the story. The prince didn't pry, unless remaining annoyingly silent counted as an invasion of privacy.

Talk about a good way to gain his trust, I thought wryly. Telling Kai about the night Mat had stolen me from Fae Canyon would forge a bond between us, one I had with few others. And only one of them was among the living. But that wasn't why I told Kai the truth. I told him because I truly trusted Kai with such a personal story.

"Fae elders fear fire moons," I began, focusing on a spot on the ceiling above me. "For a lot of reasons. Many believe they signal a bad harvest coming. Others think they're generally bad omens. I thought my father and the other elders were just old and superstitious." I laughed humorlessly. "I thought I knew better. I thought I was invincible. I snuck out with two of my friends, Sienna and Gregory." Tears filled my eyes, and I let them fall. "We just wanted to have some fun. And we did. Until the cowboys came."

Kai climbed onto the bed and curled up beside me, gently brushing the wetness from my cheeks. I could feel his dark gaze watching me, but I continued to stare at the ceiling.

"I killed one of them, and I didn't even feel bad about it. If anything, it made me feel strong. Like I could take on an army. I was so stupid, so naïve. I couldn't handle three of them, let alone an army. They caught me." Fresh tears spilled from my eyes. "I still remember when Mat— that was the leader—sank those vile fangs into my neck. I don't know if I'll ever forget."

Before I knew it, Kai's arms were around me. Holding me tightly against his chest, he stroked my hair. In the darkness, wrapped in his warm embrace, crying didn't feel weak. It felt cathartic. It didn't feel like I was telling him a secret. It felt like sharing a part of myself with him. He didn't offer meaningless platitudes, and I was grateful. I didn't want to hear them, not from him. Not from any caster.

Eventually I drifted off to sleep again, warm and comfortable in Kai's arms.

When I woke the next morning, the bed felt empty. The curtains were still drawn, but I could tell the sun had yet to rise. I expected to find a note on my kitchen counter when I plodded downstairs to make coffee. What I didn't anticipate was a freshly showered and casually dressed prince sitting on my living room sofa with a laptop open in front of him. Or Kenoa flipping pancakes in the kitchen.

"I apologize for the inconvenience. A personal matter has come up." Kai spoke into a cellphone wedged between his shoulder and ear as he typed. "I do appreciate your understanding. Tomorrow it is. Please thank Coroner Aliako on my behalf."

I froze halfway down the stairs, panic rising quickly. Kai had been in my condo all night, and I had an unregistered cell hidden on my patio—not a good combination.

The prince disconnected his call and turned to smile at me. "Good morning. I hope you do not mind, but I thought I could work from here today?"

"Um, yeah. Of course. But I have training. Botto will report me if I don't show up." My eyes darted nervously to the patio doors.

"The situation has been handled," Kai informed me happily.

"Handled?" I repeated, a slight edge to my voice.

In the kitchen, Kenoa groaned audibly. "Bad choice of words, man."

"I only meant—" Kai's dark gaze darted back and forth between Kenoa and me. The prince pointed a finger, literally, at Kenoa. "He called Botto, not me."

I arched an eyebrow at my friend.

"He expects you back at practice tomorrow," Kenoa said without elaborating further.

"What did you tell him was wrong with me?" I asked suspiciously.

Kenoa shrugged his large shoulders. "I didn't. And he didn't ask."

No, I suppose my trainer wouldn't have asked. Not when Kai's personal bodyguard called to say I was taking the day off, I thought, annoyed.

"Let it go, Brie," Kenoa said, taking the next words out of my head. "This was my favor to you. Just like you've been doing Sumi favors to get her out of the commune after curfew and without a proper chaperone."

I shot an uneasy glance at Kai, who was concentrating way too hard on his computer. These weren't serious crimes, but they were my crimes, not Sumi's. I certainly didn't want to get her in trouble.

Without looking up, the prince said, "Because I have only just escaped your wrath this morning, I would prefer we do not debate the reasons for the current restrictions placed on foreign fae and shifters beneath the dome. Please be assured, the palace is redrafting legislation as we speak to adopt a more welcoming plan of action for the newly arrived." His satisfied smile faltered when he saw the look on my face. "Pancakes?" he tried.

"Pancakes?" I shook my head, a little of my righteous fury disappearing at the abrupt segue.

"Kai normally finds that pissed off fae are less upset if he switches the topic away from controversial crap, like politics." Kenoa flipped a perfect, golden-brown pancake using just the pan. "How many?"

I'd clearly woken up with a chip on my shoulder and was feeling ganged up on. But the pancakes smelled heavenly, and my stomach rumbled. "Five, please."

"Kai?" Kenoa asked.

"The same."

I joined the prince on the couch. He filled a mug with coffee from a carafe and handed it to me.

"Breakfast and coffee? A girl could get used to this," I admitted.

Kai leaned over and kissed my cheek. "I worried you might be upset that we were still here."

I thought about the unregistered cell again. "No, not at all. I appreciate your concern."

"Now who's trying to be diplomatic," Kenoa teased from the kitchen.

I stuck my tongue out at him. "I can't tell whether you're playing peacekeeper or instigator."

"Both." Kenoa tossed the pancake one more time in the pan before transferring it to a plate. "Whichever I feel is more entertaining at the moment."

I switched my focus back to Kai and sipped my coffee. "What are you working on?"

His eyes lit up. "The disappearances. We may have a break in the case."

Suddenly, I wasn't very hungry. "Oh, yeah? What did you learn?" I asked too loudly, as though that would dull the sound of my heart thumping in my chest. I caught

Kenoa giving me an odd look, but the prince didn't seem to notice my jumpiness.

Kai's cheeks reddened beneath his golden skin. "You have heard of House of Mana, I assume?"

I made a face. "I've heard of it."

Kenoa laughed as he deposited three plates of pancakes on the coffee table, along with another carafe of coffee, a bottle of syrup, a tub of butter, and utensils.

"Thanks, Ken. I don't know what I would do without you," Kai said with a smile.

"Me neither," Kenoa said. "But I put on the apron for Brie, not you." He pulled one of my armchairs over and sat across from us. "You're long overdue for a grocery delivery," he added.

"I've been busy." I turned to Kai. "So, what's the deal with House of Mana? What does it have to do with the disappearances?" I dumped syrup over my pancakes and took a large bite, letting the cinnamon and vanilla wash over my taste buds. Kenoa was an awesome cook. "These are amazing, by the way."

Kenoa grinned around a large forkful of gooey pancake.

Kai cleared his throat. "House of Mana caters to a select portion of the caster population," he began.

"The wealthy ones," I interjected. "That place is expensive."

"It is," Kai agreed.

I washed down a bite of food with coffee. "Have you ever been?"

"I have. I will admit, I was curious," Kai said primly.

"Just curious?" Kenoa quirked an eyebrow.

"I am feeling very outnumbered." Kai glared at his bodyguard and then at me.

I laughed. "Okay, so what's the significance?"

Kai set down his fork. "We know for certain that three of the male casters who have gone missing were last seen at House of Mana. Two of them were found late last night. Or rather, their bodies were found."

Coffee nearly came out of my nose. "They're dead?"

That wasn't right. The missing people weren't supposed to be dead. *Maybe they aren't connected to the missing fae. Killing wealthy casters would be risky, and Christina isn't stupid.*

"No, worse," Kai said gravely. "They are depleted. Both have been moved to the Royal Hospital. I am meeting with the families tomorrow to ask for permission to attempt memory retrieval."

"What about revival?" I asked. "Isn't that usually the first step?"

Kai looked down. "It was unsuccessful. We are not certain how much time had passed since depletion. Too much, as it turns out."

"And you think these casters are somehow related to the missing fae?" I asked uneasily.

"I do. I have no proof, of course, just a gut feeling. That is why I am asking for the right to perform memory retrieval."

Memory retrieval is dangerous. And complicated. It almost never works, I reminded myself.

"Not many casters can perform that spell," I hedged, wishing I hadn't been so eager to devour my breakfast. The undigested bits of pancake bobbed on a sea of syrup in my stomach.

"Very few, yes," Kai agreed.

"You're not—you're not thinking of doing it yourself, are you?" I eyed him dubiously.

For a caster, Kai rarely used magic. In fact, in our time together, he'd never used magic. *That you know of*, I reminded myself.

Still, the royal family was known for being powerful. Queen Lilli supposedly possessed more magic than any other caster in the kingdom. And the prince was rumored to be an accomplished warlock.

Kai laughed loudly. "I would not attempt a spell of this magnitude. I do know of a witch in North Shore who is known to have performed the necessary spell before. If she does not agree to help, which is likely, I do have contacts in the other kingdoms. This is our first real lead. I am prepared to follow it at any cost."

"Even without the memories, we know at least a few of the disappearances are linked to House of Mana," Kenoa pointed out.

"A few of the *caster* disappearances," I clarified. "None of the missing fae are connected to House of Mana, are they?"

Kenoa studied me over his breakfast. He wasn't part of the rebellion—he'd never had an interest—but he knew of the movement.

Does that mean Kai knows, too? I wondered. *Maybe he knows you're a spy.*

The very thought made me go numb.

"In the past five years," he consulted a file on his laptop, "twelve House of Mana fae employees have gone missing," Kai reported.

Damn it. Shouldn't have asked.

I knew House of Mana fae were some of the rebellion's most wealthy clients. Christina often charged those fae double the normal price for an evacuation to cover the bribes for those who couldn't afford the cost. The money wasn't just for bribes either; Christina set up new lives for these fae and gave them money to start over.

"Um, is that a lot?" I asked. "I mean, twelve in five years doesn't sound...too bad."

"Fourteen in the five years before that." Kai shrugged. "To answer your question, no. Twelve is an average amount."

"So, the disappearances of the House of Mana fae and the two depleted casters aren't linked," I argued.

Kenoa fixed me with a piercing glare. *Watch it,* his eyes said. My gut turned to lead, and I pushed my plate away.

"Again, I have no proof, but I do believe all the disappearances are linked," Kai replied.

I took a deep breath and folded my hands in my lap to stop them from shaking. "I'm just playing devil's advocate," I lied smoothly. "I'm not sure what to believe." My eyes flicked to the patio. I needed to contact Christina.

"Do not worry, I have made it my mission to uncover the truth," Kai announced, like a detective declaring he was on the case.

Awesome. I think I just made things worse.

The day was a war of conflicting emotions; it felt both traitorous and right to have Kai in my living room. While he worked, I caught up on a new book I'd bought weeks ago. Kenoa decided to organize my kitchen, which seemed ridiculous since I only really used it to make coffee. He took it upon himself to order me a grocery delivery. I held my breath and waited for him to comment on the fact that my last recorded delivery was only three days ago, yet I had no food.

There was a family of house fae who barely had enough rations to feed their three children. For a hefty fee, the delivery were-tiger recorded the order as mine—fighters had great meal plans—but took the food to the Cleary family. I ate at Pele's mostly and could afford any restaurant.

Kenoa said nothing, but I knew a lecture was in my future. He wouldn't care that I was feeding a hungry family. It was a criminal offense to forge my food orders, but he'd think it was nice. His real concern would be all the other criminal acts I'd committed—those that he'd never asked about.

After lunch, I soaked my tired muscles in a sea salt and coconut bath while Kai made phone calls, and Kenoa put away groceries. I read the news on my phone, which was considerably less interesting than the real news happening in my condo. Classical music played in my bathroom, but I could still hear Kai talking downstairs. I switched to a site called Caster Gossip that revealed all the dirty deeds of high society witches and warlocks. Even as blind items, where the subject wasn't explicitly named, it was obvious their favorite target was Kai.

This caster hunk had his crown askew last night

at Pixie. Word on the street is that our favorite party boy was working his magic on a certain caster cutie. Is love finally in the "heir"?

Lies, I thought. Kai had been with me the previous night. Besides, who went to the club on a Tuesday? I kept reading.

Inside sources say the firstborn has been having romantic dinners with a fiery companion. Anyone else hear wedding bells?

"This isn't even a blind item," I complained to myself. "This is obvious. And it's bad." I dialed Cala's number.

"Are you okay?" she asked immediately.

"Yeah, fine." I reconsidered. "Ugh, no. I'm not okay. Have you read Caster Gossip today?"

"Excuse me? You skipped practice because of a gossip site?" Cala demanded.

I sighed. "No. I skipped practice because I'm sick. Well, not like the flu. Did you happen to look outside last night?"

"Yeah, the freakin' sun was still up when I went to bed. I had to draw my blackout curtains," Cala retorted, clearly annoyed.

"It was Night of Four Moons," I said simply. "Four fire moons."

Cala didn't know my whole story or even that Mat had kidnapped me at the beginning of a new harvest. But she did know that I preferred my condo on Night of Four Moons.

"What happened?" Cala breathed.

I filled her in on my experience on the beach and how Kenoa gave me a potion meant to relax casters when they overdosed on magic.

"Do you feel more powerful?" Cala asked when I was finished.

I took my free hand out from beneath the bubbles and watched as water dripped from my fingertips. An instant later, tiny flames replaced the droplets.

"Not really. I just feel sort of…blah," I admitted.

"How did Prince Kai react?" she asked.

I lowered my voice. "Like a prince. Really. He, um, stayed with me. I mean, he was here when I fell asleep."

"Was he there when you—wait, is he there now?" Cala sounded as if the summer solstice had come early. "Where are you?"

"I'm in the bath," I whispered. "Yes, he's here. He's working downstairs."

There was a squeal, followed by a loud clatter, on the other end. "Oh, my Gaia! Are you going to be our next princess? Will I have to curtsy to you? That's weird. But I'll totally do it just to see all those caster society girls forced to do the same."

"Let's back it up." My voice would've been inaudible to anyone besides a shifter. "I'm not really dating him. I'm spying on him." *I shouldn't even be using the word* spy *in any iteration on my regular cell,* I thought.

Cala snorted. "You're reading Caster Gossip. You're definitely really dating him."

I sank down in the water until only my head was above the bubbles—bubbles that danced with small, emerald flames.

"This is bad, Cala," I muttered. "I'm in over my head."

"It's okay to like him," she said softly. "I know I shouldn't say that. I know I shouldn't be happy that you chose a caster when you finally got back out there. But I'm happy that you seem to really like this guy."

"I didn't choose him," I snapped.

"Whatever," Cala said dismissively. "My point is, if you like him, he can't be a bad guy."

Kai wasn't a bad guy. Yeah, he said stupid stuff sometimes, but he was making an effort to understand. And I did believe that when he was king, whenever that finally happened, fae and shifters would have more rights. *The entire system is wrong. More rights don't equal freedom*, I reminded myself.

"Tell me about this gossip, since that's obviously why you called," Cala interrupted my musings.

"Oh, right. Go look at Caster Gossip. Today's blind items are particularly obvious," I said quietly.

Three seconds later, Cala laughed. "Okay, you're overacting. He was with you last night."

"I'm not jealous. Keep reading," I hissed.

"I never used the word *jealous*," Cala laughed. "Fiery companion? That could be anyone," she reasoned.

"It could be, but it isn't," I protested.

"Let's take a deep breath," Cala instructed. "Stop reading gossip. Enjoy your bath. If you keep dating Prince Kai, your relationship will eventually go public. I will be here for you when it does. Right now, you need to focus on what you can control."

"Which is what, precisely?" I asked.

"Advancing the relationship so that you stay close to the investigation," Cala replied.

I groaned. "If I'm spying on him, how can I really be dating him?" I asked.

"Everyone has secrets," she assured me.

"This is different," I argued.

"The two aren't mutually exclusive," she tried. "You can really be dating him and spying on him. I mean, I sort of spy on all the guys I date. I've been known to go through a guy's text messages."

I laughed despite my sour mood. "You're nosy. That's different." A sobering thought popped into my head. "What about Everly? What the hell do I tell her?"

"One problem at a time."

"I want to tell her that it's progressed beyond one date before our relationship goes public," I replied.

Cala sighed. "You might want to schedule a lunch with her soon."

"Why?" The flames turned to glass and shattered into millions of tiny particles that floated on the bubbles. "What haven't you told me?"

"There's a royal bodyguard outside your building— two, actually. I saw them when I drove past earlier. I didn't think much of it. There are a lot of rich casters in your building. The prince could be visiting anyone."

Freakin' hell, I thought.

After I dried off, I slipped into a pair of navy silk lounge pants and matching soft sweater. Kai was still plugging away on his laptop when I went downstairs. He moved to one corner of the couch and put a pillow next to himself. I curled up with my book, my head resting on the pillow by Kai's leg.

Your feelings don't matter. Only the rebellion matters. Hating myself, I kept one eye on the computer screen and one on my book.

The two depleted casters had families. Kai had said as much but seeing the pictures of Lono Kohue's husband and their two daughters made me queasy. That family embodied everything I hated about life under the dome. They had five house fae, which had to be a record for any household beside the palace. The eldest daughter was sixteen and ready to make her debut into society.

And yet, I felt sorry for them. *Please don't let this have anything to do with the rebellion,* I thought.

Kai absently stroked my hair as he scrolled through reports. Every so often he'd smile down at me, and I would smile back. It was nice, natural, like we'd played this scene a hundred times.

It's okay to like him, Cala had said on the phone.

I did like him. I liked him a lot.

CHAPTER FIFTEEN

KAI OFFERED TO stay the night with me again. He wanted to be there in case I incurred any lingering side effects from the potion Kenoa had given me. Besides extreme lethargy, I was fine.

Then there was the matter of the very important phone call I owed Christina. A phone call I very much didn't *want* to make.

When I had joined the rebellion, it was to help free my people. I hadn't agreed to deplete casters. That wasn't the original point of the rebellion or something I wanted to be a part of. If Christina told me that the rebellion was behind the depletions, I might have to walk away. Which would mean walking away from Kai, too. *I'm not ready to give him up*, I realized.

But I needed to know the truth. And Christina wanted a report. She'd texted me five times that day, each one more insistent than the last. I trudged to the patio, steeling myself mentally and emotionally for the impending conversation. The unregistered cell was safe in its hiding spot. My fingers shook from premature anger as I mashed the buttons with unnecessary force. Maybe she really didn't know about what happened to the casters, maybe she wasn't involved at all. It only rang once.

"Depleted, Christina?" I spat. The words were out of my mouth before I could think twice. "Please tell me that the rebellion is not responsible. Tell me that the information I gave you did not lead to this."

"Brie, calm down," she began, her tone annoyingly even. "You know what the rebellion stands for, what *we* stand for."

"I thought I did," I snapped. "But that was before I learned that you were depleting casters."

"First of all, why do you care if we are?" Christina retorted. "You hate casters."

"Because it's wrong," I practically yelled. "Have you ever seen a body that's been depleted? I have. It's not a pretty sight."

"Calm down, Brie," Christina repeated. Then, with a long sigh, she added, "The two depleted casters found near House of Mana aren't tied to us."

"Really? It's just a coincidence? Where are all the missing casters? They can't survive in the Freelands. They aren't built to withstand the cold. So, I know they're not being evacuated like the fae."

My body hummed like it did in the arena, right before a fight. A faint orange glow spread down my legs like a rash. It was late, 11:04 p.m., but the sun was just setting. As the sky darkened, my skin grew brighter.

"I have nothing to do with the depletions. The rebellion has nothing to do with the depletions. You have nothing to do with the depletions," she said slowly, enunciating each word.

I didn't know whether to believe her. There weren't supposed to be secrets between us. We needed trust and loyalty, or the rebellion would fall apart. I'd assumed that Christina hadn't told me where she was keeping the missing casters so that I'd have plausible deniability. Or, more likely, so there wouldn't be much for the vampires to torture out of me. Now I wasn't sure what to believe. My extended silence clearly read as doubt to Christina, too.

"I saw the news bulletin. Both casters were high-ranking officials. Do you think I'm an idiot?" Christina asked. "We wanted the disappearances to go unnoticed as long as possible. Males like that do not go missing without notice." Her voice rose an octave. "Plus, why the hell would I deplete them and leave them in the open? That's just asking for a royal inquiry."

I blew out a long breath, and my glow dimmed. "You're right. I'm sorry. It's just, Kai is convinced there's a connection between House of Mana and the disappearances—*all* the disappearances," I emphasized.

"Kai? You call him Kai?"

"Well what else would I call him?" I snapped

defensively. "You wanted me to pretend to date him, to get close to him, to gain his confidence. It would be a little awkward if I called him 'Your Highness' all the damned time."

"*Pretend*, Brie. That part is very important. Don't forget that. I have placed you with him for a reason. You are no good to me or the rebellion if you get emotionally invested in the caster prince."

Rein it in, Brie. "I haven't forgotten," I said calmly. "But I can't help wondering what that reason really is."

"To do just what you're doing," Christina assured me. "Listen. Report back. Steer his investigation away from us. I know he spent the day at your condo. What'd you learn?"

"How do you know that?" I asked uneasily. Of course, I already knew the answer from Cala.

"Two royal bodyguards stationed outside your building," she replied. "Didn't take a genius to figure out he was there."

Does everyone stalk me?

"Yes, he was here," I admitted. I conjured a ping-pong-ball-sized fireball in my palm and started tossing it in the air. "That's how I know about the depleted casters. There's definitely a royal inquiry."

"Did they attempt revival?" Christina asked evenly.

"Yes. It was unsuccessful." I caught the fireball and sent it skyward again. "Kai is asking the families for permission to do memory retrieval, though," I added. I held my breath and listened carefully to Christina's response. I wanted to believe her. I wanted to trust her.

"Wow, the warlock is suddenly serious about this

investigation," she mused. "Who is he using to cast the spell?"

I hesitated. "I don't know."

"Find out," Christina ordered.

"Why does it matter if this isn't your doing?" I countered.

"I'm curious. The caster who performs the memory retrieval has to be strong and knowledgeable. They have to be extremely powerful to perform that spell without depleting themselves. Only the royals and a few very elite families could expend that much magic. Whoever it is probably has a harem of fae they will use to recharge."

I squirmed in my lounge chair as I caught the fireball and held it suspended over my palm. *A harem of fae.* I didn't like the sound of that.

"So, find out for me," Christina continued when I didn't respond.

"I'll see what I can do," I replied curtly.

"Anything else to report? You've spent a lot of time with him," she hedged.

I swallowed thickly. "He asked me to be his date to the luau."

"Good. You're doing your job then."

The fireball spun in the air above my hand. "I'm assuming you want me to say yes."

She scoffed. "You haven't already?"

The fireball spun faster. "No. I didn't know what to say. I'm awful at this double agent thing."

"From all reports, you're pretty great at this. My spy network tells me the prince is smitten."

Spy network. Is she spying on me?

227

"If I say yes, my fake relationship goes public," I reminded her.

"You're a big girl, Brie. You can handle it," she insisted.

Really? Because just *reading* a freakin' gossip site with a blind item about me nearly sent me over the edge.

"How long do I have to do this?" I asked her. "What's the endgame here? Am I supposed to sleep with him? Am I supposed to marry him?"

Her pacing heels clicked a frantic rhythm on the other end. "Let's take this one day at a time. For now, just keep him interested."

Way to not answer my questions.

"Anything else?" she pressed.

The fireball started moving at dizzying speeds and then burst. Embers floated on the breeze around my balcony. "I think Kenoa is suspicious."

The footsteps halted as Christina stopped pacing. "Will he say anything to the prince?"

I shook my head even though she couldn't see me. "Not without coming to me first."

"You're sure?"

"Positive."

I wasn't, but if she thought Kenoa was a threat to the mission, I couldn't say for sure what she'd do. Once upon a time, I would've believed that Kenoa was more loyal to me than his employer. Kai wasn't just his employer, though. They were friends. Very close friends. Forced to choose between us, I didn't know who Kenoa would pick.

"Then it's a nonissue for the moment. Keep me

apprised. Anything else?"

"No, that's it," I told her.

"Next time you talk to the prince, agree to be his date to the luau." It wasn't a request. It was a command.

"Fine," I agreed. "If you swear to me that any memories retrieved from those two casters won't be connected to the rebellion.

Christina didn't hesitate. "You have my word, Brie."

CHAPTER SIXTEEN

KAI WAS WAITING for me outside the locker rooms at the training facility the following day. Lounging against the wall, he looked out of place in his navy suit and striped tie. Even in the glow of the fluorescent bulbs, Kai managed to look good. His dark eyes, which I'd thought were the color of black coffee, appeared inky blue.

As I took a moment to admire the prince, Christina's warning played inside my head: *You are no good to me or the rebellion if you get emotionally invested in the caster prince.*

As though he felt me watching, Kai glanced up from his phone. He smiled. "Tough workout?"

Following his gaze down, I realized my shirt was soaked with sweat and singed in several places from when I'd lost control of my magic. My hair was also plastered to my head, and my face was the color of a ripe tomato. Overall, it wasn't my best look.

"That obvious?" I asked dryly.

He walked over and placed a light kiss on my forehead. The gesture felt so right, so natural. It wasn't until I heard the whisperings of two female shifters nearby that I considered the ramifications of such a public display. I stepped out of his embrace.

Kai gave an embarrassed laugh. "Sorry. I was not thinking." His eyes darted to the shifter girls, and he lowered his voice. "I am happy to see you."

"What are you doing here?" I asked uneasily, keeping the shifters in my peripheral vision.

"I need a favor," he said sheepishly. "You can say no, and I will understand."

"Well, with that caveat, I'm guessing I will want to say no."

Kai chuckled. "It is a big favor. I am due to meet with Samira Duquesne in an hour. She is the witch I told you about from North Shore. She is not loyal to my family, as she does not agree with the current laws regarding fae and shifters being brought beneath the dome."

"I like her already," I interrupted.

He grinned. "I thought you might. Samira is an extremely vocal supporter of fae and shifter rights. She is reluctant to help with the investigation of two depleted casters, particularly two casters who have, in the past, wanted to further limit those rights. She did agree to the meeting, though. I thought perhaps if you came and possibly explained—"

"That you think these casters' memories could help you find the missing fae and shifters, as well as the missing witches and warlocks," I filled in. "You think she'll agree if the request comes from me?"

Kai wrinkled his nose. "Yes," he admitted. "I believe Samira will be more amenable to helping if you are present."

I crossed my arms and fixed him with narrowed eyes. "So, you want to use me?"

"Well, yes. That is one way of looking at it. I would owe you." When I didn't respond immediately, he added, "Big. I would owe you big."

I let him sweat a moment longer, then held out my hand. "Deal."

Kenoa, Harton, Makani, and a female caster I thought was named Lara were all waiting in the limo when Kai and I exited the training facility.

"Three bodyguards?" I arched an eyebrow at the prince.

"My mother protects her investments. I am her biggest investment." He shrugged. "I promise, you will not even notice they are there."

That was a lie, of course. It was hard not to notice Kenoa. Makani wasn't small, either. Lara was pretty tiny, but something told me that she might very well be the most lethal of the three.

"You're costing me a lot, Brie," Kenoa grumbled as I climbed into the back seat beside him.

"Maybe you should stop betting on what I'll do," I shot back, nudging him in the ribs.

The ride back to my condo was awkward, to put it

mildly. Kai tried to strike up a conversation with me, asking about my training and if the potion was out of my system. But with all those ears pretending not to listen, I couldn't engage.

When we arrived at my condo building, Makani remained outside, while Lara took up guard outside my door. Kenoa came inside the condo with Kai and me. I considered insisting the other bodyguards wait in my living room, but I wasn't sure how I felt about them yet. Until I was, they weren't hanging out inside my personal space.

I showered in record time. Wrapped in a heavy robe, I exited my bathroom to find Kai and Kenoa rifling through my closet. Numerous dresses were already spread out on my bed.

"Um, what are you two doing?" I asked.

"Helping, hopefully," Kai said, examining a purple sheath that I'd never worn.

Behind him, Kenoa snickered. I glared back at the bodyguard.

"By raiding my closet?" I snapped. "You don't trust that I can select an appropriate outfit on my own?"

Kai turned, eyes wide. "No. Brie, that is not—"

"Told you," Kenoa interjected.

"Out. Both of you. I'll be down in ten minutes." I pointed toward the door, and they scurried from the bedroom.

Kai had laid out several of the dresses I'd been considering for the meeting. Still, my feelings were a little hurt. Did he think I would dress like a floozy? I might not have been one of Madame Noelani's girls, but that didn't mean I was socially stunted.

Short on time, yet not wanting to leave with wet hair, I summoned just enough magic to heat my hands. I ran them through my tresses until the hair was shiny and smooth. After applying powder and mascara with a light hand, I shimmied into a green and white dress with capped sleeves and a belted waist. Though I rarely opted for heels, I pulled on nude pumps that seemed both appropriate and demure.

"Do I get your stamp of approval?" I asked, sauntering down the steps from the loft. I clung to the banister as I adjusted to the heels.

Kai grinned up at me from the couch, where he and Kenoa were engaged in a discussion about centerpieces for the luau.

"You look stunning. Perfect." He held out a hand to me. "Do not be nervous. I will do most of the talking."

"Except for the part where I explain that performing the memory retrieval would help find *all* the missing persons," I shot back.

"Yes, except for that part," Kai agreed.

"Delightful," I muttered. *Why am I doing this?* I wondered, as Kai, Kenoa, and I exited my condo. I'd barely given any thought to Kai's request before agreeing to the favor. But all dressed up in heels, reality hit me: I was aiding a royal inquiry into caster depletions.

Again, why did I say yes? But I knew it was because I needed the truth. If Samira could retrieve the memories, I'd know for sure if Christina, and by extension *I*, was responsible for the depletions.

It wasn't until I was once again in the back of the limo

with Kai and the bodyguards that I thought to ask where we were meeting Samira Duquesne.

A smile curved Kenoa's lips.

"What? Why do I get the impression you purposely didn't tell me before now?" I demanded of Kai.

Lara's eyes narrowed and her lips pursed. For a second, I thought she might scold me for speaking harshly to her prince.

"Well, probably because you are very intuitive," Kai said, fighting a smile of his own.

The partition lowered behind his head, and Harton called, "Would you like me to pull around to the back entrance, sir?"

"Yes," I replied, even though I wasn't sure where we were going. Regardless of the locale, I wanted to keep a low profile when with Kai.

Lara glared at me when I answered for him. Harton hesitated. Unwittingly, I'd put him in an awkward position. I started to apologize, but Kai spoke up.

"As Miss Maybrie indicated, the back please."

Harton smiled in the rearview mirror. "Yes, Your Highness."

Kai squeezed my hand. "Ms. Duquesne thought it best if we met at the hospital, so she could see the depleted before she made a decision."

"Samira Duquesne is one of your subjects," Lara said stiffly. "You should order her to perform the spell. Your Highness," she added, almost as an afterthought.

Kai was still looking at me when his eyes frosted over. That cool gaze settled on his bodyguard. "I will not order a caster to risk depletion for a spell. I would never order a caster to risk depletion to save the life of another. And it would serve you well to remember that I do not take orders regarding delicate political matters from you."

He didn't yell. He didn't even raise his voice. His tone was polite yet firm. Still, Lara shrank back against the leather seat. I almost felt bad for her. Almost.

Harton pulled the car to a stop at the hospital's back entrance. Makani and Lara jumped out to open the doors. Kai motioned for me to go first, and he and Kenoa followed directly behind me.

"Samira isn't going to perform the spell now, is she?" I asked as we walked toward a group of very official-looking hospital workers.

"No," Kai assured me. "The spell is too complicated, and there are several potions involved, if I am not mistaken."

I breathed a little easier. As much as I wanted answers, I didn't want to learn the truth with all Kai's bodyguards and the hospital administrators around.

Lara and Makani walked a respectful three steps behind us, but Kenoa was right beside me. It was like he sensed I needed his support more than Kai needed another shield in that moment.

"Samira Duquesne did not agree to this meeting because she intends on helping," Kenoa told me. "She won't have come prepared with the necessary herbs and tonics. In the unlikely event she does decide to help, it will be another couple of days before anything more happens." Though my friend sensed I was uncomfortable—I wasn't hiding it well—he misread the cause. "No one expects you to be present for the retrieval," Kenoa assured me, fixing Kai with a hard look. "And, of course, no one wants to put you in an uncomfortable position by *making* you see a depleted caster today."

"Oh, Brie, no." Kai was quick to jump in. "Of course not." He reached for my hand and gave it a quick squeeze. "I would never ask that of you."

I forced a smile. "Sorry, this is all just happening really fast."

The hospital administrators fawned all over Kai and, to a lesser extent, me. Kenoa chatted easily with a dark-haired caster doctor. They even exchanged a few laughs as our entourage walked to a conference room where Samira Duquesne was waiting for us. Only Kai and I went inside, though.

"Ms. Duquesne, thank you for meeting with us," Kai said politely, extending his hand as we sat across from the older witch at the conference table.

She smiled just as politely and accepted the handshake, though she didn't call him "prince" or "sir" or "Your Highness". In fact, she didn't say anything to Kai at all. The witch didn't take her eyes off me.

"Maybrie Hawkins, ma'am," I introduced myself and offered her my hand.

Samira Duquesne was eccentric, the type of witch that was depicted in fairytales. She wore heavy fur robes that were appropriate for the frozen world outside the dome but out of place in our artificial climate. Her long, gray braid was streaked with white. Gold, wire-rimmed glasses perched on the end of her long nose.

"Maybrie, you say?" Samira repeated my name with a

knowing glint in her eye. "You are the fighter. I have heard of you. They say you are second to none." Her gaze flicked briefly to Kai, and I got the impression she wasn't just talking about in the arena. "What interest does a famous pit fighter have in a criminal investigation?"

Kai opened his mouth to say something, but I didn't need his help.

"I've seen a depleted. No one deserves that fate," I told her honestly.

"Ah, yes. My condolences on your loss." From behind her glasses, the caster watched me curiously, like I was a puzzle she had yet to solve. "If I may be so bold as to ask, is Tanner the reason you don't fight with your magic?"

"No," I said with forced calm. "I don't fight with my magic because I don't need to in the arena."

"Ms. Duquesne," Kai tried to draw her attention from me. I could tell the prince was ready to end the meeting there.

"You are a powerful fae," she said to me, talking over the prince.

It wasn't a question, so I wasn't sure whether she expected an answer. I gave her one anyway. "I am. All the more reason not to fight with my fire. The majority of my competitors are shifters; my magic would give me an unfair advantage. I like my wins to be honest and hard won."

"Fascinating," Samira commented. "May I ask another personal question?"

"Ms. Duquesne, maybe we could—" Kai started to say.

"Quiet. If you want to know if I can do the memory

retrieval, the answer is yes. Whether I will depends on Maybrie." Her eyes never left my face.

I blew out a long breath. "Sure, ask away. Just know that I may not answer."

Samira laughed and cut her eyes to Kai. "I do hope you know what you have gotten yourself into. Your girlfriend has more magic than even a royal can manage. She also has more attitude than most casters care for."

"Brie and I do not...Maybrie does not...we have never...." I'd never seen the prince so flustered.

"Oh, I am aware," Samira informed him. "She has not shared her magic with you. But when she does, a word of warning: That which makes you stronger can kill you, my prince."

Excuse me? Who said anything about sharing my magic?

Samira turned back to me. "Why do you not practice your craft more, child?"

"What makes you think I don't?" I countered.

Samira shook her head as though I'd let her down. "Come now. You may not cast much now, but you are trained. You have had instruction. I know just by touching your hand that you only perform basic spells. Tell me, Maybrie, what has our one handshake told you about me?"

Under the table, Kai reached for my hand. I let him slip his fingers through mine, but my focused stayed on Samira. She held out her hand to me like a queen expecting a subject to kiss her knuckles.

In the canyon, all faelings are taught to sense and detect magic in others. Without casters around to practice on, I'd only learned to detect elemental magic.

Still, as I cupped Samira's hand in mine, I found myself recalling the techniques I hadn't used in years. I closed my eyes and inhaled deeply. The witch smelled of snow and salt and brimstone. *She's been casting recently.* Her hand felt like cool water between my fingers. *She's taken magic from a water fae.* There was a wildness to her magic, like a stud yet to be broken. *No formal training.* I squeezed her hand gently and let all my barriers fall. A wave of power hit me so hard that I actually flinched.

Samira withdrew her hand, and I opened my eyes. "Now, child, what can you tell me about myself?"

I sat up straighter. "Magic is a part of your everyday life. You use it for the most basic of tasks. You're a powerful caster, but you prefer potions and tonics. As recently as this morning you brewed a," I thought hard, "a freezing solution of some sort."

Samira smiled. "Keep going, child."

In my peripheral vision, I saw Kai watching me with wonder.

"You didn't attend a caster school; you have no formal training. You learned to cast from an elder in your community. Wait, no." I shook my head. "You learned to cast from a water fae. I'm going to guess, the same fae who gives you magic."

"My husband, Albert," she said.

I met her gaze levelly and smiled. "He was your family's house fae when you were a child. You two fell in love. That is why you, an extremely powerful caster, live in North Shore, away from the royal court and your family. It's why you are such an advocate for fae rights." That was all conjecture. I couldn't have known any of that just by touching her. Nonetheless, I knew I was right.

Samira nodded approvingly. "You are quite something, child. Particularly for a non-practicing fire fae." She turned to Kai, finally bringing him into the conversation. "I will help you on one condition." Even before the words left her mouth, I knew her terms. "Maybrie must assist me while I brew the concoction. I will cast the spell myself, but I will need to channel her energy."

"I—"

"If you will excuse us for just a moment, Ms. Duquesne," Kai interrupted. He grabbed my hand and tugged me to my feet.

We were in the hallway before I could protest. I caught sight of Samira sipping tea just before the prince closed the door to the conference room without using his hands.

"You do not have to do this," Kai said softly, so the bodyguards stationed at either end of the corridor couldn't overhear us. "We have other options."

I arched an eyebrow. "Other options? Like what? You bring in a caster from another kingdom? That takes time. And probably paperwork. I know how you royals love your paperwork."

"She is asking you to willingly share your magic with her, Brie," Kai said, a spark of anger flaring in his dark eyes.

"I know what *channel* means," I hissed. My temper was directed at him, while his was focused on Samira.

"Have you ever shared your magic?" Kai asked.

"Not willingly." I rubbed my neck and thought of

Mat.

"She has no right to ask this of you," the prince snapped.

"Why? Because my magic belongs to you? To the royal family? To some caster your mother deems worthy of my power? It's mine, Kai. I can give it to whoever I want. Or not give it to some asshole so he can perform parlor tricks." I was seething. It took all my control to keep my hands from turning into flaming mittens.

Kai rested his hands on my shoulders, flinching slightly when he felt the heat of my temper. He didn't let go, though.

"You know that is not what I meant. You are free to give or not give your magic to whomever you choose." His eyes softened. "I never meant to put you in this position. Please, just think about what she is asking of you."

"Does it hurt?" I asked uneasily.

Since I had never shared my magic with a caster, I had no idea how the transference spell worked or felt. *Am I being hasty?* I wondered. Then another thought hit me: *Is Christina going to lose her shit?*

Kai shook his head. "No, not when both parties want the exchange. It can even be, well, magical under the right circumstances."

I averted my gaze. "I…I want to do this, Kai."

Until I spoke the words aloud, I hadn't realized they were true. Once upon a time, I had studied magic religiously. I had brewed potions and cast spells that were more involved than securing my locker. Casting was invigorating. I missed that wash of power that made me feel as though I could take on the world.

"Are you sure, Brie?" Kai searched my face. His voice was barely above a whisper when he continued. "You do not have to do this for me."

I fixed him with the same blank expression I gave my competitors at the start of a fight. "Do you honestly believe you factor into this decision at all?"

At one end of the hallway, Kenoa covered a laugh with his hand. Lara looked like she was ready to shove a spike through my heart. Makani had his hands clasped behind his back, head tilted back like a movie was playing on the ceiling.

"Well, let's go tell Ms. Duquesne the good news." Kai gestured to the closed conference room door. He put a hand on my shoulder when I passed him. "Brie? Thank you."

"You owe me two favors now," I whispered. "*Big* ones."

CHAPTER SEVENTEEN

AFTER WE WORKED out the details with Samira, Kai and I picked up sushi to go for an early dinner at my condo. I invited all four of the prince's staff inside, since we'd gotten them food as well. Harton insisted he needed to stay with the car. Makani and Lara, wishing to follow protocol, politely declined my invitation and took up positions outside my door. I was most surprised that Kenoa declined to join us.

"I'm going to need a nap after all this rice," he told me. "I'll just stretch out in the back of the limo. You two kids have fun."

Kai and I ate at my dining room table and then retreated to the couch with steaming mugs of cinnamon tea. We talked about my next fight, a match against a vampire. I'd only fought two in my five years in the pits.

"I think that's part of why Botto wants me to practice my magic," I told Kai as we snuggled under the same blanket, our legs intertwined.

"You aren't supposed to kill him," Kai reminded me.

"No, but I can restrict his movements, which is the only way to defeat a vampire. They're so fast."

The prince set his mug on the coffee table, then took mine from my cupped hands and put it beside his. He pulled me close. "I have no doubt you will have one hundred and one wins very soon."

Our lips met in a kiss that deserved fireworks. But when we pulled apart, Kai's expression was serious. "I need for you to know I meant what I said earlier. No matter what happens between us in the future, you will never have to share your magic."

"When I retire from the pits, I'll have enough to buy out my contract," I replied. "So, I'm not worried about it."

He studied me for a long moment. "We both know that is not true. At least, not as things stand now. What is interesting is that you *should* have enough money, but you do not."

I started to back away.

"I believe I know why," Kai continued.

No. No. No. Just no. We can't have this conversation.

"You are helping house fae, are you not?"

I sagged with relief. My donations to individual fae weren't legal, but at least he hadn't asked about the rebellion. *Yet,* I reminded myself.

"I am," I admitted. Then, in a much more measured voice, I asked, "Did Kenoa tell you about my food deliveries?"

Kai's brows drew together. "Um, no. He did not. Are you diverting your food deliveries to house fae, as well?"

Freakin' hell. "Yeah, sort of." There was no point in lying. Plus, I preferred his focus stayed on my more minor crimes.

"How does it work?" Kai asked.

"Nope." I shook my head. "I'm not getting anyone else in trouble. If you want to charge me—"

Kai reached for me. "I have no interest in getting you in trouble. In my mind, it is your money and your food credits. You can do with them as you please."

"If you didn't know about the food deliveries, how did you know I was helping house fae?" I asked curiously.

The prince's jaw tightened. "My mother ran a background check on you," he admitted.

Breathe. You knew this would happen.

"I saw several donations appear in the account of Everly Woods. There were no direct transfers, of course. But the same amount left your account, only to show up two days later in hers," Kai continued.

I did help Everly. But those donations weren't entirely for her. She funneled the money to the rebellion via large purchases at Christina's boutique. I could've done it directly, but Christina wanted me as far removed from the transactions as possible.

"That's not illegal," I told Kai defensively.

"No, it is not," he agreed. "I would not have made the connection, except for...." Kai trailed off, eyes pinning me in place.

"Tanner. Tanner Woods was my boyfriend. Your mother uncovered that fact in her investigation," I said calmly, though my body vibrated.

Kai held me tighter. I pulled away again but just far enough that his arms were no longer around me.

The prince met my hard stare. "She did," he said carefully. "But that is not how I know about your relationship with Tanner." The way he looked at me nearly brought tears to my eyes. "His death was inexcusable. The entire situation was a debacle."

I wanted to look away. I wanted to talk about anything else. I wanted to be anywhere else. Nonetheless, my gaze never wavered when I said, "The Pit Masters killed Tanner. They forced his hand. He did what anyone would've done in his situation."

"I agree," Kai said simply. "Had the royal family been informed of his condition, which we should have been, he would likely still be alive. I could have found him help."

Tears stung my eyes as Tanner's beautiful face filled my mind. He'd been so sweet, thoughtful, loving. The ache in my chest that had been my constant companion for months after his death returned tenfold. I hadn't felt that deep stab in my heart for weeks. I wanted to cry and scream and throw things.

And then, Kai was there. Slowly, as if afraid of rejection, he took me in his arms and held me. I pressed my face to his chest and cried into his shirt. The prince stroked my back.

"I am sorry to have to bring all of this up," he

muttered into my hair. "I just felt it was best to be honest. I have never agreed with my mother on this issue. Prying into your private affairs simply because we are dating is not fair. Unfortunately, it is not my decision." He dropped a light kiss on the top of my head. "People have begun to notice the amount of time we spend together, and my mother wants to be prepared for the press that will soon begin."

I sniffled a few times and nodded. "Yeah, I get it," I mumbled against his chest. Tilting my head back slightly, I peered up at Kai, who had a line of sweat along his forehead. "This is protocol, right?"

With his thumb, Kai gently wiped away my tears. "I know you probably do not want to hear it from me, but for what it is worth, I am sorry about Tanner, Brie. I met him on several occasions and once even had the pleasure of his company over dinner. He was a good man."

More tears fell, and Kai was there to catch them.

"He was a great man," I said softly.

We sat in silence for a long time, Kai holding me while I cried over another guy. But that wasn't the only reason for my waterworks. Kai had brought up the subject because he wanted to be honest about the fact his mother had dug into my past. He wanted me to know that he knew about Tanner. I couldn't reciprocate that honesty. I was a liar and a spy. Yes, I liked the prince. But that didn't really matter when I'd been deceiving him this whole time. Our relationship was built on lies.

"I want to stay with you tonight," Kai said after a while. "Would that be okay? I can sleep on the couch."

"I'm not sure—" I began.

"There is no pressure," the prince interrupted. "I just want you to know that I am serious about our relationship. I care about you, Brie. I find myself in an odd position of wanting to protect you and understanding that you are not the type of girl who needs a Prince Charming."

Am I? I wondered. Because in that moment, I wanted his comfort more than I wanted my next breath. Did I want him to stay? Yes, I did. Was I ready to take our relationship to the next level? The answer was too complicated to unpack at this moment.

What would Christina want me to do? I wondered. *I should tattoo that on my hand.*

"I care about you, too," I said finally. "And I do want you to stay. Honestly. Just another night." *If I sleep with him, it'll be for me,* I told myself.

His thumb, wiping away my tears, then moved to trace the contours of my mouth. I closed my eyes as Kai brought his mouth to mine. His hands traveled up my back, beneath my sweater. My entire body tingled at his touch.

Kai pulled away first. Breathless, he gazed into my eyes and ran his fingers through my hair. "I should probably go," he said softly.

I nodded and gave him a small smile. "Yeah, that's a good idea."

He kissed me one more time, and then I walked him to the foyer.

"What time should I send the car for you?" he asked.

Though I acquiesced to Samira's request, Kai countered her terms with one of his own: that we work on the potion at the palace. Both Samira and I had been a little taken aback. Kai claimed it would be more private, and we would have easier access to all the materials needed for the memory retrieval. Technically, that was true, but I secretly believed this was his way of getting me to meet his mother again. Whatever the case, I was more reticent about the location than Samira.

"Six o'clock would be good for me," I replied. "I'm working the lunch shift at Pele's. I get off around five, so that gives me time to shower and change."

"Or Harton can pick you up at work, and we can have dinner first?" he countered.

"Or we could have dinner afterward?" I offered. For my first trip to the palace, I didn't exactly want to show up in work clothes and smelling like fried food—I needed the extra hour to get ready. "Besides, aren't you going over to House of Mana to interrogate fae?"

"Interview," he corrected. "I am, though I do not expect it to take long. They are unlikely to tell us much. They may donate magic to casters, but they do not trust my kind."

"Do you blame them?" I asked, my words carrying a bite.

"No, I honestly do not." Kai shook his head. "But I believe those fae know something about the disappearances, and the establishment is our only real lead. I have to try."

"You're right," I agreed. "No one deserves depletion."

Kai pulled me closer and ran his lips over my cheekbone. "You are adorable when you are lost in thought."

"I'm not lost—" I started to protest. Then his mouth was on mine, and I forgot what I was going to say.

Once Kai had left, I debated whether to check in with Christina. She would want to know about my impending work with Samira, and that I would be spending the next few evenings at the palace brewing a potion. I didn't go to the patio, though. I didn't want to hear more warnings about mixing business and pleasure. My personal feelings were clouding my judgment. I was well aware of that fact.

Instead, I muted my registered phone and curled up in bed with a mug of tea and my favorite book: *The Lioness, the Human, and the Broom Closet* by D.T. Louis. After an hour, my eyelids began to droop. I reached absently for the light switch beside my bed and knocked my cellphone off the nightstand. I leaned over the side of the bed to retrieve it, only to nearly drop the phone a second time when I saw:

(63) NEW MESSAGES
(42) MISSED CALLS

Twelve texts and twenty of the missed calls were from Cala alone. *This can't be good.*

CALA (11:23 P.M.): *Call. Me. ASAP.*
CALA (11:10 P.M.): *Where are you?*
CALA (11:02 P.M.): *VIDEO Attachment*

With trembling fingers, I pressed play on the video attachment. A sinking feeling in my gut told me that I already knew what I'd see. Sure enough, the short clip showed Kai and me at the training facility with his arm slung around my sweaty, disheveled body. As if that wasn't bad enough, the cameraperson had zoomed in on the moment he kissed me. I didn't bother reading the rest of the messages or listening to my dozens of voicemails. Instead, I dialed Cala's number and turned on the television in my bedroom.

"Are you okay?" Cala answered on the first ring.

"Jury's still out," I replied. "When did this video get out?"

"I don't know for sure. Rocko and I were out running trails when Cassie sent it to me, but it's all over the place, Brie. Your secret is out. Like, *really* out."

"Wait...your personal shopper sent you the video?" I demanded.

"Seriously?" she shot back. "That's your concern in all of this?"

I sighed. "No, but I'm trying to not freak out right now."

On the television, an entertainment reporter was speculating on the latest in "Prince Kai's long line of questionable love choices," while the video from the training facility played in the background.

"What did Rocko say?" I asked.

Cala laughed. "You know, he's Rocko. I think he's a little hurt you didn't tell him yourself."

The footage behind the reporter changed to a clip of Kai and me leaving the hospital together. A headline across the bottom of the screen read "Official Royal Engagements Already?"

In a hesitant voice, my best friend added, "But you

really need to talk to Everly now."

I pinched the bridge of my nose. This was not the way I'd wanted Tanner's sister to find out. "Yeah, I'll do that, just as soon as I figure out what I'm going to tell her."

"Want me to come over?" Cala offered.

"No. Not tonight, but I might need you soon."

"Open invitation," she promised. "Night, Brie. I love you."

I smiled. "I love you too, Cala."

CHAPTER EIGHTEEN

"BRIE! OVER HERE! How serious is your relationship with the prince?" a reporter yelled.

"Is it true you were visiting the hospital on official palace business?" another called out.

"Are you pregnant, Brie? Is that why Prince Kai is taking this relationship so seriously? Is that why you were at the hospital?" The woman wore mittens and shoved a microphone in my face.

"Are you crazy? Of course I'm not pregnant," I snapped.

Kenoa shouldered through the crowd that was gathered in front of my building. As he sheltered me beneath his large arm, cameras vied for pictures of me in my dark sunglasses and large hat, which pretty much confirmed that I had something to hide.

"Just keep your head down," he murmured in my ear.

When one ballsy reporter stepped between us and the open limo door, I felt Kenoa's magic swell. The camera popped as his lens crackled over with ice and shattered. The reporter sulked off while Harton fended off the horde and Kenoa helped me inside the car. The instant my door was closed, the driver ran to the front, hopped in, and floored the accelerator.

Letting out a shaky breath, I removed my hat and glasses. The reporters had been staked outside of my building since that morning.

"Is this normal?" I asked Kenoa.

"Yes and no," he admitted, pulling off his sunglasses. "You are sort of famous in your own right, Brie. That makes things more…intriguing. And Kai, well he's never mixed business with pleasure before."

"It wasn't like that," I protested. "Yesterday was a special situation. He needed my help."

"True." Kenoa nodded. Even as he agreed, it was clear that he didn't totally agree with my argument.

"What? Are you saying there was more to it?" I demanded.

The large fae looked as though his suit had suddenly become too tight. Fixing him with a hard stare, I waited out the pause.

"He could have asked someone else, Brie," Kenoa finally said. "In case you've forgotten, I'm also fae. And he does have quite a few friends in our community. The prince still chose you."

I turned to stare out the window, though the dark tint impeded any sightseeing. Pondering my friend's words, I felt my lips curl into a smile. *He chose you.* The thought shouldn't have made my heart skip a beat. *I'm getting way too invested,* I thought.

More reporters waited outside the palace gates, all hoping to get a shot of me arriving at the royal residence. They pressed their cameras against the windows while Harton waited for the gates to open.

"You can see them, but they can't see you," Kenoa assured me as I shrank away from the glass.

The gates finally opened, and Harton pulled through. Press wasn't allowed on palace grounds without an engraved royal invitation, so I was able to breathe a little easier once we were driving up the long road to Kai's royal home.

The prince came running down the front steps of Iolani Palace before Harton had opened my door. We'd spoken several times throughout the day, but Kai seemed determined to confirm with his own eyes that I was okay. He held me at arm's length and studied every bruise and scrape visible on my body.

"They're from practice," I assured him.

His concerns weren't completely unfounded. To avoid the training facility, and the reporters waiting for me, Botto had met me at Diamond Ridge State Park for our session. But the reporters mobbed me outside of Pele's instead. Jon was forced to close until Kenoa arrived and the two of them smuggled me out the back. Sending his personal bodyguard had probably not been the most inconspicuous move, but I was grateful for the friendly face. Particularly when most of the media I encountered that day had been either nosy or hostile.

Kai folded me into his arms. I hugged him just as tightly as he hugged me. He shivered in the brisk evening air. When I spoke next, I saw my breath.

"I'm fine. Really. It's just a lot." I pulled back but kept my arms around Kai's waist. "I didn't expect things to get to this point...ever."

"Does this change how you feel about 'things'?" he asked slowly.

"I don't know," I admitted. It was possibly the most honest response about my feelings that I'd ever given him. I couldn't imagine a life where I was followed by cameras all the time, where people felt they had a right to invade my privacy. I'd thought being a pseudo-famous fighter was hard, but it was nothing compared to the level of scrutiny that came with dating a royal.

"Well, that is not a *no*," Kai replied with a grin. Taking my hand, he led me up the steps to the palace. "Ms. Duquesne is already here."

"Were you able to get all the ingredients?" I asked as we passed through the enormous double doors and into the royal residence.

Trying to keep my expression as neutral as possible, I glanced around the vaulted foyer. It ran the entire width of the palace, ending in a sweeping staircase that lead to the second floor and the royal residences. The koa wood floors gleamed like a polished ice-skating rink. The sheer glamour of the space was overwhelming, but I vowed to keep my brain on the task at hand instead of gawking at Kai's home.

"Remarkably, yes," he replied, oblivious to my sudden stiffness. "Well, most of them. The lion heart flower is not due to arrive until tomorrow." He shook his head. "Ms. Duquesne is not pleased, but she has agreed to begin since the flower is one of the last ingredients needed."

"Yeah, lion heart is…," I trailed off, unable to finish my thought as we entered a room decorated entirely in shades of blue, from the velvet drapes to the thickest carpet I'd ever walked on.

The walls were lined with portraits of past monarchs. The largest one was a stoic woman in a black dress and blue sash with a white flower decorating her hair—the last human monarch of Hawaii. Queen Lili'uokalani's portrait was a historic artifact, and I'd assumed it would be hanging in a museum somewhere. Suits of armor stood at attention between the portraits. It felt like they were staring at me, judging me for my disloyal behavior. *But was it really disloyal when I never asked to be in this kingdom?* I pondered.

"Would you like the grand tour?" Kai asked.

"I don't want to keep Samira waiting," I replied quickly.

"Then I shall just take one small detour on the way to the casting chamber."

Through another arched doorway, we turned left. According to a sign, we were headed toward the gardens and royal tennis courts. We stepped through an exterior door, onto the wraparound porch out back, and into a setting straight from the Freelands. Snow blanketed the ground on either side of the walkway, which appeared to be heated. Frost-coated ivy snaked around trees with sugar fruit growing on the branches. Icicles formed beautiful sculptures on overhangs and benches.

A calm washed over me like warm bath water, though the temperature was below freezing. My body began to tingle. A current of raw power coursed from my head to my toes. The elemental magic and enchantments in the Winter Garden called to my fire magic like long-lost siblings who were desperate for a reunion.

Kai yanked his hand from mine with a yelp. Looking down in confusion, I saw tiny orange flames coating my palm.

"I'm so sorry," I gasped.

He looked at his own hand. The skin was red but not blistered. "I am fine," he promised. "No harm done."

"I swear that doesn't normally happen. The magic here is powerful."

Kai cupped my cheek with his unburnt palm and ran a thumb across my jaw, shaking from the cold. "It is. Casters don't feel magic quite the same way fae do, since ours does not come from the outside world. But even I find myself overpowered when I spend time here."

It's a wonder he can spend any time in here. It's awfully cold for a caster.

"Why is the magic so strong?" I asked. Kai slid his hand into mine, and we started walking again.

He looked down at me appraisingly. "You really want to know?"

"Why wouldn't I?"

"I am a little nervous to tell you," he hedged.

And because thinking before speaking was not

something I'd ever learned, I replied, "Why, is it some big secret? Do you think I'm going to report back to my spy network?" A strange noise, like a soft shivering of a dying cat, escaped my lips. I meant it as a joke, until I realized what I'd said.

"Nothing so sinister." Kai laughed. "It is sort of a secret, though, only because I wanted to see if my idea worked before making it public." He took a deep breath, very excited about his big news. "I am nervous to tell you specifically, because I think the idea is great, and I worry you might not agree."

"The suspense is killing me," I said, only half kidding.

"The different flowers in the Royal Garden were chosen because they all retain elemental magic better than most. Some, like the orange blossom, retain earth magic in much higher quantities than the average flower. Others, like the rose, are great at retaining air magic," Kai said, sounding like a sultry tour guide.

"And fire magic? Which flower holds that power best?" I asked.

"The frozen hibiscus," Kai said immediately.

Just like the flower he gave me in the arena.

"What we have done is ask willing fae to imbue the flowers with their specific magic. Normally, the strength begins to wane after about twenty-four hours. But, if a caster performs an everlasting spell, then the flower can be used as a source of power for a caster for much longer. I theorize, with a strong enough caster and a strong enough fae, the power could be, as the spell name implies, everlasting."

Thus giving weaker casters the power necessary to become

stronger casters, I thought.

"We could end the need for direct fae-to-caster transference," Kai finished, watching me expectantly.

"That's amazing. Very forward thinking of you," I told him.

Kai suddenly became very serious. "I am to be king one day, Brie. If I want my children to live in a peaceful world, I need to find a way for fae and shifters and casters to live together in harmony. Otherwise, my heir will inherit a kingdom at war."

You'll be the one to inherit a kingdom at war, I thought sadly.

I forced a smile. "Well, this could be a solid first step."

"We plan to unveil it at the luau. Well, just the garden itself—I am not ready to claim my idea a success. I would like a few more months of data first." He ran a hand through his hair. "But my advisors think we must do just that: claim success. They hope it will counteract the rise in tensions between casters and non-casters, in light of the disappearances."

"No way. Bad idea. If you do that, and your experiment doesn't work, fae will be very upset. We'll feel like you've lied to us," I said automatically, never once considering that my advice was just as out of line as Lara's had been earlier.

"Precisely what I told my advisors," Kai agreed.

Hand in hand, we meandered along a stone path lined with rose bushes. The petals were covered in a thin layer of frost. Cherry blossom trees ringed a koi pond, which was the only attraction without ice.

"Does this remind you of home?" the prince asked softly.

"Yeah, a little," I admitted. "Not in a bad way, if that's what you're wondering. I don't think fae would be upset that you chose to make a Winter Garden."

"I am mostly worried about *you* being upset I chose to make a Winter Garden," he replied.

"Oh." I laughed, and heat rushed to my cheeks. "Me, personally? I love it. That's why I keep the condo so cold."

"That is what gave me the idea, actually. Originally, we had planned another summer garden. Then I spent time in your chilly condo and wondered if maybe part of the reason everlasting spells do not actually last forever was because fae magic is stronger outside the dome, in the Freelands."

"That's pretty smart thinking. So, you're going to credit me if this works like you think?" I teased.

Kai laughed. "Definitely."

We exited the Winter Garden and entered a much warmer hallway.

"Magical barrier," the prince explained when he saw my confusion. "It was the only way to prevent the entire palace from feeling like the Arctic."

He turned right down another corridor and climbed a back stairway with two guards posted at the bottom.

"We aren't going to run into your mother in her housecoat or anything, are we?" I asked uncomfortably.

"No," Kai promised. "This is my wing of the palace."

Oh, lovely. He doesn't have a suite, he has a wing.

"What kinds of rooms does one have in a wing?" I asked. "Do you have a secret magic room where all secret magic is performed?"

Kai looked down at me. "I know you are making fun of me, but the answer is yes. I do have a secret magic room where secret magic is performed. That is where we are headed now."

CHAPTER NINETEEN

A LOT OF casters had specific rooms where they performed spells and brewed potions. Kai's chamber was different, though. For one, we accessed the staircase to it via an opening in the hallway that seemed it might disappear when closed. But it was more than the covert entryway that made it feel special. Magic wasn't just performed there; the room itself contained a great deal of energy.

It's like ghosts of spells past in here, I thought with a rush.

Samira's robes hung on a hook beside the door. She was busy examining the ingredients spread out on a long work bench in the center of the circular room.

"Good evening, Ms. Duquesne," Kai said, as the older witch dipped her finger in a pile of red powder and tasted the contents.

"You aren't needed here," she said without looking up.

"I thought I might observe," the prince replied tightly.

"You thought wrong," Samira snapped.

Kai glanced between the witch and me, looking as though he worried that leaving us alone together could go wrong in many ways.

"I'm fine," I assured him. "Where can I find you once we're finished?"

"I will be in my library," he replied pointedly. "Back down to the second floor, first door on the right."

"See you soon," I called, admiring the lines of his back as he walked away.

Samira cleared her throat, bringing my attention back to the task at hand.

"So, what should I do?" I asked her with a tentative smile.

The witch stared at me from behind her glasses and gestured to the table. "If you want to see that boytoy princeling of yours before summer solstice, you better intend on helping." Samira held a mortar in one hand, while the other hand grabbed leaves from the various plants in front of her. The caster shoved the mortar and a pestle at me. "Muddle these. Make sure they're completely broken down. We need the true essences."

"I can do that."

Samira selected a blade from a rack of utensils and started slicing slimy, peeled-grape-looking objects in half. The first one she cut sent an arc of brown juice squirting back toward her. A musky, fishy scent filled the room. I gagged when it wafted over to me.

The caster chuckled. "The newt eyes aren't to your liking?" she asked, practically cackling.

Rolling my eyes, I shot her a glare. "Can't say I've had a lot of interaction with them."

Samira's face broke into a wide grin. "Grab the haladian flower."

I spotted an enormous purple bloom with white accents set off in the corner of the table, away from the other ingredients. The interior leaves were turquoise and dotted with orange splotches.

"And do what with it?" I asked Samira.

"Add the entire flower to the leaves and keep muddling." She resumed slicing eyeballs.

The first press of the pestle on the delicate flower drew a blood-like substance that ran crimson and thick.

"Is this normal?" I demanded.

She didn't look up. "Yes, yes. Perfectly."

An hour later, all of the ingredients mixed, smashed, or otherwise decimated, Samira began adding them to a cauldron. Some items needed to stew much longer before the next ingredient could be stirred in. Others needed to enter the cauldron together to avoid an explosion and the need to start all over.

Finally, after we added the blood-like substance from the haladian flower, the witch stepped back to admire her work. Samira wiped perspiration from her forehead with her sleeve. "Ah, yes. Smell that tang? That means we're progressing. Had there been more of a sweet smell, we'd know we needed to begin anew."

I sniffed the air. Definitely tangy.

The witch gestured for me to move closer to the

cauldron. "Look inside. What do you see?"

Crimson bubbles formed and popped on a swirling surface of steaming liquid. "It looks like boiling blood," I said.

"Very good," Samira replied, as though I'd made some grand observation. "Now, are you ready to begin, Maybrie?"

Haven't we already begun? I thought. *If not, what were the last three hours about?* "Begin what, exactly?" I asked, shifting from tired foot to tired foot.

"The first incantation," Samira explained. "Now that we have mixed the first round of ingredients, we must cast the first spell; then, the solution needs to boil for exactly sixteen hours, forty-two minutes, and twenty-eight seconds; then, it will need to be chilled to just above freezing for another three hours and twenty-nine minutes; we will then let the solution return to room temperature in its own time, which could take anywhere between two and six hours. While all of this is happening, we will prepare the second round of ingredients."

"Followed by another incantation?" I guessed.

Samira held up her index and middle fingers. "Two more incantations in total. One after the second round of ingredients, and one when we actually cast the memory retrieval spell."

I forgot how tedious and time-consuming casting could be.

"For tonight, just a short incantation." Samira held out her hands to me.

"If it's a short incantation, why do you need to channel me?" I asked, slipping my hands into hers across the work table.

Samira closed her eyes, and I did the same. "Short does not mean simple, Maybrie, and short does not mean what you think it means. We're casting a spell, not merely performing a card trick."

No, I realized an hour later, *short did not mean what I thought it meant.*

The witch had been very clear that I remain silent while she cast, so I couldn't ask how much longer we had to go without ruining the spell. I was starting to fatigue, though. Channeling and transferring magic were different. I was channeling my magic through Samira, who was just a conduit that recited the spells; she wasn't absorbing or using any magic, so I was the one sweating profusely and unsure if my legs would give out.

"You should practice more," Samira scolded me when we broke apart finally, and I sagged on the counter for support. "Tomorrow will be harder. Rest up."

If tomorrow is any harder, I might be depleted before this over, I thought as the witch began packing her belongings.

"Tell the prince I'll need a car to take me home," she added over her shoulder.

Kai must've been spying on us, because he opened the door before my hand touched the knob.

"Samira says she's ready for a car to take her home," I relayed.

"Gianni is on his way now," Kai promised. "And Harton and Kenoa are waiting for you whenever you are ready."

"Kenoa, too?" I asked. "Are you that worried about press outside my building at this hour?"

Kai offered me his arm as we descended the steps of the magical room. "Paparazzi never sleep. I have learned that the hard way more times than I care to count. Since I know you will not agree to staying at the palace, I have asked Kenoa to stay with you."

"No," I said flatly. *How am I supposed to call my contact in the rebellion with your bodyguard sleeping on my couch?*

"Just until this interest blows over," Kai continued.

Christina will love not getting a report until next harvest season, I thought wryly. "No," I repeated.

"How about he stays with you tonight, and we can negotiation terms on a daily basis going forward," he tried.

Just tonight? I thought about the reporters shoving their cameras in my face. *I'd rather not tackle that alone. Christina can hold off another day.*

"Deal," I agreed.

Kai looked stunned. "Really? I thought that would be a harder sell."

"Someone took a picture of the inside of my nose today. I'd rather not have a second one taken. Ever," I replied honestly.

The prince laughed. "I have had that happen as well. Those never turn out well."

We walked for several moments in companionable silence before Kai cleared his throat uneasily. "I was wondering if you might do me another favor."

"I'm starting to feel like the fountain of favors," I teased. *It would serve you right—you're spying on him!* "What do you need now?"

"I met with several House of Mana workers today," he

began.

"Let me guess, they didn't tell you anything?" I interjected.

Kai shook his head. "No, they literally said nothing. Well, maybe not *literally* because a very spirited air fae named Tonya did, I believe, hex me. She muttered an incantation the entire time I spoke."

I laughed so hard I snorted. "Sorry to hear that. I hope you don't grow a third ear or something."

"I guess only time will tell. But as there are no fae on the police squad—"

"You mean fae are not allowed on the force," I piped in.

"Yes, currently that is the law," Kai agreed as if he'd anticipated I would make this argument. "That will change in the future. For now, I do not have any fae officers to interview House of Mana employees, and those employees have no desire to answer my questions. Can I persuade you to help?"

"Hmm. Persuade me how?" I asked to buy some time.

This request was a lot different than the last one. I wasn't sure if Kai even understood the magnitude of what he was asking. Helping with Samira was one thing—she was one caster, and she advocated for fae rights. House of Mana employees were all fae who would probably not take me asking questions much better than Kai. It was going to take a lot to persuade them that I hadn't sold out to the casters. And even more to persuade them that the royals cared about the missing fae.

"Name your price," the prince challenged.

Great, now you're bargaining with him like you actually want him to grant you some favor in return.

"What is something you really want?" Kai added when I didn't answer right away.

Freedom. The ability to leave the dome.

That wasn't on the table. Even if Kai had the power to grant it to me, I didn't know if I'd take it. Why was my freedom more important than someone else's? *Exactly, and there is someone else's, relative, freedom that could be on the table.*

"I want Sumi to have twenty-four-hour sign-in and sign-out privileges at the commune," I said evenly. "Unrestricted. No chaperones. You can do that, right?"

"I can," he agreed carefully. "But you do know there is an interview process and an evaluation that normally comes before a decision like that is made."

"I know," I said, remembering the whole degrading process.

The prince took a minute to consider. "Would you vouch for her, if I sped this through the pipeline?"

"Definitely," I agreed.

"You would certify that beyond any doubt she is not a member of any rebellion or anti-royal movement?"

I swallowed hard. "Yes. I'm positive. Sumi just got here a few weeks ago. She hasn't had time to form a rebellion."

"There is a reason we watch new arrivals so closely," Kai informed me. "We have found in the past that some of them are tied to a faction that seeks to upend our kingdom."

"I didn't know that," I admitted uneasily. *The royals know about the rebellion.*

"It is also why we scrutinize those applying for inter-kingdom fights so carefully. One in ten is a messenger for one rebellious group or another," he continued.

I'm going to be sick.

"You denied my application. Does that mean you think I'm part of some rebellion?" I asked evenly. *Gaia, get me out of here.*

"No, not at all. If you really want to know the truth, which I think you do, it is because your association with Tanner makes you a high flight risk. We find that when a loved one has passed, many people want the chance to start over. This dome is only one island, with a very small population."

Am I relieved? I was too numb to decide.

"I see. Um, so, do you need me to sign something that says I vouch for Sumi, or were you just getting my hopes up?" I asked.

"I will do it," Kai said. "If you say she is not planning a coup, that is good enough for me."

Oh, Sumi definitely isn't. How do I know? Because I am.

"And in return you will accompany me to House of Mana tomorrow and interview fae, yes?"

"Yes," I said with a smile. "House of Mana tomorrow. I'm there. No promises they'll talk to me, but I'll try."

"Wonderful. Now that you have agreed to my small favor, I have one last big one. My mother would like an audience with you before you begin your work with Ms. Duquesne tomorrow evening," he said, all in one breath so I wouldn't have time to make some snarky remark about his laundry list of favors.

"An audience with me?" I asked frantically.

"Well, technically the queen has granted you an audience with her at her behest, but that is just wordplay, really," Kai replied nervously.

"Can I say no?" I asked.

"You can," he said quickly. "Though she might just end up inviting herself to your home for tea, instead."

"Delightful," I answered with a sigh. "Bring on the audience."

CHAPTER TWENTY

HOUSE OF MANA was an unsettling establishment and not simply because of my own personal feelings regarding the purpose of the business. Despite the lavish furnishings, plush carpet, and distinct air of wealth, there was a coldness that made me wary of the building's occupants. Kai and I sat together on a red chaise lounge in the corner of the room, more a boudoir setup with canopied curtains than a public reception area.

A heavily perfumed woman appeared from behind the velvet drapes. "Welcome to House of Mana," she sang in a husky cadence that belied no worries. "How can we fulfill your magical dreams today?" Her heavily lidded eyes fell on Kai. "Your Highness, how rude of me."

"Not at all." The prince stood and gestured to me. "Maybrie Hawkins, this is Madame Sheila. She has arranged for us to speak to the employees again."

"It's nice to meet you," I said politely.

"If you will both follow me." Madame Sheila waved us through the velvet curtains. "This way."

Stunning fae, both male and female, in extravagant clothing drank and laughed with casters in golf clothes in a casino-like atmosphere. The more senior fae opted for tuxedos and gowns and were adorned with sparkling jewels—the real deal, too, no cubic zirconia there. A group of young female fae in tennis attire spun the roulette wheel alongside a beautiful warlock in a pricey business suit. I saw a few fae dressed in lingerie dealing at poker tables, three mimes entertaining a warlock, and a creepy clown playing craps. *A clown?*

"You are always welcome to stay afterward and take a closer look at all that our fae have to offer," Madame Shelia said as we exited the casino floor. "House of Mana has many private rooms to choose from, the least of which is the one I am about to show you."

Thick carpet gave way to marble floors. My nude heels clicked softly on the polished ground. Madame Shelia showed us to a small room at the end of the main hallway. Two male fae and three female fae were already seated inside on a wraparound couch. Kai and I sat together on the far end, while Madame Shelia took the middle like a referee. She made introductions and then turned to me.

"Well, I guess you guys know why we're here," I began, wringing my hands in my lap. I'd known this was going to be awkward, but sitting across from five fae, none of them happy to see me, was even harder than anticipated.

"You want to know about the depleted casters," Tonya, the hex-casting air fae, snapped. "We're going to tell you the same thing we told the prince. Nothing."

"Prince Kai's manners are much better than mine. I'm not going to go away so easily," I shot back. *That is not how you practiced this,* I reminded myself. *Be nice. Pleasing. Diplomatic. That is how you practiced it.*

"Lono Kohue is one of your regular clients, Tonya. Both he and his husband come to you at least once a week for magical donations. And you'd given Pika Tau magic six times in the month before he went missing. You know something," I continued in a much less hostile tone.

"Why should we tell you, even if we do know anything?" an older male fae named Duke asked. "Why do you care about depleted casters?"

I took a deep breath and launched into my carefully planned speech. By the looks on their faces, it didn't endear me to the House of Mana employees.

"Fine. Look. You want to know why it matters? Because the prince is determined to figure out who depleted those warlocks. If he doesn't hear the truth from you guys, he might hear lies from someone else. Innocent parties may get blamed, and the whole mess could get ugly."

"Brie." Kai placed a hand on my arm. "She does not mean to make this sound like a threat."

I met each fae's eyes, studying all five sets for a sign.

No, I wasn't making threats. One of them, I was certain, worked for the rebellion. I didn't know which one, but Christina had too many contacts inside House of Mana for the odds to be against me. Whoever that was, I hoped, would pick up on the hidden meaning in my comment. *Or the rebellion really is involved, and no one here is going to talk.*

"I was the last to see Lono," Tonya said finally. "He came in alone," she added. "He usually prefers that. The husband isn't big on indulging; only comes in if he's real low."

"Was there anything weird about that last time?" I pressed.

"Not that I—wait, this last time I saw him, he was sort of different. Lono didn't ever come to me because he *needed* magic, only because he *wanted* it. This last time, though," Tonya shook her head, "he was low. Real low."

"Pika was the same way," Duke admitted, though I didn't know if he spoke up because Tonya had, or because he too understood the larger implications. "Sometimes his eldest daughter would come with him, but as far as I know, she didn't that night. She's not one of my regulars, so I can't say for sure. Pika was definitely low on magic, though."

"Mr. Tau's daughter was not with him," Madame Shelia confirmed.

Kai looked troubled, though I couldn't say why exactly; maybe because we hadn't really learned anything new; maybe he thought Duke and Tonya were lying; or maybe, there was more going on behind the scenes than I appreciated.

The prince asked a few more questions, which the fae grudgingly answered. And when our hour was up, it was hard to know who was most eager for the interviews to be over. Though polite and respectful, Madame Shelia seemed to think Kai and I were bad for business and led us out and around the casino, instead of through it again.

"Thank you again for all of your assistance," the prince gushed at the back exit, where Kenoa and Makani were waiting to escort Kai and me to the car.

"Hey, Brie," someone hissed.

I looked down the darkened hallway and saw Tonya's face poking out from behind a gauzy curtain. She waved me over, one eye on Kai and Madame Shelia.

"Yeah? What's up?" I asked softly.

"This isn't, you know, *us*, right?" Tonya mumbled. "Or is it?"

I shook my head. "No, the depletions have nothing to do with us," I said carefully.

"Good. Good. It's already been a nightmare here. The madams don't want me, or any of us who were in that room, working until you guys figure out what happened. I need the money."

"*Everyone* wants this figured out." I emphasized the first word, so she knew that I meant Christina and the rebellion. I was getting nervous having this conversation with Kai down the hallway. "That's why the sooner Kai figures out who is responsible, the better," I assured her. "If there's anything else you can tell me that would draw attention away from this place...?"

"I don't know. Lono told me he felt like he was being followed. Not the night he went missing, specifically, but in general. Then there's this woman, Sita Latani, who's another of my regulars. She was worried about Lono and Pika even before they were found depleted. She thought she might be next," Tonya informed me. "She's hired extra protection."

The missing casters had been of more and more concern to the witches and warlocks of the community, which was only natural, given the staggering number of people who'd disappeared. Still, for Sita Latani to believe she needed more bodyguards suggested there was a connection between her and the two depleted casters.

"Brie?" Kai called from the other end of the hallway.

"Be right there," I called back. To Tonya, I said, "We'll get this figured out. In the meantime, I'll transfer over some money to your account. If you need more, just get me word."

Her big, round eyes studied me for a long moment and then nodded toward the prince. "Is he really as big of an ass as they say?"

I laughed. "He can be."

Apparently, leaving House of Mana via the back entrance didn't matter—the press converged on Kai and me immediately. Kenoa shouldered our way through the throng of reporters on one side, while Makani tried to hold back cameras on the other. The questions hurdled at me were even more invasive than the previous day.

"Did you share your magic with the prince, Brie?" someone yelled.

"Were you here to supervise the exchange of magic? Does that mean you're officially engaged?" called another.

"What? No!" I snapped.

"Don't respond, it only makes them hungrier," Kenoa muttered.

"You've never dated a caster, Brie. Is it different than dating another fae?" a cheery witch wanted to know.

"Have you met the queen?" a large man in a puffy coat asked.

"How do you respond to concerns that your relationship is a publicity stunt?" demanded a shifter wearing a beret.

Are there concerns my relationship is a publicity stunt? I wondered.

Wrapping an arm around my shoulders, Kai guided me inside the limo. Kenoa hopped in as well, but Makani stayed behind to keep the crowd back from the car. The partition rolled down, and Lara stared back at us from the front passenger seat.

"The mob's worse in front of Maybrie's building," the bodyguard informed Kai. "We should return to the palace immediately."

"I'm not hiding out in the palace," I snapped.

"No one is suggesting that," Kai said calmly, placing a hand on my knee. "Samira is already at the palace tending to the memory retrieval potion. I know she would appreciate your help."

"How is being holed up in a room with her inside the palace any different from hiding?" I countered.

Kai's dark eyes softened. "The intent. Besides, what were you planning to do until your audience with my mother?"

"Honestly?" I smiled cheekily. "Practice my hex work. Just in case."

CHAPTER TWENTY-ONE

THE PALACE HAD an official throne room, where the monarch conducted affairs of state and met with visiting dignitaries. That was not where I met with Queen Lilli. Fifteen minutes prior to our appointed meeting time, I stood outside of the queen's private library with Kai. He reassured me that it was just a friendly chat.

"If it's just a friendly chat, why does she want to talk to me alone?" I hissed.

"Her Majesty will see you now," Angela, the queen's senior advisor, called. She stood in the doorframe and waved me inside. With my heart in my throat, I squared my shoulders and followed her gesture. Other than the enormous desk that the queen sat behind and the bookshelves that lined the walls, the room was sparse and no-nonsense.

Kai squeezed my hand and whispered, "Good luck."

"Hello, Maybrie." The queen greeted me without looking up from the pile of papers on her desk. She waved dismissively at her aid. "Please find my son something to do besides lurk outside the door, Angela."

"Yes, ma'am." Angela curtsied and backed out of the library with an encouraging wink and smile for me.

"And now," the queen scrawled her name across the bottom of the document she'd been reading, "you have my full attention, Maybrie." She smiled up at me with eyes that reminded me of her son.

I bobbed a quick curtsy, since Kai had told me that it was customary. The queen's smile widened. "Please, sit." She gestured to the chair across from her desk.

"Thank you. It is very nice to meet you," I said politely.

"We have met several times." Queen Lilli studied the navy pinstripe pantsuit I still had on from House of Mana. If the queen's dove-gray skirt suit was any indication, she preferred her work clothes a little more classic. "Is that from Ivy's?"

"Excuse me?" I stammered.

"Your outfit; is it from Ivy of the Avenue?" the queen clarified.

Kai had warned me that his mother would ask a bunch of get-to-know-you questions. But asking about my clothes had caught me off guard.

"It is," I said. "Um, do you shop there?"

"My daughter, Sarah, she is a patron. I am afraid I have found, after a certain age, all of my clothes need to be custom made, or they do not flatter me."

I smiled politely.

"I understand you have been helping the prince with the depletion investigation," the queen continued smoothly.

"I have," I confirmed. Kai mentioned this would come up, but he had no way of understanding just how uncomfortable the topic was for me. "Along with Samira Duquesne," I added for good measure.

"What do you think of Samira?" The queen folded her hands on the desk and stared at me expectantly.

"She's, um, different than most casters I've met," I admitted.

Queen Lilli chuckled softly. "She is. Just as you are different than most fae I have met." Her expression hardened, though she didn't come across as unfriendly. Not exactly. "Which is why I have been so eager to meet you. My son has dated other fae, but none quite so outspoken about the disparities between casters and non-casters."

She hadn't asked any questions, yet she clearly expected answers. I swallowed uncomfortably. "I don't see a point in pretending that there aren't disparities," I said cautiously.

"I agree," the queen said, just as carefully.

"That doesn't mean I think there should be disparities," I added quickly.

"I would not imagine so. Is that your interest in my son? Are you hoping this personal relationship will turn in to a political alliance that would strengthen ties between our races?" A slight crease formed between the queen's brows.

She is genuinely curious as to what I think, I thought, slightly amazed. Until Kai, no caster had cared about my views on caster-fae relations.

"Ultimately, if we decide to take our relationship to the next level, yes. I would hope a marriage between the caster prince and a fae would improve relations. But that's not why I agreed to go out with him."

"And why was that?" Queen Lilli pressed.

I laughed uneasily. "Truthfully, because my friends thought it would be interesting," I admitted, which was as close to the truth as I could get without risking execution.

To my surprise, the queen smiled. "I thought it might be something along those lines. You have been out together several times now. Surely your curiosity, and theirs, is appeased?"

"Yes...." I looked down at my hands. "I guess somewhere along the road, I actually started to like Prince Kai. I enjoy spending time with him."

When I met the queen's blank expression, I wasn't sure what to expect; definitely not for her to say, "Good. I was hoping you would say something to that effect."

I'd come to this meeting thinking she didn't like me or the fact that I was dating her son and heir to the throne, but that didn't appear to be the case. She reminded me more of a lioness protecting her cub's heart than a shrew thinking her son deserved better.

"I know the press is already giving you trouble," continued the queen in a frank tone. "That kind of exposure is not easy for most to handle. You, at least, are not unfamiliar with fame."

"Oh, I'm not famous," I protested.

"Modesty does not suit a royal," the queen advised me.

"I'm not a royal," I pointed out.

"Not yet." The queen smiled. "My son cares about you, though. You are the first companion he has not tired of after two dates. I am treating your relationship as very serious unless there is a reason you think I should not."

We aren't really dating, I thought. But I shook my head, "No, ma'am."

"Wonderful." Queen Lilli stood. I followed her lead, and we walked to the library door together. "I look forward to more of our talks." She opened the door and gave her son a small wave. "Hello, darling," she said right before she closed the door.

"How did it go?" Kai asked anxiously.

I shrugged. "I don't think she hated me. She may even have liked me." I looked up at him. "How do I know if she liked me?"

He laughed. "Let me just say, if she hated you, you would definitely know."

<hr />

The second evening with Samira was much like the first. She had me slice and dice flower petals, grate herbs to a fine powder, and drain leeches that had been used to collect blood samples from the depleted casters. Samira checked the potion every half hour to see if it had warmed to the correct temperature.

"It is time," she declared. "See that wonderful sunflower-yellow color? That is how we know. I only use the thermometer to erase any doubt."

Samira added the remaining ingredients according to the recipe in her casting book while I stirred the entire concoction. We had an hour to kill before it was time for Samira to cast the second spell.

"I saw you were at House of Mana today," Samira broke the silence between us.

"Yeah, Kai thought I might have better luck interviewing the employees," I said absently.

"Did you?"

"Yeah, a little. For all the good it did—they didn't know much. Now we really need the memory retrieval to work," I lamented as the potion turned the color of fresh grass. "One of the girls, an air fae, told me another one of her regulars is worried about being the next caster to go missing." I shook my head. "So, there must be a connection between her and the two depleted casters."

Samira considered my logic for a few moments. "What was this other caster's name?"

"Sita Latani," I replied, noticing the spark of recognition in the witch's eyes. "Do you know her?"

"I do…well, *did,* anyway. We are about the same age. Our families were friends growing up." Samira tapped the tabletop thoughtfully and mused. "So, Sita, Lono, and Pika. Interesting."

"Did you know all of them growing up?" I asked.

"In one capacity or another," Samira admitted.

That doesn't sound like a coincidence. "Then maybe you can tell me—what's their connection to one another?" I asked.

"There are probably a lot of connections. They're all from old, rich caster families. I think Lono is married to

Sita's brother, or maybe her cousin. I can't remember exactly, but there's some familial connection. And, if I'm not mistaken, all their families have something to do with maintaining the dome."

My ears perked up. "What do you mean 'maintaining the dome'?"

Samira's gaze narrowed. "The magical barriers that keep out the elements. Casters create those. Very specific Casters. They act as magical tentpoles to keep the dome up. Don't tell me you didn't know?"

No, I didn't know. And why didn't Kai tell me? I wondered.

"You didn't, I see." She smiled grimly. "I suppose your prince isn't as honest with you as you thought."

The words stung, because they were true.

"Is that why Lono and the others need so much magic?" I asked. "Is that why they go to House of Mana a lot?"

"If I had to guess, yes." Samira nodded. "The spells are very involved, so it would make sense that they consistently needed to power up their magic with fae." Glancing in the cauldron and finding the potion had turned milky-pink, she brightened. "It seems we have been successful. Are you ready for the second spell?"

I offered her my hands across the table. As Samira chanted, I considered what she'd said about the dome's magical protections. I should've known that was the case, or at least suspected as much. Still, I was irked that Kai hadn't said anything. He had numerous opportunities, like when we commented on the temperature drop, or when he'd told me the royal family was fiddling with sunset and sunrise times to compensate.

When Samira and I finished the potion well after midnight, I felt even more drained than the previous spell. I wasn't up for a fight with Kai; not about the dome's magical protections and not when the prince insisted Kenoa spend another night on my couch. A part of me was curious about what the water fae may know about my newfound knowledge of the connection between the depleted casters.

Of course, had I known someone would be waiting outside my front door, I might've put my foot down about Kenoa staying with me.

"We need to talk," Everly snapped as soon as she spotted Kenoa and me. "Alone."

"I'll take a walk. Stretch my legs," he offered.

"Yeah, thanks," I muttered.

Neither Everly nor I spoke until we were inside my living room. Tanner's little sister was so mad she was crying, and I didn't blame her.

"You said you were doing this for Christina," she accused, her face the color of an eggplant.

She's been holding this in a while, I thought. "I am," I said calmly.

"Seriously? You're going to stand here, and lie to my face?" Everly demanded. "I've seen you all over the news with him, Brie!"

I started to sweat despite the air conditioning. "It was only a matter of time before our fake relationship gained a real press following," I mumbled.

"You loved my brother," Everly snarled, her rage seeming to cause the very foundation of my building to shake. "I know that look on your face right now. I know your feelings for the prince aren't fake!"

I couldn't keep lying to her. She deserved the truth, even if I really wasn't up for the discussion. "No, they aren't," I admitted finally. "I'm sorry. I should've—"

"Yes, *you* should've told me!" she hollered.

It was a good thing my place was soundproof, otherwise the police would've already been on the way.

"I'm sorry," I repeated, my own temper flaring. "Do you think I meant for this to happen? Do you think I wanted this to happen? I tried to back out. Many times. Christina wouldn't have it."

Everly rounded on me. "Does she know? Does she know you're one kiss away from tattooing his name on your ass?"

I glared at her. "No. Well, I don't know. If she does, I'm not sure she cares as long as I'm more loyal to her than him." I lowered my gaze. "Just let me be the one to tell her. Please."

"Like you should've been the one to tell me?"

She didn't wait for an answer. Everly stormed from my condo, slamming the door so hard behind her that I wondered whether there would be structural damage. I flopped on the couch, annoyed with myself for handling the confrontation so poorly.

"Way to go, Brie," I said aloud. "And two days before the big luau and your first public date. Awesome work."

CHAPTER TWENTY-TWO

BECAUSE THE LUAU was only two days away, and I couldn't be certain whether Everly would contact Christina, I took advantage of Kenoa's absence and called her myself.

"I don't have a lot of time, so just listen," I said as soon as she answered. "First of all, the royals know about the rebellion. A rebellion, at least. Kai says that's why they watch the new arrivals so closely and restrict fae and shifter access outside the dome."

"Yeah, I know about that," Christina replied impatiently.

"Really? Why didn't you say anything?" I asked, pacing around my balcony to burn off the frantic energy racing through me.

"You shouldn't be calling me anymore," she responded, ignoring my question completely. "The royals are watching you too closely. Where's your bodyguard right now?"

I looked around uneasily, as though a royal spy was watching me at that very moment. "He took a walk. He'll be back soon."

"Anything new to report before he returns?" she asked.

I sighed. "I think there's a connection between the two depleted casters and the dome itself. They both had something to do with the dome protection spells." Silence fell on the other end. I couldn't even make out her breathing.

"Christina?" I prodded after a minute.

"I knew about the protection spells," she said finally. "I suspected anyhow. But I didn't realize those two warlocks were involved. Did the prince tell you that?"

I bit my lip. "No, he didn't. The witch doing the memory retrieval, Samira, she did."

"What did the prince say when you confronted him?"

"I didn't confront him," I admitted.

Christina sighed. "Brie."

"I know," I retorted defensively, even though I'd specifically called to tell her about my feelings for Kai.

"Then why are you upset?"

"I'm not upset," I protested, sounding *very* upset.

"Look, I'm not surprised you like him. He's charismatic. Even my spies inside the palace say he comes off like a nice guy. He's not, though. His family is the reason we have to share our magic. They're the assholes." She paused to let her words sink in. "I need you to remember that."

I slumped into a lounge chair. "I know. I know."

"You don't have to do this much longer," Christina continued. "I can get someone to replace you if you'd like. I just need a little more time."

Did I want someone replacing me in Kai's affections? No, I definitely didn't. Did I want someone to replace me spying on him? Yes, very much. But I couldn't have my cake and eat it too; I couldn't continue to date the prince if I refused to spy on him. The rebellion wasn't kind to traitors. And, apparently, like I'd told Everly, as long as I was more loyal to Christina than Kai, the rebellion wouldn't consider me a traitor.

What do I consider myself, though? I wondered.

"We can talk again after the luau," Christina continued. "Until then, do not contact me unless it's a life or death situation. And even then, get word to Elton first. He'll pass along your messages."

"Yeah, okay," I agreed. "I'll see you there."

"Not if I see you first," she said and disconnected.

What does that even mean?

CHAPTER TWENTY-THREE

CALA CALLED EARLY the next morning while I was
still half-asleep. I sent her to voicemail three times before
I finally answered.

"It's my one day to sleep in—this had better be good,"
I groaned.

"I thought I might come over for breakfast," my best
friend said cheerily.

"Now?" I grumbled.

"Well, yeah. It's almost noon."

I bolted upright. My curtains were still drawn, and the
bedroom was pitch black. "Seriously?"

Cala laughed. "Late night with the prince?"

"I let that witch channel me again last night. Her spell

must've taken more out of me than I thought." I swung my legs over the bed and plodded toward the bathroom. "Plus, Everly showed up at my place."

I could practically feel Cala cringe through the phone. "I know. She called me. That's sort of why I thought you might like some company. And Cassie wants to know if your dress for tomorrow fits."

I splashed water on my face. "I haven't tried it on yet."

"I'll be over in thirty," Cala promised.

"Fine. But bring a lot of food. Kenoa's here."

Cala arrived with egg sandwiches from a bakery near her house. I didn't feel much like eating, but with the final memory retrieval spell only hours away, I needed the energy. Cala insisted I model the dress for her, which luckily fit since there wasn't a lot of time left for alterations.

"You'll be the belle of the ball," Cala assured me as she studied my jewelry case with a critical eye. She pulled out something gold and held it up. "Is this the bangle he gave you? Because, if so, you should definitely wear it."

"I'd rather blend in with the decorations," I muttered, snatching the bracelet and trying it on my wrist for the first time.

"She won't cause a public scene." Cala held up a pair of gold hoops. "Let's go with studs. That'll be classier."

I slipped out of my luau dress and hung it on the back of my closet door. "You didn't see her, Cala," I explained as I shimmied into a pair of jeans. "She was so mad."

My best friend poked her head inside the closet. "She's just hurt. Give her time."

"I don't know if there's enough time in my life for

Everly to get over this," I insisted.

Cala handed me a sweater. "Wear this. It's freezing outside."

Should I tell her why it's so cold beneath the dome? I decided against it. I didn't want to get into how I was feeling hurt because Kai had lied to me. *You lied to him, too. A lot.* That reminder didn't make his omission sting any less.

I slid on a pair of boots that I never got to wear in this tropical island temperature; they were perfect for temperatures just above freezing. Then, I grabbed the only real jacket I owned, a neon-pink raincoat that I'd never worn.

"Want me to come with you to the hospital?" Cala asked. "I can be moral support."

I smiled. "Thanks. But no. It's going to be a long evening, and you'd just be bored. Want to come to the palace to get ready for the luau tomorrow? I'm sure it would be fine."

"I thought you'd never ask," Cala told me happily.

"Really? You want to be there earlier than required?"

She rolled her eyes. "I've been wanting a glimpse inside Prince Kai's personal wing for years. Does he really have a pet dingo?"

I stared at her blankly. "No. I mean, I don't think so. What's a dingo look like?"

Cala shrugged her shoulders. "I was hoping you could tell me."

We found Kenoa waiting on the couch, tapping his foot somewhat impatiently. We said our goodbyes, and Cala sauntered down the front steps of my building, while Kenoa and I snuck out a side door. Cala distracted the reporters just long enough for us to get into the limo. Harton was already pulling away from the curb when the first camera snapped a picture.

"You okay after last night?" Kenoa asked me.

I fidgeted with the belt on my raincoat. "It's not like I didn't know she'd be pissed that I was dating the caster prince," I mumbled.

Kenoa's dark eyes narrowed. "That's why she was at your house last night?"

My heart skipped a beat. "Yeah, obviously."

"It's just that I thought she already knew."

Oh, Gaia. No good. "I had told her I said yes to a *date* because I was curious. She didn't know I was *dating* him." *Stick to the facts. If you don't actually lie, he can't catch you in one.*

"Why did you say yes?" Kenoa watched me so closely that I was sure he noticed the first bead of sweat on my forehead.

"Because I was curious," I repeated. "But not about Kai so much as why you seemed to like Kai. It never made much sense to me."

That seemed to mollify Kenoa's curiosity enough— for now. My lies were catching up with me, though. Honestly, I wasn't sure how much of what came out of my mouth these days wasn't a lie.

Outside of Lono Kohue's hospital room, Kai and Samira were having a very spirited discussion in the hallway. They both looked like they wanted to rip their hair out. Then again, they had spent all morning with the depleted casters' families getting all the paperwork handled for the memory retrieval procedure.

"Another caster could contaminate the spell," the

witch argued. "I'm sorry, but only Brie and I go inside the room. And if I didn't need her power, I'd be going in alone."

Kai's jaw tightened. "I would feel better if I was present. In case something goes wrong."

Samira laughed. "Like what? You can't give her magic. And if her power isn't enough for the spell, yours certainly won't be either."

"I'll be fine alone with Samira," I interrupted their bickering.

The prince turned to me. "Brie, you have not seen a depleted since—"

I held up my hand to cut him off. "Yeah, I know," I snapped, still annoyed with Kai. I didn't need or want his support at that exact moment.

He misread my agitation and placed a comforting hand on my arm.

I shrugged out of his grip. "I'll be fine."

"Good. We should start soon." With that, Samira slipped inside Lono Kohue's hospital room.

The prince started to reach for me again but thought better of it when he remembered all the eyes on us. In a low voice, he asked, "Is everything okay, Brie?"

"Fine." I stepped out of his reach. "I'll let you know what we learn." I followed Samira into the hospital room.

Samira was standing over Lono, tipping a vial of the memory retrieval potion down his throat. I closed the door softly behind me. The witch turned and gave me a strange look but didn't comment on my attitude.

"The spell won't take long, but I will need a lot of power. I hope you got more sleep than it looks like you did," she said.

"I got plenty," I promised. I averaged four to five hours a night, and I'd slept close to twelve when Cala's calls woke me.

Samira arranged two chairs on either side of Lono's bed. She sat on one side and motioned for me to take the other seat. She held her arms out, straight across the depleted caster, and offered me her hands. I took a deep breath and for the first time dared to look down at Lono Kohue. His eyes were closed, his hands clasped primly at his waist. Someone had dressed him in a pair of well-worn pajamas, as if worried about his comfort.

Probably his kids or his husband, I thought.

The caster's complexion was the color of dirty snow. His left cheek looked as though he'd been on the losing end of a fight. Angry red scratches streaked the back of one hand. I'd spent enough time in the arena to know those were defensive marks, as if Lono had tried to shield his face.

"Are you ready, Maybrie?" Samira asked softly.

I nodded. My hands were numb where her wrinkled fingers curled around them.

"Clear your mind," she said in a voice barely above a whisper. "We need to make space for Lono's memories."

"Okay. Clearing my mind," I promised and closed my eyes.

Samira began to chant beneath her breath. A trickle of power crackled between our joined hands.

"Concentrate, Maybrie," Samira snapped.

I pictured an endless black sea and felt the magic swell in my chest. Slowly, like the sun was rising, the landscape brightened. Samira chanted louder. I called more magic forth. Flames erupted on the obsidian waves. The witch was practically screaming, but I could barely hear her over the roar of my own pulse.

This was much more power than she'd channeled the last two times. My breathing became heavier, like Samira was sucking the air out of my lungs. I gasped as a soft moan escaped her lips. An explosion of light nearly made me break contact. The witch's grip tightened on my hands until the pressure was painful. I had the odd sensation of being yanked from my body, like an evil spirit at an exorcism.

Suddenly, I was looking down on the scene from above. Except, I didn't see myself or Samira. I saw Lono and Tonya. Then, like a sardine in a can, I was stuffed inside of Lono's body. I saw Tonya through his eyes.

"You're topped off for now," she said, leaning back in her window seat. "Don't wait so long next time. You were really low."

Lono shrugged into his suit jacket. "Work has been busy," he said with a smile. "I'll make more of an effort, though."

"You better," Tonya teased.

She likes him, I thought. And Lono seemed to like her, too. Not romantically on either end, but there was a friendship there.

"Are you still coming over for dinner tomorrow?" Lono asked as he poured Tonya a glass of wine and handed it to her. "The girls are really looking forward to seeing you."

Tonya smiled and sipped from her glass. "I'll be there.

Don't forget, you promised fish tacos."

One hand on the door, Lono grinned. "I didn't forget. Have a good night."

Tonya waved and the warlock went on his way. Lono stopped to chat with a few fae, including Duke, before finally leaving House of Mana via the same back exit Kai and I had used.

He left, I thought, relieved. *Christina has been telling the truth.*

The caster walked with a slight wobble in his step, though he became more stable once in the fresh air. He didn't have a car waiting for him, nor did he hail one of the passing taxis.

I could see through his eyes, but I couldn't read his thoughts; I didn't know if he was just walking off some of Tonya's magic before returning home or if was meeting someone else.

Either way, the caster didn't make it far. Within a block of House of Mana, a mewing sound caught his attention. He rerouted his course down a side alley bathed in shadows. Strong hands closed around his upper arms from behind and dragged him backward. Lono's arms flailed but a cold, white hand clamped over his mouth and muffled his cries.

My own breath caught in my throat. I didn't need access to Lono's thoughts to know the guy was scared. I was scared, and if Samira's shaking hands were a clue, she was terrified.

The unseen assailant dragged Lono through a doorway and threw him into a chair. A hand darted out and slapped him across the face.

"Shardinam holis!" a female yelled.

I didn't recognize the voice, but the air of confidence behind it told me that the caster was no novice. The spell itself was unfamiliar.

It soon became apparent that it was an incapacitating incantation, because Lono was out for the count. The caster stepped into view, and I realized she was actually a vampire/caster hybrid.

Just like the fanged beasts who'd captured me.

In three long strides, the hybrid had her fangs out and plunged into Lono's neck. After the pinch of fangs and the incandescent draw of blood, the caster's world slowly plunged into darkness.

The end of his memory was the end of our vision.

The relief was nearly crippling. Vampires were depleting casters, not the rebellion. There were a few casters who worked with the rebellion in more than just a bribe capacity, but there were zero vampires among our ranks.

Why would vampires turn on their co-conspirators, though? Vampires worked for casters, capturing and delivering fae and shifters. The casters paid them a lot of money and blood, and they even pretended as though the pointy-toothed life-ruiners had a place among polite society. Vampires could forcibly drain a caster of their magic, but the vamps couldn't do anything with the magic itself. They probably got a nice little energy rush, but nothing that would be worth treason and the threat of getting staked over.

The blood of a fae was a million times more valuable to a vampire. It was a power that could be replenished, and therefore tapped at innumerable intervals. Draining a caster seemed nonsensical when there were fae at the House of Mana right around the corner.

There's no incentive for a vampire to drain a caster, and a lot of incentive not to. *So, what's the motive? Is it personal? This particular caster, these particular vampires? Or is it bigger than I could even imagine?*

It took me several minutes to reacclimate to the real world. Samira's face came into focus first.

"Vampires," she said plainly, leaving no room to wonder if it was my own interpretation of the memory. "An immortal stole the life from him, just after he had magic transferred from a fae. Is that poetic? I'm not sure."

"I…I don't know," I stuttered, trying to adjust to the air on my skin. In the world of the living and present, it felt too cold, too icy to be reality.

Samira shivered, the temperature clearly affecting her as well. Was it the real world, or was it the fact she'd been trapped in the depths of Lono's memories with me?

Either way, her lips turned a faint shade of blue as she spoke. "That was a different situation than I was prepared for," Samira admitted. She reached up and examined Lono's neck for bite marks. "Looks like someone took the time to heal the bites. She didn't want to leave evidence of her crime."

"Why would a vampire/caster hybrid want to commit this specific crime? Even after his magic infusion, Tonya had way more power than Lono. So, if the hybrid wasn't after power, why'd she do it?" I asked.

"Why does anyone do anything? Magic isn't the only

currency. Money is a strong motivator. Revenge, even stronger. Love, maybe the strongest of all." The witch smiled sadly. "Or, because we're dealing with vampires, the answer could simply be because she's evil."

"You don't think they were targeted because they have something to do with maintaining the dome?" I asked.

"Possibly, though the only advantage I can possibly see in that is because any caster working on the dome would have much higher levels of elemental magic than the average witch or warlock." She shrugged. "No use forming wild theories. At least not until we see what's in Mr. Tau's memory."

As it turned out, Mr. Tau's memories were nearly identical to Lono Kohue's. I knew even before the fangs came out that the last face Mr. Tau would see was the female vampire/caster hybrid who'd depleted Lono. And it was. The rebellion was not responsible for the depletions. I should've felt more relieved.

So why don't you? I wondered as I wandered out into the hallway to find Kai. *Why does something feel…off?*

"Hey, Brie." Kenoa hurried over. He looked past me to Samira and lowered his voice. "Kai got called away. They found another depleted caster."

"What? Who?" I demanded.

"Um, Sita Latani, I think is her name."

I felt cold all over. "I need to talk to Kai right now."

Kenoa sighed. "I can try to get him, but he's going to be tied up for the rest of the night. Not to mention all the increases in security this will mean for the luau tomorrow."

"It's really important," I pressed.

"Okay, I'll call him. Let's just get you home. Unless you'd consider staying at the palace? I know that would make Kai feel better," he tried.

I considered it because Kai really needed to know about the vampires' involvement. But so did Christina. She'd told me not to contact her, but this was the sort of life or death exception to her rule.

"I'd rather go home. But if you do get through to him, tell him to call me right away. And remind him that I'm getting ready for the luau at the palace, and it would be nice if he could stop by and see me."

"No way. I'm not playing messenger boy. I'll tell him you want to talk to him. That's it. You two can handle it from there," Kenoa protested with a firm shake of his head.

"Handle what? There's nothing to handle."

"Come on, Brie. You don't think I can tell you're pissed at him? Just tell him what he did and move on. If it's not worth mentioning to him, it's probably not worth being upset over." He placed a large hand on my shoulder and started marching me forward.

"Sometimes I wonder where your loyalties lie," I grumbled.

Kenoa waited until we were outside the hospital before whispering, "I could say the same about you, Brie."

CHAPTER TWENTY-FOUR

I DIDN'T HEAR from Kai that night. With Kenoa in my guest room, I decided against reaching out to Elton or calling Christina. I told myself I couldn't make the call because Kenoa was already suspicious of me; I couldn't risk him overhearing my conversation. That wasn't entirely true, though. The truth was, I didn't completely trust Kai because he'd failed to tell me about the dome protection magic, and I didn't completely trust Christina because it seemed she'd failed to tell me the truth about a lot of things. *Or maybe you're just paranoid.*

Kai didn't call the next morning either but rather sent word through Kenoa that he'd see me at the palace. I was a little annoyed that Kenoa was playing messenger for

Kai but had refused me the same courtesy. I showered at my condo, and then Kenoa and Harton loaded my garment and toiletry bags into the limo. We stopped to pick up Cala and all of her things, which made for quite the tight fit for the drive to Iolani Palace.

Angela, the queen's advisor, met us in the entranceway to the private residences. She showed us to a suite of rooms in Kai's wing. To my dismay, Kenoa came too. I really wanted some time alone with Cala to discuss the memory retrieval spell from the night before and Lono's memories about the vampires. I wanted to ask her who she'd go to first: Kai or Christina.

Instead, we played music and danced, and I tried not to think about all the unpleasantness weighing me down. But the more time that passed, the more I felt like I was sitting on a ticking time bomb of a secret. Someone needed to know about the vampire situation immediately.

Calm down. You're overacting. You're just very sensitive where vampires are concerned, I told myself. Still, I couldn't shake the shadow of impending doom that seemed to grow darker as I watched Cala write our names in the condensation on a glass window.

Kai never came by before the luau. Kenoa offered no explanation except to say that the prince would explain when he saw me. For the first time, I felt like Kenoa was more Kai's bodyguard than my friend. He didn't make any more cryptic comments, though he did give me enough appraising looks that I knew my truth couldn't be a secret forever. I had to tell Kai about working with the rebellion. Soon.

"You ready to go down?" Cala asked, ten minutes

after the luau had officially started.

"You go ahead. I just need another minute to myself before the shitshow starts," I told her.

Cala threw her arms wide. "They're going to love you, darling," she said dramatically.

"I'll take you down," Kenoa offered. He met my gaze in the mirror. "Don't be too long, Brie. Everyone else has gone down. You shouldn't be away from security tonight."

"I'll be right behind you guys," I promised, forcing a smile.

For several long minutes after they left, I sat at the vanity and stared at my reflection. The room behind me was simple yet elegant, all bright whites and sunflower yellows to make the room as light as possible. It was the little touches—crystal chandeliers, platinum candlestick holders, an emerald and pearl perfume bottle—that made the suite fit for a princess.

A princess. What I'd be if I married Kai.

It wasn't as though I sat around planning our wedding, but it was hard not to even consider the possibility when I was getting ready for a big party at the palace. Especially when the prince was about to introduce me as his date.

Moot point. Once Kai finds out the truth about me, I'll be lucky if he doesn't have me drained.

Kenoa hadn't been exaggerating when he said everyone was already down at the luau. Kai's wing wasn't just devoid of any dingo, there weren't any guards either. A chill ran through me. I'd spent most of the day resenting Kenoa's presence, but I would've welcomed two of him on the walk down to the party.

Finally, I reached the atrium and relaxed slightly as I joined the small crowd of people entering the Winter Garden. I couldn't recall ever being so happy to see a group of casters. I passed the royal household staff handing out furry, white coats to anyone wishing more layers for their walk through the frosted wonderland.

It really is beautiful, I thought, admiring the twinkling strings of bulbs that danced flames on the snowy surfaces.

The chill in the air made it so everyone in the Winter Garden breathed out small white clouds. Some of the older casters appeared to have a hard time breathing at all. Is it too cold for them already? I wondered uneasily.

"How long until they notice you, do you think?" a familiar voice whispered in my ear.

I spun to face my trainer.

"Bold choice with the white, by the way. If you're not careful, they're going to say you brought this freeze."

"I'm not an ice fae. Fire is the opposite."

He grinned cheekily. "I meant the dress. Isn't white supposed to be a bad omen? Oh, or maybe the fire moons the other night brought the freeze. That's where I'm putting my money."

Personally, I was starting to equate fire moons with vampires. It seemed if four of those fiery suckers hit the sky, the next thing I knew I had a fanged foe problem.

"Um, I'll be back, Botto," I said. "I really need to find someone."

Kai or Christina? I still didn't know for certain, and I couldn't seem to locate either one. After a lap around the perimeter of the Winter Garden, I continued my search in the Summer Garden. As ukulele music played, a group of hula dancers acted out the mythological story of Pele, the Hawaiian fire goddess. I stopped for a moment at the edge of the crowd to enjoy the show.

Finally, I spotted the prince across the room at a table surrounded by press. Kai's expression was pleasant enough to a casual observer, but I noticed the tight lines around his eyes that belied his somber feelings. He didn't look as though he'd slept, and his uncharacteristically drawn appearance made me wonder whether they'd found a fourth depleted caster.

The crowd was denser than it had been in the Winter Garden. Making my way across the room took several minutes of apologies and promises to circle back around to catch up with people. Before I reached Kai, a shock of emerald tresses caught my attention: Christina.

She was ten feet away, working her way through the revelers in the opposite direction. Pausing, I warred with whether to follow her or keep heading toward Kai. This was it, the moment of truth: Where do my loyalties lie?

Kai got up from his table, and the decision was clear: him. I needed to tell him about the vampires.

You're in way too deep.

Pushing the thought aside, I brushed past the edge of the dance floor as Kai shook hands with the people he'd been sitting with. When we locked gazes, I pointed to a path lined with rosebushes that meandered away from the masses. A nod told me he registered the gesture. A minute later, he wrapped an arm around my waist and pulled me around the bend in the path.

"You are stunning," he breathed, dipping his head to

brush a gentle kiss across my lips.

"I really need to talk to you," I said in a low voice.

Stepping back, he kept hold of my hand and spun me in a circle. The white tulle skirt flared out as I twirled, and I laughed despite myself. Kai's warm eyes raked me from head to toe, taking in the low neckline and even lower back. Heat rushing to my cheeks, I ran a hand over the embroidered bodice to smooth nonexistent wrinkles.

"I really need to talk to you," I repeated.

Kai pulled me close again. I ran one hand over his chest and the perfectly tailored gray suit. The feel of the soft and supple threads on his rock-hard chest caused a shiver to run down my spine. Focus, Brie, I reminded myself.

"Vampires, Kai," I hissed. "That's who depleted those two casters."

The measured look in his eye told me that he already knew. "The warlock found just after dawn this morning had bite marks."

So, they did find a fourth depleted caster. "Do you know anything about the vampire or why she's doing it?" I asked.

Kai shook his head. "No. We did not know she was female. Did you see this during memory retrieval?"

"I saw her. She's a vampire/caster hybrid."

He arched an eyebrow. "Do you think you could describe her?"

"Probably," I agreed.

"Tomorrow, first thing, we will speak with the officers assigned to the case and get a sketch," he promised. Then, with a forced smile, he added, "There is someone

I would like for you to meet. Do not mention vampires. I do not wish to scare her."

Before I could object, Kai raised his arm and waved someone over.

"Sarah! Come meet Brie," he called.

Turning, I followed his gaze to the path behind me. White-blonde hair and silver sequins emerged from the darkness.

"Sarah, this is Brie." Kai slipped an arm around my waist and pulled me to his side. "Brie, this is Sarah, my little sister."

"Hardly little," she said, rolling her eyes at him. "It is so nice to finally meet you, Brie. I've heard so much about you."

Her light-blue eyes sparkling, the princess pulled me into a hug that surprised me. Something furry and warm wriggled between us. When a small, pink tongue lapped at my bare arm, I yelped and jumped backward.

"Sorry!" Sarah said, giggling.

What I'd thought was a furry bag draped over one arm turned out to be a small, white creature with curly hair and curious, dark eyes.

"Did you have to bring that thing here?" Kai asked, patting it on the head affectionately.

In a perfect counter to her regal presence, Sarah's lower lip jutted out slightly. "She cried at the door when I tried to leave. Fifi wanted to come to the party."

"What is that thing?" I asked, immediately realizing how rude I sounded. "I mean, I've never seen anything like it."

"This is Fifi," Sarah replied. "She's a poodle. The

French royal family sent her as a gift last week."

The creature wriggled in the princess's arms, pawing at the air between us. Stretching a hand forward, I held my breath when the animal bumped at it with her nose.

"She's adorable," I said, smiling when Fifi licked my hand again.

"You'll have to come over to play with her sometime," Sarah said. "It was really nice to meet you. I hate to rush off, but duty calls."

Kai looked down at his watch and narrowed his eyes. "Is it already time for Mom's speech?"

Sarah nodded. "And you know how mad she gets if we miss one."

Kai leaned in and brushed a gentle kiss across my cheek. "This will not take long. I will come find you as soon as it is done."

"Of course," I stuttered, feeling plain in the company of the glamorous princess. "It was great to meet you too, Sarah."

She squeezed my forearm as she headed toward the party. "Let's grab a drink afterward, okay? I have plenty of stories for you about this guy."

Kai followed Sarah but turned back to me a few steps down the path. "Do you want to come with us?"

Despite his earnest expression, I laughed. "I've had enough of photographers and gossip this week. Definitely find me afterward."

Kai nodded. "You have my word."

And in the meantime, I'll deal with Christina, I thought.

CHAPTER TWENTY-FIVE

HAVING TOLD KAI about the vampires, I had the very strong urge to look Christina in the eye and tell her the same. I wanted to see her reaction in person. Tonight, while Kai listened to his mother's speech, would be my only chance for a while. When I saw Christina earlier, she'd been heading toward the hallway between the gardens. That seemed like the best place to start looking for her.

Just as I reached the portico of the Summer Garden, a scream rang out in the crowd. Pushing against the people suddenly rushing toward me, I hurried closer to the noise. Only a few revelers remained in the Winter Garden, all in various states of shock. One guy with magenta hair and a powder-blue suit had tears pouring down his face. Without a word, he pointed to a frosted pathway.

"A vampire," his companion said, trying to fill in the blanks. "She took someone down the path. Are we safe here?"

This can't be a coincidence, I thought. "Get the authorities," I snapped. Instead of waiting for help to arrive, I rushed down the pathway after the vampire. Bile rose in my throat when I saw a pair of drag marks in the snow that led beyond a wall of frozen hedges.

Sharp branches bit my skin as I pushed through a gap only a foot wide. My eyes strained to follow the tracks in the darkness, but the coppery sent of blood in the air left no doubt that I was on the right track. Then, in the light of the twinkling bulbs, I saw the ghoulish pool of crimson with a corpse in the center.

The vampire had taken care to heal the bite marks on her first two victims and presumably the third; Kai had only mentioned that the fourth warlock, found that morning, had them. Meaning by the fourth victim, the vampire no longer cared whether the authorities connected the crime to one of her kind. And now, leaving a dead caster in nearly plain view at a social event, she no longer cared whether anyone connected the crime directly to her.

This is not good, I thought. What if she's planning to deplete someone high-ranking for her finale, like Kai?

Cursing under my breath, I spun on my heel and ran back to the party to find Kenoa. He would make sure the prince was safe. But Kenoa wasn't among the crowd of people who hovered at the entrance to the Winter Garden. Kai's voice boomed from the speakers, signaling the beginning of the presentation. At the same time, a murmur swept through the crowd.

No, no, no. Kai needs to be somewhere safe. Is Kenoa with him?

Realizing that I needed a better vantage point, I dashed onto the wrap porch between the gardens and climbed atop a riser next to the bar.

From there, I could see above the heads of people in both gardens. I spotted an emerald bob at the edge of the room. A pit formed in my gut, telling me to go after her. Only, she darted away before I could reach her.

I followed her jewel-toned tresses and the scent of her signature perfume down a hallway that was not open to the public. Where are you going? But I didn't call out to her. Christina never once looked over her shoulder to see if she had a tail. Odd. Unless you aren't expecting a tail. She clearly wasn't expecting to see any security either. And there wasn't any. Because everyone was in the gardens listening to the royal speech or telling anyone who would listen that vampires were attacking partygoers. Almost like she planned this.

Christina disappeared around a bend. By the time I rounded the same curve, she was nowhere in sight. Standing perfectly still, I listened for her footsteps. Instead, a low moan echoed down the hallway. I ran toward the sound, my heart hammering in my chest.

I found three empty rooms before I located the source of the moans. My friend, the leader of the rebellion, was inside. So was a familiar vampire and one very recognizable caster. Well, she definitely picked an impactful person for her finale, I thought as I met Queen Lilli's defiant gaze.

"Close the door!" Christina hollered.

I held the older caster's eyes but spoke to Christina. "What's going on in here?" The door slammed shut behind me, and I spun to face Christina, who fixed me with her amber gaze, a challenge in her eyes.

The vampire hissed. I flinched as I took in her gleaming white hair and dull, gray eyes. Blood was smeared down her chin and throat, and her teeth were tinged red.

"So, you are working with the vampires," I said evenly.

I saw the moment of understanding in Queen Lilli's eyes as she realized that I knew one of the two women holding her captive. It wouldn't be Kenoa who ratted me out, it would be Kai's mother. I wanted to say so much to her in that moment but none of it mattered, not if there was a chance of getting her out of that room alive. For that, I needed to play this smart.

"Why are you guys doing this?" I asked, attempting to sound more curious than disgusted.

"You wouldn't understand. You've never truly understood the point of the rebellion," Christina said with a laugh that made me wonder how I hadn't noticed years ago that she had crazy eyes. "You dream of a place where fae can be free. But what about payback, Brie? Don't you think the casters should pay for how they've treated us?"

"What about the vampires?" I countered, taking a step closer to the queen. "They've been pretty shitty to us, too."

"They're not so bad," Christina said, gaze sweeping to the female vampire.

What did Samira say about love being the strongest motivator of all?

"I see. So, what? You want to kill Queen Lilli to make a statement? Is that what this is all about? No one's safe, not even the royal family?" I asked, the frenzied quality of my voice underscoring my otherwise calm demeanor.

"You really haven't figured it out yet?" Christina's expression was amused, but her forehead crinkled into lines. "I want to make a statement, for sure. But not simply by killing her." She sent a powerful wave of air toward the queen, forcing it down the caster's throat. "She's just the cherry."

Is it mandatory to sound like the villain in a bad movie when discussing evil plots? I wondered.

"We plan to kill them all," the vampire added, sliding over to put her arm around Christina's waist.

The air fae sent another gust toward Queen Lilli, who wasn't holding up well under the torture.

"Stop! You're going to kill her," I snapped.

"That's the point," the vampire said, practically salivating with bloodlust. "I want her power." Her fangs dropped, and she licked her lips seductively.

"If you want power, take mine," I said, my mouth moving faster than my head.

"Maybrie, no!" Queen Lilli gasped as I met her gaze.

"I'm like an endless battery. The vampires can have me. Just let the queen go," I said firmly.

Christina cocked her head to one side and grinned at

the vampire. "Brie really is a self-sustaining power source, Alyssa."

"And twenty times as powerful as a caster, at least," I pressed, naively believing that my words were getting through to her.

"You are," Christina agreed with a nod. "But killing you won't bring down the dome."

Her words didn't make any sense. Why would the rebellion want to bring down the dome? Why not just leave and be free? And then Christina's previous statement rung in my ears: What about payback? Fae and shifters, even vampires, could survive the frozen world beyond the dome. Casters could not. If the dome collapsed, they would all die. That was how Alyssa and Christina planned to kill them all.

"The depleted casters didn't place protections on the dome, they powered the dome, didn't they?" I asked. "You've been systematically depleting them—that's why it's been getting colder. And that's why Lono and Pika were visiting House of Mana so often. They weren't overindulging on magic, they were simply keeping up their supply."

"They're called tentpoles," Alyssa explained, squeezing Christina affectionately. It was the same term Samira had used for the casters whose magic supported the dome. "I should know. My caster father was a tentpole forty years ago; my sister after him. The queen's the only one left from the current lot," the vampire finished.

Her bloodlust turned to another kind of lust when she glanced over at her paramour. The vampire was completely sprung. She'd probably been putty in the hands of a powerful fae as manipulative as Christina. I was, and I don't even want to sleep with her, I thought, glaring daggers.

"Maybrie?" The queen's voice sounded like she was uttering her dying breath.

"It's…it's okay," I promised. Fixing the full weight of my stare on Christina, I casually called a fireball to each of my hands. "Let Queen Lilli go."

Instead of shrinking from the threat, Alyssa edged closer to me. "You will not fight," she rasped, holding my gaze.

My amusement was short-lived and came out as a snort. "That's adorable, fanger. Don't even waste your breath."

Alyssa's eyes lit up, as if the challenge excited her. "Wanna play, little girl?"

I couldn't release a fireball without endangering the queen, but it took every ounce of my willpower to hold back from attacking the cocky vampire.

"You and I need to talk," I said to Christina. "But before we do, you need to let Queen Lilli go. Security is already looking for her. It's only a matter of time before they find you in here. They will kill you, no questions asked. Is that how you want this to end?"

Christina took several steps toward me. The hypnotic draw of her amber eyes held my attention. "Are you with us?" she challenged, enunciating each word. "Or are you against us? Last chance, Brie. Pick a side."

Knowing what she wanted to hear, I edged closer. The queen would be within arm's reach if I could just distract

Christina long enough to slip between the two women. Alyssa was still in the way, but I had a feeling she wouldn't enjoy the wrath of fire I was going to rain upon her at the first opportunity.

"I'm not your enemy, Christina," I said evenly. "But I was kidnapped by a vampire, so hopefully you understand my reluctance to trust her." I nodded to Alyssa.

"I'm not the one you need to worry about," the vampire hissed.

"Alyssa won't hurt you," Christina promised. She smiled at her girlfriend. "Will you, my love?"

I realized too late that the fae wasn't actually looking at Alyssa but rather at a second fanged creature in the shadows. He was tall and broad shouldered, with mesmerizing eyes. He had an air of confidence that would've told me he'd been a caster before he was turned, if I hadn't already known that to be true.

It had been five years since that night on the beach in Fae Canyon, but I remembered Mat's face like it was yesterday.

His movements were instantaneous, faster than my brain could comprehend. The crimson line across Queen Lilli's neck could've been a dainty choker. Mat dug a single sharpened nail into the queen's carotid artery. The arc of blood spray only lasted for a moment before the vampire's lips closed around the wound.

I sprang forward to rip his face away from the neck of Kai's mother, but Christina caught me in midair. Still holding fireballs, I let loose a wave of power that could've levelled seven kingdoms, all directed at a single person.

Unfortunately, that person was super-humanly fast. Mat was across the room before the queen's lifeless body slumped to the floor. My scream was half raged and half heartbreak as I stared at her waxy lips and hollow gaze. But no one left was alive to hear me.

Christina and the vampires were gone.

I was no match for vampire speed, but I never considered that fact. Just as Samira had said, revenge was a powerful motive. And I wanted revenge more than I wanted my next breath. For myself. For Queen Lilli. And for Kai, who didn't even know he'd just lost his mother.

You want payback, Christina? See how you like being on the receiving end.

CHAPTER TWENTY-SIX

CHRISTINA, ALYSSA, AND Mat had fled back through the party and out the front entrance of the palace, leaving a trail of terror in their wake. Few pursued the trio beyond the relative warmth of the main hall. Outside, for the first time in centuries, snow blanketed the lush lawn of Iolani Palace. My breath wasn't only visible, it practically turned to ice in the frigid air.

They're getting away, I thought frantically.

Heels and icy conditions made for a dangerous combination. I skidded down the palace steps and fell to my knees in the snow. My legs went numb instantly as chunks of ice soaked my skin. The dome really is falling, I thought.

I was ill-equipped in my current outfit for the rapidly falling temperature, but the casters who'd run screaming from the palace were turning to popsicles like they'd been flash frozen. They were all going to die. Kai was going to die.

I stared up at the sky. Think. There has to be something you can do. The tentpole casters, as Alyssa had referred to them, all used fae magic to create and power the dome. Could fae take over the duties, with possibly just one caster to perform the necessary spell? How many fae would that take, though?

What had I told Alyssa? I was as powerful as twenty casters. That might've been a slight exaggeration but not an outright lie. I just needed a few other very powerful fae like me, maybe one for each of the elements.

Kenoa was the strongest water fae I'd ever met, including those I'd known in Fae Canyon. And I had a feeling he was even more powerful that I knew. He had kept Kai alive when the duo was lost beyond the dome for two days. That wasn't survival skills—that was magic.

Unfortunately, Christina was the strongest air fae I knew. My mind went to Sumi. Even Kenoa had commented on her incredible power. Let's hope it's enough, I thought.

That left the earth element, and there was only one earth fae I trusted: Everly. The others were too closely associated with Christina to know where their loyalties lied. Everly was a good person; I couldn't believe she would stand by and do nothing while casters dropped dead.

They wouldn't be the only ones either, I realized as I

shook violently from the cold. Fae under the dome were soft compared to those in the Freelands. We'd grown accustom to our comfortable way of life. Even I, who had lived the majority of my life without the dome's protection, was not going to last long in a frozen world.

I stumbled back up the palace stairs and pulled out my cellphone from my dress pocket. I worried Everly wouldn't answer, but the call was picked up after the third ring.

"Hello? Brie? Can you hear me? What's happening? Have you been outside?" she rambled breathlessly as though running.

"Where are you?" I asked.

"The Winter Garden," she replied automatically. "There's a dead caster, Brie. People are saying the queen is missing."

"She's dead," I said bluntly. "The rebellion killed her. Vampires working with Christina killed her."

Tanner's sister didn't reply. Only the rustling of the crowd and shouts to get inside told me she was still on the line.

"She wants to bring down the dome, to kill all the casters," I added. "Please, Everly, we have to do something. I know how you feel about them, but we can't let them die. And if they do, a lot of us won't be far behind."

She didn't hesitate this time. "What do you need me to do?"

"Meet me at the staircase. Don't go anywhere else. Just wait." I hung up the phone without waiting for a response.

Dialing Sumi's number, I elbowed my way through the stream of luau guests clogging the entryway. As I barked the same instructions at Kenoa, I spotted him muscling his way to the base of the stairs with Kai and Princess Sarah. Makani and Lara were with them, too. Both caster bodyguards looked like they were already struggling with the cold temperatures. And they're probably in much better shape than a lot of the witches and warlocks on the island, I thought dismally.

"Brie!" Kai shouted from the first-floor landing. He broke away from his guards and bolted down the steps toward me. Grabbing my hand, he tried to drag me back to Kenoa and the others. "Hurry! We need to get somewhere safe!"

Nowhere is safe, I thought.

Kenoa turned, and our eyes locked. Something in my expression must've tipped him off that whatever I needed, it couldn't wait.

Kenoa barked at Makani and Lara, "Get them to the panic room. Don't open the door for anyone besides me or Brie."

They didn't argue. Kai tried to protest, but Kenoa wasn't having it. "We still can't find your mother," he told Kai in a low voice. "Right now, you are the most important person in this kingdom."

The prince started to protest again.

"Please, Kai. Go." I took his hand. "Your sister needs you."

He held my gaze for a long moment before finally shaking his head. "No. I am sorry. You clearly need me more." Calling to Makani and Lara, the prince gestured to Princess Sarah. "Take care of my sister. Protect her with your lives. And dear, Gaia, someone find my mother." He turned back to me expectantly.

I looked back and forth between Kai and Kenoa. "The dome's falling, in case you didn't notice. But I think I might know a way to get it back up, at least temporarily."

"Go on," Kai prompted, as Sumi and Everly shouldered their way through the crowd.

I waited another moment until they reached us before explaining my idea. "I think we need a powerful fae in each element. And a powerful caster, since I assume there are spells involved," I finished hurried.

"I can do it," Kai offered immediately.

"No," Kenoa and I said in unison.

Though Kenoa was clearly reluctant to voice his concern, I was sure he suspected that Queen Lilli was dead. That was why, like me, he didn't want Kai risking his life to resurrect the dome.

"I'm sure Samira already knows the spells," I added quickly. "She seemed to know a lot about all of this when we spoke the other night."

Like the leader he was, the prince started delegating responsibilities. "Kenoa, go find her, and bring her to the casting chamber."

Both Sumi and Everly looked like they wanted to ask a lot of questions, but there would be time once the island was no longer under the curse of winter.

Kai led our group up the stairs and past the guards keeping the masses from invading the residence wings. The four of us moved fast, Everly even ditching her heels after a ground tremor sent her tumbling down the hallway. Kai helped her to her feet as Sumi aimed a gust of wind at a falling chandelier headed for Everly.

"We can access the chamber through there," Kai called to me, pointing to a section of wall at the very end of the hallway.

Another quake rumbled the palace floors. The prince hurried over and tugged on a panel of wainscoting. The wall itself slid up like a garage door. A staircase lay on the other side, and he took the steps two at a time. I followed Kai, Everly and Sumi clambering up the stairs behind me. The room at the top was dark, save for two burning torches and the moonlight shining through a hole in the ceiling. Large, fat flakes drifted through the opening to land on my upturned cheeks.

"Brie? A little help?" Kai held one of the torches to me as he held the other to a trough along the wall.

Realizing his intention, I called forth a spark and sent it flying. The flame ignited the fire pit that ran around the entire room. Within moments, we were surrounded by a ring of fire.

"Now what?" Sumi asked, frightened but determined.

Everly spun in a circle, taking in the full experience of the room.

"We need Samira and Kenoa," I said.

"Do you think Samira is strong enough?" Kai asked doubtfully. "Normally we have quite a few casters involved in the dome maintenance spells."

"Normally, but this situation isn't normal, and we're fae. We'll provide the power, she just needs to perform the spell. Besides, she's the strongest caster alive that I know." I spoke without thinking.

"My mother, the queen. She is the most powerful caster in the kingdom. If we could only—"

"I'm so sorry, Kai," I said simply.

"What are you talking about?"

Please don't make me say it, I thought. But I did. Because he deserved the truth from me.

"Your mother is dead, Kai. A vampire murdered her. I tried…I wanted…I'm so sorry I couldn't save her," I finished lamely.

He shook his head like he couldn't quite wrap his head around the truth.

"I'm so sorry," I repeated again.

"That is why the dome is coming down. I thought maybe…maybe she simply could not power it herself. I thought…," he shook his head. "I knew. On some level, I must have. I just didn't want to believe the truth."

"Sometimes it's easier that way," Everly told him stiffly.

They exchanged glances, a small bond forming over their respective losses. But commotion from the bottom of the stairs interrupted the moment. Samira appeared a few seconds later, followed immediately by Kenoa.

"The dome is—," I started.

"The bodyguard told me. Besides, I'm not blind, child. I can see the dome is falling. Hurry. I need you four to form a circle around me."

"What about me?" Kai asked. "What can I do?"

Samira leveled him with a hard look. "Pray to Gaia, my prince. We will all need her strength." She moved to stand in an empty pool in the center of the chamber. "Air," she snapped and pointed to a spot on the floor. Sumi hurried to obey the command.

Reluctantly, Kai moved to the top of the stairs in an attempt to be out of the way yet still observe. "My sister?" he called to Kenoa.

"The queens guard is stationed outside the panic room. She is the safest person in the kingdom," he promised.

"If you want her to stay that way, come here." The witch pointed to a spot opposite where Sumi stood. Kenoa got into position without delay. "Brie, there. And you, earth child, just there."

Once Everly and I were in the right places, Samira yelled, "Call the water!"

Water bubbled up from the ground beneath the witch's feet, filling up the shallow pool.

"Air!" Samira shouted.

Sumi raised her right hand and spun it as though screwing in a light bulb. Wind whipped around us, causing the flames in the fire pit to flicker but not die. Water and air collided to form a swirling tornado of liquid. The effect of their combined powers was awe-inspiring.

"Earth!" Samira screamed to be heard over the cyclone.

Everly closed her eyes and held up her arms parallel to the ground. Dust and dirt flew across my field of vision. I thought I heard a loud crack, like the wall breaking under pressure, but I couldn't say for certain.

"Fire!" Samira hollered her last command.

Without any real direction, I went on instinct. I embraced the heat of the flames at my back. My skin warmed considerably until I wondered if I wasn't part of the blaze.

"More, child!" Samira insisted. "You have it in you. Dig deep. All of you, give this every ounce of energy you have. We only have one shot."

The sounds of the blowing wind, churning water, and flying debris mixed together into one long cry for help. I blocked the outside world and its distractions, focusing instead on the fire burning hotter and brighter inside of me.

The flames were intense, a whitish blue in my mind's eye. I'd never summoned something so alive, something so volatile and powerful. A steady stream of energy poured from my body into the elemental tornado. Samira chanted at the top of her lungs. My hands shook and sweat beaded my forehead. Sumi was so pale, it seemed she would collapse at any moment. Kenoa, with his fierce stoicism, dropped to one knee, but the power he output never dimmed.

The words Samira spoke were other-worldly and nonsensical, unlike any spell in any language I'd ever heard. The fiery cyclone jutted sideways, barely missing Everly. As I began to lose doubt that Samira had any idea what the hell she was doing, the elemental funnel began climbing toward the opening in the ceiling.

"Do not stop!" the witch yelled over the screaming winds.

It sounded like the island itself was moaning, and the ground shook beneath our feet. My vision flashed with bright spots, quickly followed by long blinks of darkness. I didn't know whether the room was spinning or just my head. Either way, I stumbled. The ground rushed up to meet my face, but I didn't move my hands to catch myself. Instead, I let my skull take the hit while I kept my palms pointed to the swirling vortex.

Blue flames darted through the water and ignited the dirt. As the energy ball broke through into the night air, I had time for one last thought before darkness claimed me.

We're all going to die.

CHAPTER TWENTY-SEVEN

MY HEAD THROBBED like I'd spent a week binging cocktails from the Hideout. My eyes felt swollen and crusted over. How many blue punchbowls did they give me? I wondered. Cala is going to pay for this.

A groan escaped my parched lips. I was beyond dehydrated. Water. I need water.

Cursing the fact my kitchen was so far away, I rolled to one side. It might take me a whole day to get there, but my need for hydration wasn't going away. If I kept rolling, I would eventually end up on the floor, and I could crawl to the sweet, glorious water my body was screaming for.

I am never drinking again. I heaved several times, but

nothing came up. Never again.

After two rolls, I should've been at the edge of my bed. Instead, the damned mattress went on for what felt like miles. Had my bed become an infinite plane while I slept? With another loud moan, I fought to open my eyes. When my eyelids didn't work on their own, I physically lifted one with my forefinger.

The reason I hadn't reached the edge of my bed? I wasn't in my bed. Nor was I anywhere in my condo. My place was nice, but these unfamiliar surroundings were a definitive five levels up from nice.

The sunlight that poured in the single, uncovered window stung my retinas, and I squeezed my eyes shut again. Rolling onto my stomach, I resigned myself to lay face down on the fluffy pile of pillows until my head exploded.

A soft knock on the door sounded like a jackhammer to my skull.

"No," I moaned.

A soft click told me the door had opened, but I didn't have the strength or the desire to pull my head from its feathered nest.

"Brie?" Kai's voice sounded panicked. Without warning, he rolled me over so my face was no longer buried in the downy fabric.

"No," I repeated my protest.

"No what? Can you breathe?"

"I can't live," I groaned in reply. My head was starting to clear enough to realize what a baby I was being. It was just a hangover. It wasn't the end of the world. I didn't even remember going to the palace, but I must've made my way there at some point after the Hideout.

"What can I do?" Kai asked.

"Water. Dark. Quiet."

When he closed the curtains over the only source of light in the room, the pressure inside my head lessened. A moment later, a hand slid around my back and pulled me up. I slumped against Kai and eagerly gulped from the cup he held to my lips.

"Easy," he cautioned. "Not too fast."

The glass disappeared, and I grumbled for more. It was quickly replaced with a small vial. Assuming that he must've gotten me a healing tonic, I snatched the bottle from his hand and downed it greedily. Before I could utter my thanks, I passed out again.

The next time I came to, my eyes no longer felt superglued shut. Running my hand over my face, I struggled to put together the pieces. When the memory of the cyclone crashed into my mind, I struggled to sit up. In the darkness, I could make out Kai's slumped form in a chair beside the bed.

The queen. Tears pricked my eyes as they adjusted to the dark room. Kai must've sensed my waking, because he stirred when I moved.

"What can I get you?" he asked, his voice thick with sleep.

"Come here." The bed tilted down on one side when he stretched out beside me.

Kai took my hand gently, like I was a porcelain doll that might break at any moment.

I squeezed his fingers reassuringly. "How are you holding up?" I asked softly.

"I have been better. I never quite imagined this was how I would become king."

"I am so sorry," I whispered into the darkness. "I am so, so sorry." Tears pooled over, but I swiped them away immediately.

"Shhh," Kai soothed.

Anger flared within me, directed only at myself. I'd let him down. I should've been comforting him, instead of the other way around. He was the one who lost his mother. I was the one who hadn't saved her.

Once I trusted my voice again, I tipped my head down to look him in the eyes. "Kai, I'm sorry. I tried to save her. I swear, I did."

"I know. I saw the tapes," he replied.

My heart skipped a beat. Tapes? Did he know about my relationship with Christina?

"You did everything you could." He placed a light kiss on the top of my head. "I could not hear what you said to those fanatics, but you were able to keep them talking for much longer than I could have managed."

Thank Gaia for small favors, I thought and hated myself just a little. Kai deserved to know that it wasn't just that I couldn't save his mother, but that I had a hand in the queen's death. It didn't matter that I hadn't dealt the final blow. Queen Lilli died because of a group I funded, because of a cause I'd thought just.

You didn't know what Christina was planning.

Nothing I told myself assuaged the guilt. Probably because, while I might not have known what Christina was planning, I'd suspected she wasn't telling me everything.

"I could've done more," I protested weakly.

Kai ran a finger along my jawline. "You did do a lot, Brie. You saved everyone on the island."

That got my attention. The last thing I remembered, a swirling vortex of elemental magic had flown through the opening of the casting chamber.

"It worked?" I asked, my brows curling together. "Really?"

Kai chuckled, though the laughter sounded forced. "Thanks to you and the others, the dome is back to full power."

"Permanently?" I asked.

"I am afraid we do not know. The tentpole casters were continually channeling magic into the dome. They needed to in order to sustain the ecosystem. Samira channeled all four of your elemental magics into one spell, in tremendous amounts, to create a new dome. This is uncharted territory for us."

"How is she? Samira, I mean." I asked.

His laugh sounded more genuine. "I think the polite term is crotchety."

I smiled. "I'm pretty sure she won't recover from that."

"No," Kai agreed. "Physically, she is weak, but her spirit is growing stronger each time she orders my staff to do something ridiculous."

"What happens now, Kai?" I asked after several minutes of silence.

"A lot of meetings to discuss how we move forward with the new dome, I suspect," he said.

"Okay, but I mean now that you're king?"

"You mean now that I have inherited a kingdom at war?" He squeezed me tightly. "I suppose now I find a warrior queen to stand by my side."

EPILOGUE

THE RAIN THAT fell on the day we laid Queen Lili to rest was aberrant. When I glanced at Kenoa, I knew the source of the precipitation. With so much of himself woven into the dome, the sky couldn't help but shed tears as well. Dark clouds hung low overhead as a kingdom mourned their monarch.

I felt oddly detached from the proceedings, though I had a front row seat as Kai gave his mother's eulogy. He spoke of his mother's strength and her kindness. He shared her resilience and empathy. Tears flowed freely from my eyes as I watched him struggle to put his love for her into words.

I'd spent so much time with the rebellion, and let

Christina fill my head with so much crap, that I'd never realized that most people liked Queen Lilli. No, she wasn't all that beloved among a lot of fae and shifters, but those whom she'd employed at the palace cried harder than anyone besides her children.

Stoic and beautiful, her white-blonde hair flowing wildly, Princess Sarah reached over and gripped my hand wordlessly. The clutch felt like desperation, and I squeezed back. I knew what it was like to lose a mother. It was the lowest, darkest, and most despairing place I'd ever been. Even being ripped from my father and Ilion hadn't scarred me like losing Mom.

Together, the princess and I watched as her brother, King Kai, reassured his people that their kingdom would triumph over tragedy with nothing more than a determined stare and hard-set jaw. A nation would continue to look to him for guidance, especially in the coming months, to be their strength, to bear their burdens, and to make decisions for the good of all its people. It was a heavy responsibility for any one person, but particularly for someone his age.

When Kai finished, he gestured for Princess Sarah to take his place. The siblings shared a brief hug as they passed one another. Kai sat in the empty seat beside me, back straight and shoulders squared. He reached for my hand and leaned close enough that our arms touched.

If he had to be strong for his people, I would be strong for him. Kai deserved that much from me. I was part of the reason his mother was dead, after all.

If I lived to see an entire millennium, I would always wonder: if it had been any other vampire besides Mat, could I have saved Queen Lilli? Had I become immobile, unable to protect her, because of our history? Or had it simply been shock at seeing a second vampire? Would I have really sacrificed myself for the caster queen that I'd spent a quarter of my life hating?

Kai slid his arm around my waist. With the entire kingdom at our backs, he pulled me to his side. Even at such a somber event, I heard the whispers rippling through the crowd. I was officially dating King Kai. Because our relationship wasn't complicated enough when he was just a prince.

After Princess Sarah's eulogy, the funeral attendees filed past the coffin, dropping leis of plumerias, tuberose, and jasmine. The red and yellow feathers that were also thrown into the sarcophagus were Hawaiian tradition— they were symbolic of the monarchy's history. The coffin was then moved to its resting place. Kai bit back heavy sobs. I felt the agony wrack him as his chest rose and fell.

Finally, Kai and I walked hand in hand back to the car. Princess Sarah was on my other side, looking like a lost child. Though I barely knew her, I felt that I'd deceived the princess, as well as her brother.

Kenoa hadn't alluded to the rebellion, or my involvement therein, since the day of the luau. He will, I told myself.

That was a problem for tomorrow. I wouldn't sour Kai's last day with his mother with unpleasant truths. One day soon, he and I would sit down, and I would tell him everything—about Christina, about the rebellion, and about my role in the queen's death.

For now, I gripped Kai's hand as the limo sped back

to Iolani Palace. When he turned to me, his expression a mixture of sadness and hope, I saw a whole future within his eyes.

"I know everything is happening very fast right now. Thank you for coming to this reception dinner with me. Not that I feel like eating, but duty calls," he said.

"Of course," I said quickly. "Whatever you need."

The sadness lifted from his handsome features quickly, replaced by anger like I'd never seen in him before. "What I need is to find that vampire and rip his head from his shoulders. What I need is that vampire's head on a spike."

Swallowing over the lump in my throat, I nodded. I hadn't even told him that Mat was the vampire who'd kidnapped me from Fae Canyon. Was it a coincidence? Or was it fate that had brought him into my life a second time? Either way, I was all in. And this time, I believed I was on the right side.

I squeezed Kai's hand. "Something tells me that's just the sort of thing a warrior fae gives her caster king for Cupid's Day."

He stared into my eyes for a long minute. "I wish my mother could have gotten to know you better. I think you would have been great friends."

Curling into Kai's side, I tried to send every good vibe within my body into him. It wasn't much, but he needed the light. Kai stroked my side, the gesture both familiar and exhilarating. I didn't know exactly what I was getting myself into, but I knew that I wanted it. I knew that I wanted him.

The details would have to sort themselves out later.

Until then, I just wanted to be the girl Kai thought me to be. Maybe if I could prove my feelings to him, he would understand that this—what we had—was real. It always had been.

THRONE OF WINTER

SOPHIE DAVIS

DEAR READER,

Thank you for taking the time to read Throne of
Winter. Reviews are the lifeblood of all authors. Good,
bad, or otherwise, if you could take a minute to review
Throne of Winter, we would truly appreciate..

ACKNOWLEDGMENTS

HUGE THANKS TO...

Tabitha, because she's the greatest.

Kerry, for always being there, and for editing the hell out of our crazy ideas.

Kim, for showing us what strength and faith truly are. Our hearts are with you always.

Alyssa and Christina, for being sunshine and fun inspiration.

Sarah, for being an ice princess and a cheerleader.

Shayne, for being the kind of friend who will scale your balcony when necessary, and the type of friend we can call when a stranger does the same thing.

Kylie, for being so encouraging and amazing.

Mat, for reading our books, being so supportive, and of course being our big bad.

Robbie, Andre, and Bryan, for coming up with amazing Fire and Ice drinks, and for being so damn supportive while we're working.

Our author friends and the YA author community, for the support, love, and the spirit of lifting each other up.

Our parents, as always, for being exactly who you are, and for everything you all do for us.

Sophie Davis

For more information on Sophie Davis, visit Sophie's website, www.sophiedavisbooks.com
To contact Sophie directly, email her at sophie@sophiedavisbooks.com.
You can also follow Sophie on:
Facebook: @SeeSophieWrite
Twitter: @SeeSophiesWrite
Instagram: @SeeSophieWrite
Tumblr: officialsophiedavis
Pinterest: https://www.pinterest.com/sophiedavisbook/

SOPHIE DAVIS

MORE BOOKS FROM THIS AUTHOR

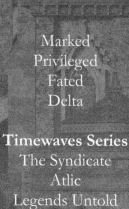

THRONE OF WINTER

Marked
Privileged
Fated
Delta

Timewaves Series
The Syndicate
Atlic
Legends Untold
Dust Into Gold
Remember Me

Blind Barriers Trilogy
Fragile Façade
Platinum Prey
Vacant Voices

Shadow Fate Series
Pawn
Sacrifice
Checkmate

THRONE OF WINTER

Made in the USA
Las Vegas, NV
08 November 2023